T...
PROMISE

KT-158-930

ALSO BY TERESA DRISCOLL

THE
PROMISE

TERESA DRISCOLL

Text copyright © 2019 by Teresa Driscoll
All rights reserved.

Published by Thomas & Mercer, Seattle

www.apub.com

Amazon, the Amazon logo, and Thomas & Mercer are trademarks of Amazon.com, Inc., or its affiliates.

ISBN-13: 9781503905078
ISBN-10: 1503905071

Cover design by Ghost Design

Cover photography by Eduardo Diez Pozas

Printed in the United States of America

For Maggie and Christopher

The Promise is a standalone story set *before* the events of *I Am Watching You.*

PROLOGUE

'I think I put my hand over her mouth . . .'

'Don't say that. Don't even think that. You *wouldn't* have done that.'

They sit very still in this room full of blood and sorrow – girls whose pulses burst in their veins and boom inside their ears. Their heads. Somewhere a clock ticks. A bird calls . . .

Three girls. One dead.

She looks up at the mirror to see her reflection, face white and terrible – just below it, the line of shells on the blue-painted shelf. She can't take it in. The shock of the familiar. The shells . . .

She gathered them on holiday just last summer, washed them very carefully at the kitchen sink and polished each until it shone. She remembers the sand between her toes, the smell of the sea and the salt on her lips. She remembers her father and her mother waving from their red-and-white-striped chairs on the beach and she remembers the feeling deep inside her – the sweep of complete happiness.

'Oh my God. What are we going to do? *Will I go to hell? Will I burn in hell?*

Her friend's voice travels as if through water, muted and strange. She looks at the other girl – lips blue – and all of the blood, and she realises that the happiness on the beach was just a trick. A fleeting moment – gone now.

Like their childhoods.

Gone forever now.

CHAPTER 1

BETH - 2008

You know that strange thing where a sound from the real world filters into a dream? *That . . .*

I'm staring at this huge red plastic phone ringing in my dream and I know it's a dream because the phone is so ridiculous. But at first I just can't shake myself awake so I pick up the phone. Still the sound of ringing. I replace the receiver and try again. And again.

Finally I open my eyes to hear the real phone ringing alongside the bed. But there's no relief because the alarm clock is blinking bad news: 3 a.m. My next emotion is panic. *Has someone died?*

And so I do the headcount. I glance at Adam snoring softly beside me. I think of Sam next door – arm lolling from a bed of rockets and stars – and Harry, just a baby in his cot. But there are others that I love and, cold now with dread, I press the phone to my ear.

It's Richard – his voice low and fast. 'It's Sally. Can you come, Beth? She's lost the baby.' A pause in case I haven't heard. '*She's lost the baby.*'

The bed creaks as I sit bolt upright. Too late I put my hand to my mouth but the sound has already escaped – a noise so alien that Adam wakes also, his eyes instantly afraid. Harry stirs momentarily in his cot but then turns and settles again, making the little snuffling noise we know so well.

I let the receiver fall away from my face to repeat the news, whispering now. 'Sally's lost the baby. It's Richard.'

Adam closes his eyes and winces, first with a pain for Sally and then with a guilt I recognise. That short pang of relief that it's not our loss – one of our babies gone.

I put the receiver back to my ear, eyes shut tight. 'So what's happening? Where are you? At the hospital?'

'We're still at home. There's an ambulance on the way but she's locked herself in the bathroom. She won't let me in, Beth. She wants you. She won't let anyone else in.'

I mutter that I'm on my way, slam down the receiver and jump from the bed. I find jogging pants and a jumper slung over a chair, not bothering with underwear, and tell Adam that I have to go to her. He does not question me, does not say anything – except to drive carefully.

Which I do not. I drive like a madwoman, hardly able to see through eyes burning with angry tears, bashing my rage at the steering wheel.

At first when I pull up behind Sally's car on the drive, I forget the handbrake and the car begins to move with the slope of the drive so that I have to jump back inside and stamp on the brake. I scrape my leg as I get out for the second time and there's the warm stickiness of blood just above my ankle but I feel no pain. Feel nothing.

On the doorstep as I wait, one ring, two rings – *oh Jeez, where is he?* – three rings, my breath spreads clouds of mist like dragon's breath in the night air, and when Richard finally opens the door I find the dragon cannot speak to him. I long for real fire on my breath to roar my anger, to burn him to ash so that I might step right over him. For me, in this moment, this tragedy has nothing to do with him. I hate him. I hate him for his infidelity, for his arrogance and for not wanting this baby which is now gone.

At last inside, I brush past him to head upstairs, tripping in my haste. There's a mirror on the landing and I can see a reflection of Richard opening the door to the ambulance crew, the emergency lights flashing on the drive. I try the bathroom door but it's still locked.

'Sal darling, it's me – it's Beth. You have got to let me in.'

I hear Sally sobbing and then some kind of shuffling.

'Please, Sally.'

Finally there's the sound of the door being unlocked. At first I can't open it and realise she must be slumped against it on the inside. I coax her gently to move away but as soon as I'm in the room, she closes the door and begs me to lock it again. Which I do.

She's sitting on the floor, staring wide-eyed like a frightened child after a bad dream, wearing a flannelette pyjama top which is white with little red hearts. No trousers, just a towel wrapped around which is stained heavily with blood. She's white and shaking and I'm very afraid. I put my arms around her but find that I'm shaking too. And then we draw apart and she just looks at me.

'It's gone, Beth.' Her voice trails away but the word lingers. *Gone* – the vowel extended like a hand stretching out but unable to hold on.

Next comes the sound of footsteps on the stairs and voices at the door. The ambulance crew. I ask them to wait and tell Sally that we should let them in, that I don't know what to do and she must let them in. But Sally is shaking her head. Not listening.

'Give me a minute with her. *Please.*' I shout through the door to the ambulance staff. Sally is now rocking gently and then she reaches across to the bath where there's a pale blue facecloth wrapped into a tight bundle and stained with streaks of blood.

'There was something, Beth. I'm afraid to look.' At first I'm confused, not following, but she coaxes me with her eyes, fixed on the cloth, and I'm suddenly appalled. I don't want her to say it out loud, to think it even. She is clearly mistaken in her grief – gone mad in her grief.

'It's OK. It can't be, darling. It's much too early. There would be nothing. *Nothing.* I promise you.' But her face is tortured, her eyes huge.

'But we can't just leave it. In case. Can we, Beth? *In case?*' Her hand is trembling and I see she's beyond reassurance. She's lost too much blood. Has lost too much. Again she rocks, to and fro, and I don't waste any more time trying to reason with her. Instead I move the hair back from her face, take the cloth gently from her hand and promise that no one will leave it behind. I'll take care of everything if she will just let the ambulance crew in. *Please.* And so she nods. And I do not know which frightens me most – the bundle in my hand or the trust in her eyes as I open the bathroom door and they rush to take care of her as I cannot.

She's resigned now, not even protesting when Richard insists on accompanying her in the ambulance. I tell the crew I'll follow in my car and nod to Sally, the stained cloth still in my hand, so that she knows I will keep my word. Which I do.

I put the little bundle into an empty toiletry bag from the bathroom shelf, feeling sick, and place it in the boot of my car so that I can follow the ambulance. It seems an appalling thing to do, even though I feel sure Sally must be mistaken.

At the hospital there's a lot of waiting and a lot of tests. Sal is reassured there should be no complications. Still she cries and cries. I smooth her hair and want to stay with her but am made to go to this horrid waiting room while she talks to Richard. It's a cold space which smells of disinfectant and forbidden cigarettes. In the corner sits a drinks machine with a dent along the bottom and an OUT OF ORDER sign dangling from a piece of brown, shrivelled sellotape. I'm tempted to try it for the excuse to add my own boot mark. Instead I pace. And think. Which is not good.

I picture the cardboard box in the corner of our spare room where I've already started to collect Sam's baby things. Tempting fate.

I kick the drinks machine anyway and then, after two hours, I'm allowed back to learn that Richard has left. Sally has sent him away – not for the first time, but for the last. So finally I take her home with me, driving more slowly this time, and because there is nothing to say I just hold her hand between the gear changes.

It's no real surprise that she's ended it with Richard. Sally found out about his latest affair just after the positive pregnancy test. No reason left now to be brave; to try.

I remember so well the night we found out about his first affair, how I watched as she sat on the cream carpet of their bedroom floor and cut up his clothes – his Armani suit, his Hugo Boss jacket. *Snip. Snip. Snip.*

She stays with me for two weeks and I buy a magnolia tree – a cliché and a crutch, which in its black plastic pot does not look special enough but is the only thing I can think of.

There was the most beautiful magnolia tree at the school where Sally and I met. She always loved that tree, sitting against the trunk in the shade to read – her face in camouflage from the light dancing through the leaves.

I dig a large hole and she just nods – her face in camouflage from darker shadows now.

We both know that there's nothing in the toiletry bag. That, of course, being the problem. The *nothing.*

So we bury the bag anyway, deep below the new tree in my garden, knowing her own beloved garden will be sold. And we say a prayer, and not much else.

The tree now stands tall and quite beautiful – magnolias blooming briefly but magnificently, like Sally's happiness over her child. Every spring when I watch the petals lost to the wind, I think of the fragility of our dreams.

It's the hardest thing I have helped Sally through but not the hardest thing I have done.

For there is another friend – a ghost of a friend – waiting in the shadows.

With more yet to ask of me.

CHAPTER 2

BETH - NOW

Seven springs pass before our letters: two identical cream envelopes delivered to two very different homes. Sally opens hers in the tranquillity of a flat with white carpets and white sofas.

I lose mine.

The postman hands it to me through the window of the car as we sit on our drive, all set for the chaos of a half-term family holiday. It's taken two hours of bikes, boxes and the boys' bickering to get to this point. I glance at Adam and wonder if he's thinking what I'm thinking.

Before the kids, he liked to surprise me. 'Pack warm, Beth,' he would say, grinning. Or 'snow clothes', refusing to confirm where we were going until the airport.

And now? I watch the rain tracing a little river around the windscreen wiper. I thank the heavens that Forests for Families has an indoor 'swimarium'. But then I take out the booking sheet for the sat nav code.

'Oh Lord, Adam – what's the date?'

'The sixteenth.'

I stare at the holiday paperwork in front of me as if staring may change it, but no.

Back in the house all is very soon bedlam.

'We've missed the holiday! You're seriously telling me we've *missed the holiday?*' It's Adam's turn now to stare, white with shock, as the boys hurl themselves on to their backs on the carpet, wailing in stereo and cycling their legs in the air like bluebottles hit by insecticide.

'How can anyone get the dates wrong for a holiday? The *wrong week!*'

This from the man who has not booked a holiday, let alone a surprise, since the boys arrived. For a nanosecond I consider pointing this out to him but reconsider just in time. I'm in trouble enough.

Adam's tone matches his face, which says he does not yet believe it. I don't, to be fair, entirely blame him, hardly believing it myself. Even the woman at bookings HQ can't believe it.

'You've actually *missed . . . your week?*' she says.

I know, I know. I grip the phone under my chin as she checks the computer records and wave my arms for the boys and Adam to *hush, please* so I might plead my mitigation more effectively.

I confess that it's my fault, that I am indeed hopeless. That I must have been in a muddle over the half-term dates when I booked. That I'm very, very sorry but surely they can offer us something. *Anything. Seeing as we're regulars?*

The line goes quiet for a moment. I've already been reminded that the resort is *always full in the school holidays, madam.* I've tried offering more money, which they have politely declined. Then I ask plaintively why they didn't notice that I didn't turn up last week. *Who was in my fully paid-up, luxury two-bed last week?* This seems to help. The bluebottles still their legs to listen.

Finally the bookings lady is back, offering me a lodge with a slightly faulty patio door. 'Technically out of service for an upgrade, you understand.'

I tell her that she's saved my life and my marriage. I take down the new reference number, put the phone down triumphantly and punch the air.

Which must be when I drop the letter. And it falls behind the radiator. Which explains why I don't know about the event that is to change all our lives so desperately and darkly and irrevocably until Sally phones on our return.

◆ ◆ ◆

'So what on earth are we going to do?'

'About what?'

'Beth, don't play around, please. This is serious.'

'I'm sorry, Sal. But I'm not following you. I've barely unpacked . . .'

'The school, Beth – the school closure.'

I am now eating a tuna mayonnaise roll in the kitchen, surrounded by a mountain of holiday washing, talking to Sally through mouthfuls. Today I've shaped the washing as Kilimanjaro to remind myself of the days when I did not know that my mountains were to be made of washing – and molehills. I can't believe that we have worn all these clothes in just four days. Come to think of it, I don't even recognise some of these clothes.

I turn away from Kilimanjaro as an unfamiliar yellow sock falls from the peak to concentrate on Sally. I have absolutely no idea what she's talking about but these days this is not an altogether unusual state of affairs. Much of the time Sally has no idea what she's talking about either.

'I don't know what you're talking about. Which school?' A picture of my boys' school flashes into my mind but she must have it wrong – I'd have heard something before she did, surely? I reach across to flick the switch on the kettle.

There's a long pause, and the silence feels odd. Next, Sally is talking too fast.

'The *convent* closure. Didn't you get your letter? Christ, Beth, you need to swallow your bloody pride and get back on Facebook. This is serious. It's everywhere. All over Twitter too. The convent is out of nuns. They're selling the site and the whole place is being demolished. Senior school, boarding bit – the lot. They're having some big farewell bash. Jeez, you're on the school website. I can't believe you didn't get your letter?'

It's only now, as the kettle grumbles into action, that I remember the cream envelope with the postcode from Sussex – which, yes, I was holding in my hand as we marched the boys back into the house through the rain.

'Sorry. Been chaotic. Must have lost it.'

Sally tuts. Her life since the divorce could not be more different from mine. I had rather hoped she would have met someone nice by now. But it hasn't happened. So she lives an orderly existence in a flat that is too tidy and too quiet, and apart from losing her marbles long ago (in my fond opinion) she never, ever loses anything.

I pop the final piece of tuna roll into my mouth and feel the beginnings of an involuntary frown. There's a strange sensation in my stomach also. I have not allowed myself to think of the Convent of St Colman. Not in years.

Sal pauses and I make a break for milk from the fridge, by which time she's babbling on about the nuns. How many will still be alive? She's still talking much too quickly, her voice unnaturally high, while the stirring in my stomach is getting more and more uncomfortable.

'Oh, for Christ's sake, will you say something, Elizabeth.' Her voice is lowered now, the faux jollity abandoned.

Elizabeth? She never calls me that . . .

'So what the *hell* are we going to do?' Sally's voice is barely audible.

And now it comes. A single wave, first of cold dread and then a stronger, creeping realisation like an anaesthetic wearing off through each and every muscle, so that I stop dividing the washing into piles and stand suddenly very, very still.

I'm so used to *not* thinking about this that the shock is now truly physical. Tingling. Chemicals through the blood. Yes, a creeping through my entire body as if all the nerves are reawakening.

'So, you're thinking that she'll have seen all this?'

I do not say her name.

Carol.

The name we do not say.

'I don't know, Beth. But – possibly. So what do you think? We just do nothing. Yes? Just leave it to her?'

I pause for longer this time to listen to Sal's breathing – also my own pulse in my ear, louder and louder as I press the phone closer to my head.

Carol.

I close my eyes as if this will cut off the sound, the breathing and the pulse. But it does not.

'You really think she'll have seen this?'

'I don't know. I don't know. But with social media – possibly. Probably. So you agree, yes? That we do nothing? Yes?'

I sit down. Christ.

Carol.

All these years.

'Beth. Will you please, please, just *say* something.'

◆　◆　◆

It's three days before Sally and I can face each other, three days in which I go through all the day-to-day motions like a sleepwalker. Automatic pilot. Breakfast. Load the dishwasher. Lunch. Unpack the dishwasher. To. Fro. To fro.

Each evening I watch the news and find myself looking across at Adam. I imagine footage of diggers and workmen and stinking mud, then a newsreader saying it: *A body has been found . . .*

12

'Are you all right, Beth? You look white as a sheet.'

'I'm fine, Adam.' A lie. So many lies.

At night I do not sleep and so am exhausted when finally Sally says she's ready to meet. She suggests Julio's on the High Street and I know precisely why. It's for the comfort and the reassurance of being regulars there, for the noise and the bustle and the sense of normality which is so at odds with how terrible this now feels.

Julio's is the very best of its kind – dated and endearing with candles dripping wax down empty Frascati bottles and faded prints of Italy in cheap frames around the walls. There are lots of photos too of Julio with his beloved family and his favourite customers. A few also of half-forgotten stars who call in over Christmas, playing panto at the local theatre in the twilight of their careers. And there in the middle of the display is a picture of me and Sally with pink eyes from the flash and Julio beaming alongside a matching pink birthday cake.

In the photograph Sal is all smiles and larks but not today as she arrives, late and awkward – waving through the window but refusing to quite meet my eyes, shaking her umbrella nervously and gossiping just a tad too long at the front desk before she will join me.

I plug the gap with too much gin and tonic, rereading the letter found amid the cobwebs behind the radiator. The Order of St Colman, in the latest downturn, is out of both money and nuns. It was an order originally based in Belgium, which came to run the convent school near Rye decades back, but apparently there's a problem with too few young women joining the Order and too few girls enrolling in the school. The upshot renders it impractical and uneconomic to continue with the boarding wing of the school, which makes the whole secondary school unviable. So it's over. The teaching is to continue for primary pupils only on a new, smaller site across town but there is to be no more secondary school. And no more boarders. The entire site is being sold for redevelopment. The existing boarders are already under transfer to other schools as they complete their exams.

The tone of the letter is sad but promises a spectacular curtain call. Not a reunion, this – a goodbye.

Sally is clutching a printout of the website message as she sits down while Julio pours her wine, knowing better than to ask for our order yet.

'No wonder they can't get enough nuns.' Sally's tucking her hair behind her ear. 'No sex – what a way to live.'

I remember then that Sally has not in fact had sex for the best part of three years herself but will not say this.

'So, then.' She's still feigning brightness but is fiddling with her hair. Tuck, tuck, tuck. 'Look, I've done a lot of thinking.' She pours herself water, lowering her voice, and re-tucks the hair. 'The way I see it, nothing has changed. We made a promise, Beth. And this doesn't alter anything. Not really . . .'

I examine her face. Her eyes are as tired as mine. 'Look, Sal. I understand why this is especially hard for you—'

'*No, Beth. Please* . . .' She's raised her voice so that a couple glance across from the other side of the restaurant. 'Sorry, I'm sorry,' lowering her voice again and fiddling with the cutlery, straightening first the knives and then the spoons. Moving the bread plate slightly to the left. 'I'm not going to talk about it, Beth. I can't. It's not that I don't care. You know that. But you ask me to talk about it and . . .'

I want to talk. I burn to talk. I want to tell her that I worry we'll be found out and the husband I love will leave me. My family will implode.

Instead we sit for a long time in silence, Sal's lips tight and her eyes closed while I think what to do next. I think of Pandora's box. I think about loyalty. I think about a promise that I wish with every ounce of my being I had never, ever made . . .

I think about a room of blood. A girl with blue lips . . .

But most of all I think of Carol.

For the last three nights I've lain in bed awake thinking about nothing but her. I've tried so hard to picture her in some entirely new and normal life – painting, house, kids, watercolours.

I pick the lemon slice from the dregs of my gin and tonic, put it into my mouth and suck really hard. 'You know I'm not going to say anything. Not after all these years – not to anyone, Sal.'

'So we leave things?'

'We can't. Not this time. It's too risky – when you first phoned me, you *knew* that . . .'

'I was just panicking. I've had time to think now. She would want us to leave it. It might still be OK.'

I don't want to be the one to say it and so I look away to the door to the kitchens and then back. I picture them knocking the convent down. Bulldozers and stinking mud.

'This is her call, Sally. I'm sorry, but I need to hear it from her. This time we have to find her.' I say it very quickly and with my eyes closed as if this will somehow make it less dangerous.

When I finally open them, Sally does exactly what I've been dreading. She stares for a long time at the tablecloth and then up at me with an expression that goes beyond sadness and darkness – a look of abject wretchedness and bleakness.

A look I had hoped never to see on her face again.

CHAPTER 3

BETH - BEFORE

I was eleven years old when I first set eyes on the Convent of St Colman and I have never forgotten my disappointment. It was like finding out about Father Christmas. A childhood dream shattered.

I blame Enid Blyton, to be frank, for on the long drive through the patchwork of orchards and undulating farmland of Kent on to Sussex, I had conjured up a fantasy of jolly japes and midnight feasts in a real-life version of Mallory Towers. I had drawn a clear picture in my head of some National Trust treasure – an imposing manor house with cream stucco walls, pale pink roses growing up the front and ponies grazing in the paddock.

My parents were almost bursting with pride at the prospect of their daughter going to boarding school and for two weeks had been reminding me daily what a grand step *up* in the world this was to be. So it had occurred to none of us that the school itself might be falling *down*.

As we turned the corner and swept into the little drive to the large car park in front of the convent, I knew that my mother was as shocked as I was by the crumbling façade that greeted us. I knew it from the little look she exchanged with my father and from the little cough as she cleared her throat before speaking.

But my mother was a spin doctor before they were invented. All her clouds came with silver linings and I watched her eyes perform their familiar scan for something to talk up.

'*Beautiful garden*, Beth,' she pronounced finally and I watched her fondly then as she raised her eyebrows in the familiar high arch that was a signal to my father to help buoy my spirits. I watched her point out all the plants and admire the views as I struggled with the ache deep in my stomach – my first taste of homesickness – the fear suddenly of how I would manage, away from my mother's spectacular optimism.

Later I would remember that moment often and with great fondness because my mother, as usual, was right. The garden was the very best thing about the Convent of St Colman and in time I grew to love it – a breathtaking jumble of roses and cottage garden plants, elbowing each other for space in a blur of colour. Years on, I would lie on the grass with Sal and Carol, revising for exams, watching butterflies drift from buddleia to buddleia. Soothed and safe.

But that first day, I was blind to it all. Blind to the magic. Nothing but nothing could distract me from the horrible truth of the boarding house itself.

The Convent of St Colman was a wreck. It had bits missing. And it smelled.

I should deal with the smell first since it's the thing I remember most about that initial visit. The school was made up of one large modern building linked via a dilapidated orangery to an old manor house converted into the boarding accommodation. This original Georgian house, flat-fronted and painted a strange shade of salmon, was where our tour began. The odour hit you the moment you went through the large entrance lobby – a sort of sweet, pungent dampness. The popular myth among the boarders, I was to learn, was that it was the smell of a decaying nun who'd been bricked up alive in the walls a century back as punishment for breaking her vows and falling pregnant.

My father always preferred the less exotic explanation of rising damp.

But whatever the cause, to disguise the whiff, the nuns filled the old boarding house with flowers from the gardens. Fresh blooms in large vases and dried petals in bowls. This had the effect of making the boarding section seem very homely (despite being smelly) and I could see that my mother approved of this touch.

As for the bits missing? A simple question of mathematics. The Convent of St Colman, despite its fees, was in perpetual financial crisis. So when a chunk of stone fell off a balustrade, or a piece of carving gave up its battle with the damp, it would simply be swept up. And when another crack appeared in the salmon plasterwork outside, the nuns would plant yet another vigorous climber.

The end result was a fantastic garden, but a school that appeared to be supported entirely by plant life. Too much pruning of the ivy or clematis and I rather suspected the lot would come down.

'It's horrible,' I managed to whisper eventually as we followed a tall, slim nun through the hall.

'Nonsense, dear. Let's give it a chance.'

My father said nothing at all, leaving the jollying to my mother who led the way, following a series of arrows drawn in red ink on sheets of white A4 paper taped to the wooden panelling. They led us eventually to a dining room where we were divided into smaller groups for a full tour – ours directed by the same tall nun who had greeted us and who now introduced herself as Sister Veronica. She was far too attractive to be a nun and I began to suspect she'd been hired in from some agency. Yes – like a nun from central casting to impress the parents and distract the eye from the school's very obvious failings. The tour was swift. The boarding wing first. Dormitories. Bathrooms. Dining hall. Common rooms. And then through the orangery to the school block. All passed me in a blur as I noticed only peeling paintwork. And the smell.

I was measured for uniform and we were given glossy brochures – realising only then why the illustration of the school on the front was a line drawing and not a photograph. In the car on the way home, I wished for the first time that I had failed the entrance exam.

'So what did you think?'

'It's not what I expected.'

'Never judge a book.' My father took in a deep breath. 'Just think – our Beth at boarding school.' And he said it with such pride, such hope and apparent belief that this would be my *big chance*, whatever the state of the premises, that I did not have the heart to back out.

And so just two months later, we repeated the journey for my first term proper. Bags in the back. Bags under my eyes. Mum in the front sniffling into a handkerchief.

I had been so dreading the final goodbye that in the end I waved them off rather too quickly, keen not to cry. I remember so clearly the immediate regret and vivid temptation to forget the whole sorry idea and run after the car.

Instead I was shown to my dormitory by the now familiar Sister Veronica, who introduced me to the other girls, who were already unpacking. The three on the opposite side of the room were obviously and enviably well acquainted, huddled up gossiping. They smiled but then returned immediately to their holiday stories.

My name was drawn neatly in black ink on a label stuck to my headboard on the other side of the room and the two girls alongside me – Carol and Sally, according to the same slanted handwriting – looked as awkward as I did.

We were not yet in our uniforms so the differences between us were clear. The huddled trio wore their wealth and privilege casually. Their suitcases were well travelled, their clothes expensive, their summer holiday conversation of another world.

On our side of the room things were very different. All with shiny, virgin suitcases – mine in pale blue plastic from a cheap catalogue.

There were more labels with our names on the little dressing tables alongside our beds and on large painted wardrobes in the corner of the dormitory. As I unzipped my first case, the established trio chatted more loudly, confirming my worst fear – that they had all been at the convent's primary school together.

Sal, Carol and I exchanged nervous smiles as we began to unpack – clothes first, which wasn't too bad, but then the pang in my stomach returned as I realised we would all have to make up our beds. I had been secretly dreading this. Duvets were not yet allowed – something to do with the laundry routine – and the inventory had demanded two blankets and four sheets. A week earlier my mother had set aside two dark grey army-issue blankets and I was mortified. I'd guessed (correctly) that everyone else would have the soft and fluffy coloured blankets edged with shiny ribbon that I'd seen in adverts for smart hotels and I'd pleaded with my mother to buy some new ones. I'm embarrassed now to think back on how much it mattered to me to have ribbon-edged blankets but Mum, in her silver-lining voice, explained the army grant would cover the fees only. The uniform had stretched their budget to the limit. There was nothing left over for new bedding. Not this term. *Maybe next term, Beth.*

I was a lucky girl to be going to boarding school, remember.

So I stalled over the bed-making for as long as possible, leaving the dreaded blankets in the bottom of my case and pretending to reorganise my clothes as the others drifted downstairs for tea. Carol was genuinely behind so was left in the dormitory with me so it was Carol who found me out. And it was Carol who first saw me cry.

'It's OK,' she soothed. 'We'll get used to it.'

'I'm not homesick. It's not that.'

I rubbed the bridge of my nose and looked directly at her face – taking in for the first time just how beautiful she was. Straw blonde hair, long and straight, and bright blue eyes – one of them with a tiny beauty spot just below the eyebrow as though someone on the production line had decided on a miniscule flaw to ensure she looked real. I rubbed again at my nose, too miserable even to be jealous.

'It's the bedding.' I was blushing now, feeling stupid. Wretched. 'Mine's horrid. I didn't want anyone to see.'

Carol looked puzzled and so I showed her the grey army-issue blankets.

She paused then for no more than a couple of seconds, her forehead relaxing with the decision, and quite matter-of-factly did something that said everything about the person she is. She didn't try to persuade me that my blankets were anything other than ugly. She just whipped the pink blankets off her own bed.

'We'll share. One grey one on the bottom and the pink on the top. With the eiderdown, no one will see anyway.'

I genuinely couldn't believe it. My humiliation spared. My life *saved*. By this complete stranger.

And do you know what? I loved her instantly for it. For surprising me. For being nicer than me. For being more generous and giving than you dared hope of someone whose looks could so easily have afforded less effort, and as we walked down to tea together, with her beaming encouragement, I felt a wave of complete relief – a realisation as welcome as it was surprising that the Convent of St Colman was going to be all right after all.

Over tea and cakes, Carol explained that she was only at boarding school because her mother had got lucky on a lottery. 'Oh heavens, not a *big* win.' She was teasing as our eyes widened. 'I was all for blowing it: cruise, flash car – something like that. But Mum gives me this big lecture about education and *opportunity*. So here I am.'

Sally said she was on an armed forces grant also – her parents believing, like mine, that it was time to stop school-hopping with the military postings and to settle in one place to work towards exams. She told us her mother had cried for the whole journey and we each rolled our eyes, pretending to be exasperated by our parents, but each secretly missing them.

And as I looked from one to the other – Carol and then Sally – I just *knew* that something important had begun.

So that when I lay in bed that first night, sniffing the pillow which smelled of home and made me picture my mother, smiling at me from the ironing board, I traced my fingers across the pink blanket to soothe myself and thanked God for my new friends.

And to this day when I see the colour pink it makes me feel good.

And it makes me think of Carol.

CHAPTER 4

CAROL - NOW

Tuesday

Here in France they now call me Carole.

Car-OLE. Car-OLE. All the emphasis wrong. But I'm used to it now. Used to everything now.

These days we live mostly in the south, which I find too hot though I love the garden – not the pool with its huge fat fish motif, mouth gaping at the pale turquoise tiles, and not the terraces which Ned had designed by that dreadful architect friend from Lyon, but the plants. I love the shade of the vine and the colours in the borders.

It's where I'm sitting today. To calm myself.

There's been another message on the school website and on the Facebook page too – with pleas to get in touch, just a whisper short of desperate this time. Get your tickets, girls. Book now . . . Carol – where are you? Blah de blah.

I'm trying very hard not to think of them. Beth and Sally.

No.

Keep busy. Plan supper . . .

I must remind Pierre that the Hayles are coming to eat and that Ella is a vegetarian.

Pierre always threatens to quit when I request vegetarian food. He has no time for people who will not eat meat, he tells me. It will serve them right, he says, if he puts foie gras or horsemeat in their casserole.

I pretend to laugh each time but fear secretly that he's serious.

I have flattered. Cajoled. Suggested his mushroom dish, which I assure him no other chef could prepare so well.

For now he's humming. And not yet drinking. Both good signs.

And there's plenty of time. Ned will be early. The Hayles will be late. Even now I can see Jonathan in the distance on the tractor working the largest of their fields. They've been here just a few months and still dream of being farmers, too new yet to know that here the sun bakes dreams to dust.

I'll watch until he checks the time and realises he needs to shower away this heat – this dust. And when he goes inside, I will go inside. To check the table, check the wine, check the mushroom dish for foie gras.

To wear my new name.

To be a good girl.

CHAPTER 5

BETH - NOW

I haven't told Sally this, but I've looked for Carol before. Not seriously – not like this. Tentative inquiries which when they bore no fruit I put aside. Excuses. The boys. Work. Adam. *Her choice. Her right.*

And now?

One solid week of trying every trick in the book (and heaven help me, I know a few) and too late I'm confirming what deep down I already knew. That Carol does not want to be found, that nothing is all right. That the builders who are going to knock down the Convent of St Colman are going to knock down our whole lives with it.

Back in Julio's I'm wondering how to tell Sally what I've been up to when—

'Ah! Miss Houdini.'

Damn.

'I was rather hoping I'd find you here. Didn't you get any of my messages?'

'Sorry?'

'The *gay parents*, Beth? Really need to know where we're at?'

Heads turn our way. Dear Lord. The latest politically incorrect aberration for the cable television series my boss, Stella, laughingly calls *The Meeting of Minds* – a show she insists is about empathy, bringing six people together to share a common experience, but which in reality is a painful, low-budget and dated version of the worst talk shows long since jettisoned by the main networks.

'I'm wondering if we've had any luck with the cross-dresser?'

'Working on it, Stella.'

'Good. Good. Look – I know you have reservations. And I know you all think we should be moving into all this reality nonsense but talk shows are coming back, I just know it. Empathy is what people want – trust me, Beth – *empathy*.'

I stare at the empty seat opposite.

'Oh, for heaven's sake, don't stress, darling. I'm not joining you. Gonna eat and run. But you will get back to me on this? The cross-dresser? By tomorrow – latest?'

'Yes, of course, Stella. Working on it, I promise you.'

'Good. Good. *Buon appetito.*'

And then she's gone – back to her iPad at a table soon heaving with food that she tucks into greedily, unlike the poor studio guests, hand-picked by me, who are forced to sit around an oversized coffee table laden with cakes that they're forbidden to touch.

Do not eat the cakes we warn at the beginning of each recording, the litigation from our pilot programme still unresolved after the floor manager's inexpert attempt at the Heimlich manoeuvre allegedly broke two ribs of a woman who'd choked on a macaroon.

I snap breadsticks as across the room Stella shovels Julio's veal in cream sauce into her mouth. It occurs to me that I'd love to shove her job there also. But I'm forgetting myself, forgetting the post's bittersweet trump card. *Convenience.* That I can work from home. That the horror of the studio is only twice a month. And that, as a freelance researcher, I badly need the money.

'No Sally yet?' Julio has brought over a gin and tonic and stands as a temporary shield, using a tilt of the head towards Stella by way of a question.

'The mad boss. The one we call Cruella.'

He winces in sympathy, signalling for the waiter to top up my drink to a double on the house before heading off to the kitchen.

I check my watch, then stare at our birthday picture on the wall; stare and stare until my eyes are smarting, my mind on walkabout.

◆ ◆ ◆

Another restaurant. Another birthday. Candles. *Make a wish, Beth. Close your eyes.*

But it's not the pink cake now. Chocolate. A more elaborate affair.

It's Essex. My thirtieth. The last time we arranged to see Carol. Can it really be so long ago? Sam a toddler and Harry just a baby. No money back then but still the fuss. Balloons and bunting. And – yes, Italian food. Though I remember that I'm not enjoying myself because it's nearly midnight. Still no Carol.

In the background, I can hear Adam trying to jolly me along. Sal too. 'Maybe their hire car broke down. Or the plane was delayed?'

'She would have phoned.' I'm staring through a gap in the louvre blind covering the restaurant door, the melee behind me pounding at my headache. The blind is covered in dust and every time I stretch the gap wider for a better view of the road, particles are dispersed, tickling at my throat.

I think we should call someone. Her mother? The hospitals? 'She said she'd come, Adam.'

'I know, love – but all the way from France. Anything could have held her up.'

'She said she'd be here.' My throat is still parched by the dust.

Sally, next to Adam, is wearing her brave face. 'Come on, Beth. We have a surprise.'

I let them lead me away and they produce a cake shaped like a grand piano – a masterpiece of sponge and cream – and I'm touched by Sally's thoughtfulness, having kidded her that I'll take lessons again.

I have my picture taken with that cake – me pretending to play the keys of cream and chocolate with Sal beaming alongside, and only when the photograph is developed and framed on top of Gran's hand-me-down piano, its keys still dusty and neglected, do I see just how strained we look. Me and Sal. The smiles so false. Our first milestone picture with Carol missing.

And then at half past midnight I'm back at the door, the first to see them – the car a shiny BMW convertible which finds a space right outside the restaurant, parking very carefully so that the tyres are just shy of the kerb, the car perfectly straight.

Carol's new boyfriend is driving – Ned, whom we have met only a couple of times. Tall and very smiley. Rich too, apparently. For a moment my spirits lift. I imagine they'll rush in with mortified apologies, and there will be hugs and kisses and champagne. And we'll retake the picture. But they do not. They just sit there. No row. No rush. Nothing. They just sit there.

And then, unaware that I'm watching, Carol takes a long, deep breath before she opens the car door. I have replayed that moment so many times, taking in the breath myself to feel it. Trying to excuse it. To explain it. But there's no mistaking it. It's the kind of breath you take before a driving test or a job interview, to pull yourself up to face something unpleasant but unavoidable.

I remember feeling angry at first – fearing she's just humouring me from her smart new life. But no. It's worse than that.

On the doorstep Carol wears a false smile. She mumbles lies about airport delays and problems with the hire car. Ned all the while beams.

Never mind – we're here now, Carol. Just look at this cake. Wow! Who made this cake?

Within twenty minutes Carol is complaining of a headache. Ned says that we should maybe try an aspirin. *Give it half an hour. See how it goes?* He takes her aside and seems to be pleading with her. He touches her face ever so gently as if encouraging her, but Carol shakes her head. Fetches her coat.

So sorry, Beth. A disaster. But this headache is a bad one – it'll turn into a migraine if I don't lie down . . .

Standing back in that doorway, Carol says she'll call me, but I know from the look on her face that she won't. And I realise in a panic suddenly that she has come not to humour me, but for something else entirely. And I don't understand.

To say *goodbye*? After all we have been through, all of these years. The thing that we did. The secret. The promise.

Our promise.

Why now? Why is she ending it now?

◆ ◆ ◆

'You OK, Beth?' Sally is right beside the table, two menus in her hand. It takes me a while to pull myself back to the present. Julio's. A glance to remind myself that my boss is still here.

'Sorry. Yes. No. Jeez – I don't know.' My hand knocks the flower vase and Sally lunges only just in time to prevent it spilling. She sits down slowly, moving the vase to a neighbouring table.

'No joy then? Trying to trace Carol?'

I shake my head, whispering that I have tried everything. Brick wall. No social media presence. Nothing on her mother. Tried everyone I can think of in Brighton. Post office. Dry cleaners. Gyms. They moved but no one knows where. It's as if they just disappeared.

'Could be she's just fine. Moved on and doesn't want—'

29

'—to be found.' I watch her face. 'Sorry. I didn't mean it to come out like that.' I direct her gaze across the room. 'Stella's here. Making me tense.'

Sally pours wine and for a moment it's very strained, neither of us wanting to take the lead. Get it wrong. She looks like me. Exhausted.

'You not sleeping either, Sal?'

'So – what about Ned. I mean, he was successful. Property portfolio. Guy like that must have his own company, surely. Website? LinkedIn?'

'Without a surname?'

'Mattings? Mattlings? Matthews? Oh heavens – I don't know.' She shakes her head. Carol hadn't been with Ned for long before she disappeared. Her boyfriends rarely lasted long, so checking his surname hadn't seemed important.

I take out my phone and call up the page. 'Look, I don't want you to get upset, OK? And it may seem drastic. But I always assumed we could find her if we really needed to.'

I pass her the phone and she begins to read, her eyes instantly narrowing. 'Have you gone completely mad, Beth? A private investigator?' Her voice is a panicked whisper as she hands the phone straight back.

'Look, Sal, I know what you're thinking and this is hard for me too. But I really need to know what she wants to do.'

'She won't want to do anything, Beth. You know that.'

'So I hear that from her. And I stop this. OK?' A pause during which my heartbeat is quickening. 'In any case, we may not get to choose . . .' I think again of the building work. I think of a policeman at the door and Adam's shock. My whole life crumbling around me.

For a moment I lock eyes with Sal but then she takes a deep breath to look first up at the ceiling and then at the table. Between us is a candle, flickering in the draught from the door to the restaurant kitchen. I stare into the glow and as the air settles I can see those other tapers – the three candles in a church. Steady flames that we lit together in the stillness on that terrible day so long ago. I imagine in her dreams that Sally sees them too. Though I dare not ask. We're both looking into this new flame – dancing once more, as a waiter carrying a large tray swings the door open with his foot.

Finally Sally reaches out for the phone again. This time she reads more carefully and I can see her pupils dilate. 'You realise, don't you, that a private investigator will ask a lot of questions?'

'I'll think of something. And we can split the cost, Sally. Also, if you're worried about taking time off work, I don't mind taking the lead on this—'

Sally's expression changes again and I know from her new face that she has something to tell me.

I know all Sally's faces.

'What is it, Sal? What is it you're not saying?'

She takes a large mouthful of wine. 'I've lost my job, Beth.' Her tone is of complete surprise, shaping each word ever so carefully as if she's hearing them for the first time. As if the words themselves are fragile and may shatter. 'As if we haven't enough to worry about, the bastards have just made me redundant.'

CHAPTER 6
CAROL – NOW

Thursday

I don't know whether to be angry or just sad. Another con artist. Madame Bouvoire, it turns out, is no more special than I am. The gift? Don't make me laugh.

I had such high hopes too this time. Eloise, who lost her mother at Christmas, spoke so highly. Such comfort, she said. Such a clever, genuine woman. She found her through some spiritualist church. 'Carole,' she said to me, 'you must see her. She'll bring you such peace.'

I believed her.

But no.

I'm only glad now that I did not use my real name. Ned worries so much about this stuff – it's why I have to keep all this scribbling so secret. He would fuss and fret and cancel his work and try to make me see a doctor about my eating . . .

I can't see any more doctors. I won't.

In any case, the way I see it, it shouldn't matter whether you use a real name or not if these people are genuine.

I guessed the worst as soon as I saw where she lived – a cramped second-floor apartment with a budgerigar in a cage in the corner.

And so many questions. Question after question as the blessed bird hopped about, biting the wire of its cage. And I'm thinking – why so many questions if she has the gift? It's answers I want, not questions.

In the end she told me it was my grandmother who was trying to contact me. On my mother's side.

A long rambling charade about cancer and crochet.

I paid her bill but threw the CD away. Gran didn't even knit.

It makes me so very angry – all this. Do people honestly not realise how much this means? That if I can't find someone who can really do this, how the hell am I supposed to work out how to go forward?

I guess I'll just have to start looking again and be more careful. Yesterday Ned almost found this diary. I can only imagine how much he would worry. I normally keep it carefully hidden away but I've been so distracted – so much on my mind with all the messages, stirring it all up – that I left it on the bedside table. Dear Lord.

He's away again for a week – Ned. Left after breakfast. Another of his property deals. I don't ask questions any more. Rationalisation, he likes to call it – sounds so much more respectable than asset stripping.

'Just another bankrupt builder, darling,' he said at the airport. 'Look, it's nothing for you to worry about,' as if the misery that goes with it all is of no consequence. The trouble is I do worry. I worry about everything, which is why he doesn't like me to be so involved these days.

I can see his face now – completely baffled. 'It's not our job to rescue them, Carol. I know this seems harsh but we don't make them bankrupt. They make themselves bankrupt. We don't make the mess, we just clear it up.'

I so wanted to say it: Who will clear up our mess? That thing we did all those years ago. Me and Beth and Sally.

But I can't ask, can I? There's no one to ask.

CHAPTER 7

BETH - NOW

'I need a favour.' Sally's voice is a whisper in my ear. The bedroom is dark, the curtains still drawn. I hold the phone away for a moment to check the display.

'Sally. It's six o'clock in the morning.'

'Six? Really? Sorry – I thought it was later. I'm a bit wired.'

'Hang on.' I glance at Adam alongside me who rolls over, apparently still asleep, and so I pad from the bed, across the hall to the box room I use as an office.

'Right, fire away. I take it you've decided on a tribunal?' Another glance at my phone confirms twelve new messages – they're bound to be from Cruella. Just four days until our next filming and I'm still one guest short.

'Nope, no tribunal, Beth. Sorted it all last night – compromise agreement. Listen, can you take some time off?'

'Today?' I'm yawning, thinking once more of Stella. I need to find a woman whose husband has had an affair with the au pair and is prepared to talk about it on camera. *By Wednesday.*

'I'm still very behind, Sal.'

'Please. Just a couple of hours. I can pick you up after you've done the school run. Say, ten?'

'I suppose.'

◆ ◆ ◆

Later, as her car draws up, radio blaring, I know for certain that things are even worse. It's raining and Sally, who hates the cold, has the car roof down. Also she's wearing no make-up – unheard of – along with her decorating trousers. Baggy overalls splattered with the colour for her kitchen. MEMORIES OF LINEN on the paint pot label – bog-standard magnolia on the walls.

'I told you to wear old clothes,' she says.

'I am. According to my husband, I always do.' Not a smile. Nothing. Instead she turns the radio up even more – Adele. I like Adele, but not this loud in an open top on my drive.

'So what's going on, Sal? Why the mystery and where are we going?' But still she can't hear me. As we pull away it's almost as if she's in some kind of trance. I wonder if raking up the past and the job loss is simply too much, has tipped her over the edge?

Our village is not far from Plymouth where Adam teaches history in one of the largest secondary schools. Sally heads in the opposite direction towards the South Hams, eventually taking one of the narrow roads towards Bigbury.

'So we're going to the beach?'

'What?'

'Bigbury. Are we going to *Bigbury*?'

'Sorry. Can't hear.' She's tapping the steering wheel to the beat. Justin Bieber now.

'Can we turn it down a bit, Sally?'

'Sorry?'

I give up, signalling with my hand that it doesn't matter. We have to pull into the hedge several times to let traffic past on the narrow stretches, and I'm just thinking how it would drive me to road rage, living in such a place, when Sally suddenly turns the car off the lane and pulls up in a narrow bay outside a row of cottages.

Finally she snaps off the radio, gets out of the car then takes off her sunglasses. 'So what do you think?'

'Sorry? I'm not following. Think about what?'

'The cottages.'

Sally picks her way through a patch of nettles to stand nearer the properties, which are set back about twenty feet from the lane. She signals with her head that I should follow her.

There are four cottages in the row, completely ramshackle. Some of the windows are boarded up with wood and much of the remaining glass is cracked. They are small, thatched and potentially cute in the chocolate box sense, but clearly uninhabitable.

'So what do you think?' Sally repeats as she fires the car lock.

'I don't understand the question.'

'Don't you think they're fabulous?'

I look back at the cottages and try to work out what the hell is going on.

'Could be lovely, I suppose. But a lot of work. Why?'

'I've bought them, Beth. All four.' And deliberately turning away to avoid my first reaction, Sally is off through the brambles and nettles, fighting her way around to the back of the cottages.

I follow, wishing I had taken her advice on old clothing seriously now.

'You've *bought* them. But you've just lost your job, Sal. What on earth do you mean, you've bought them? What with?'

'My redundancy money. Savings – plus the chunk of money Dad left me. Fantastic investment, don't you think?'

The view of the cottages from the rear is even worse. There are small back gardens with tumbledown outdoor toilets. Part of the thatch is missing at the back and I can only begin to imagine the damage caused by the damp inside.

Sally, who lives in a purpose-built flat with a wine cooler and two wet rooms in the Barbican area of Plymouth, has clearly gone mad. Maybe she's drinking again, like in those terrible weeks after losing the baby. Sure, in a buoyant market they'd be a good buy for a developer, but not now – with the market still precarious. Stricter rules over buy-to-let have seen landlords in a panic. Everyone is saying low interest rates can't last.

'Come on. We can get inside through here. I've got a key but there's no need, quite frankly.' Sal eases her way through the gap created by the back door hanging off the middle of the terrace of cottages, wiping cobwebs as she goes.

'I'm surprised there aren't squatters,' I say. 'They should have boarded the place up properly.' I pick my way through the cobwebs to join Sal inside where I realise why squatters are out of the question. The floor is soaking from the leaking roof and there's a smell that is distinctly familiar.

'Jeez, what a stink. Smells like—'

'—school.' Sal is grinning now. 'Yeah, but I've had it all checked out. It'll be fine once we fix the roof.' She pats the wall. 'All stone. Rock solid.'

'We?'

'I'm going to use the builder who sold them to me to do the major work.' Sal leads the way through the back kitchen to the front room. 'Check this out. The original bread oven. I can't believe no one has been in and nicked it – look!' She rubs away at the thick layer of dust covering the oven, set back in a deep hearth. 'The other cottages have had their fireplaces boarded over. Horrible modern ones put in years back when they were let but they probably have great hearths as well. We just have to knock through and have a look.'

Sal sounds as if she knows what she's talking about. Which is odd. OK, so she's a surveyor; she knows about property. But she has never shown the remotest bit of interest in property development herself, especially period property. She specialises in flats: buy-to-let and student blocks. High-rise and leasehold.

'So – why's the builder selling? I don't get it?'

'Borrowed too much. In too deep. He's got cash-flow problems so he needs to get rid of this project to save a couple of bigger ones.' Sal explains that the cottages previously belonged to a farmer who couldn't sell them because of a complex family dispute until his wife died. That's why they weren't snapped up in the more buoyant times. She's perched in the window seat now, swinging her legs.

I can feel my pulse in my ear. 'But – Sal. You of all people know how the market is at the moment.'

'Exactly. The only reason I can afford to do this. If things were more solid, I wouldn't stand a chance. The builder was going to go to auction but I heard about it on the grapevine and put in a cash bid.' Sal is grinning from ear to ear.

'But this will take all your inheritance. It'll cost a fortune to do them up. And *thatched roofs* – aren't they completely impossible to insure? You'll have to sit on this project for ages to stand any chance of . . .'

'Oh, Beth.' Sally is gently shaking her head at me. 'Don't look so worried. Be excited for me. *Please.*'

I try to force a smile, but Sal's right. I'm worried, big time. I have visions of her losing all her redundancy money. Savings. Inheritance. The lot. My mind is already racing ahead to a conversation with Adam, persuading him we should convert the loft into a little flat for her once she's destitute. Bankrupt. Homeless.

Sal swings her legs again to use the momentum to jump down from the window seat. 'Come on outside again. You can see the sea from the gardens. Look, Beth. Isn't it fantastic?'

I follow her around the side of the stone outbuilding. And that's when I see it. Not the sea, but the tree. A neglected but nonetheless beautiful magnolia tree – set back from the outdoor toilet. Not visible from the front of the cottages.

And now I get it – all my fears and disapproval slipping away as I picture her viewing the cottages just to pass the time, the idea a harmless pipe dream. Nothing serious, nothing dangerous – a distraction. And then seeing the tree and believing it is fate.

She looks at the tree now herself, knowing exactly what I'm thinking. And I remember a thousand pictures of her with my boys, the laughter and the love she brings into their lives. The whoopee cushion she bought Sam for his third birthday. The day she turned up with tickets for Harry's favourite band when he was just six and I argued he was too young and the decibels would harm his ears and she argued that I needed to *chill, for Pete's sake.*

I remember the day I was called to a shop to find Sally had been caught shoplifting. A pack of romper suits. Three weeks after she lost her child. Thank the Lord the security guard had a family himself, had a heart. Let her off . . .

The truth is, she would have made such a fantastic mum, Sal. Better than me.

I look towards the cottages then back to the tree, kidding myself it's the wind making my eyes smart. 'It's a brilliant project, Sal. Brilliant.'

A lie. But how can I blame her for needing this distraction? A project to keep busy, to shut out the pictures that are haunting our lives again.

The candles. The girl with blue lips . . .

'So you'll help me? Plan it all, I mean.'

I nod, following her gaze then to the sea, where distant white horses roll and crash as if applauding her courage.

CHAPTER 8

MATTHEW – NOW

Matthew Hill leans forward to part two slats of the duck-egg-blue blind – just enough to see without being seen. Across the street there's a woman in a long mac checking her watch and glancing up at his window.

He waits a few moments before sneaking another look to find she's disappeared. So not his new client? The ever so slightly strange woman Beth Carter, who on the phone yesterday was especially nervous, gabbling in a high-pitched tone, clearly well out of her comfort zone and clearly not telling him the truth.

Matthew feels himself frown and checks his own watch before sitting back down and tapping his left foot. Beth Carter is now ten minutes late. Will she turn up at all? It's still a shock to him how many people are shameless time-wasters.

Nearly two years since he left the police force and Matthew wonders daily if he'll ever adjust. He had imagined naively that the work of a private investigator would allow him to pick and choose his cases – to do something positive while avoiding all his triggers. But no.

Very quickly the reality of having no job security and no police pension has segued to this appalling new routine. Most of his week is spent on surveillance to snap photographic evidence in divorce cases – demeaning work he had never imagined he would have to say 'yes' to. The rest of the time he sits in his office, pretending his non-existent secretary is out as he answers the phone to a succession of mad people.

As well as the call from Beth Carter yesterday, he spoke three times to a man called Ian Ellis who believes miniature people are following him with a plan to kidnap him. *Like Lilliput. Will you take the case?*

No, I'm sorry, I can't.

This new line of work has confirmed what Matthew already knew in the force – that there are far too many people living right on the edge without the support they need. And while he sympathises more than he can ever say, he's no social worker; can't take them all on to his client list.

The intercom buzzer sounds and Matthew is startled, having given up on Beth Carter. He checks his watch yet again before bolting across the room to answer, running his fingers through his hair.

'Beth Carter. I'm sorry I'm a bit late.' Her voice crackles from the little speaker and Matthew feels his eyes narrowing, wondering if this is the woman he saw hovering outside after all.

'It's fine. Do come up.'

Matthew's office is up one very steep flight. Not ideal. He fears someone will one day slip and sue him. He lets out a sigh of relief, holding the door open as Beth Carter appears. 'I always worry about those stairs. Should put a sign up really.' He shakes her hand and remembers to smile. Yes – the woman who was hovering outside earlier, now hitching her handbag higher on her shoulder. 'Can I take your coat?'

'No, I'm fine.'

He signals for her to sit down and enjoys her surprise as she takes in the room. Matthew follows her gaze. A trip to Ikea and some careful shopping online allowed him to kit out the place very reasonably; he's pleased with the result. Stainless-steel shelving and matching desk with aqua blue chairs to go with the blind, plus huge art deco prints in beech frames around the wall. His particular favourites are the two filing cabinets on angled legs with circular feet, which give the impression of little robots. Good job no one knows how few files there are inside.

'Goodness. This is nice.'

'Not what you were expecting. Most people say that.' Matthew is now beaming. 'My attempt to put people at ease. People watch the movies and expect a rickety old desk and a chain-smoker.'

There's now a pause and she fidgets with a button on her mac. Matthew waits. In the police he took the lead on interviews. Now he prefers the client to go first so he can watch and wait, weigh up what he's *really* dealing with.

'I was a bit nervous coming here. I actually changed my mind twice. Walked away but then thought it would be terribly rude and also a bit ridiculous so I came back.' She's blushing and talking quickly, just as she did on the phone.

He likes her now – nice that she's being more honest. 'I guess people don't know what to expect, approaching a private investigator.'

'True. And it's quite a leap. Deciding to involve someone, I mean . . .' Still she plays with the button.

'So, this missing friend of yours. You said on the phone that it had been – what, nearly a decade?'

'She's not *missing*. Not really. I didn't say *missing*. We're just out of touch and it's important we find her.'

'Important?' Matthew pauses deliberately. 'Important – why?' He notices that Beth Carter's eyes are now darting from left to right and so he swiftly pulls back. 'I'm sorry. Rude of me. Would you like coffee before we talk about this properly? I have a pretty decent machine.'

Beth Carter breathes in deeply and her features for the first time soften slightly. 'Smells like it. I am rather fond of a good coffee. That would be lovely – thank you.' She then glances around the room with a puzzled expression, evidently searching for the machine.

'Flat next door.' Matthew tilts his head towards the door at the far end of the office which joins the two spaces. He moves across the room and into his kitchen, raising his voice so she can still hear him as he further explains his own passion for great coffee. He shares that he has just discovered a new bean, grinds his own mix and will be interested to hear what she thinks. He leaves the door between them at a deliberate and well-practised angle so that he can just watch Beth Carter through the crack. Unaware that she can be seen, she taps her foot up and down for a bit and then removes her coat after all. Good, she's relaxing. By the time he appears with the drinks plus a jug of foaming milk, she's smiling.

'I haven't told anyone I'm here. Was worried they'd disapprove.'

'Disapprove?'

'Well, it's a bit extreme, I suppose – ridiculous even – hiring a private investigator just to find a friend.'

He's pleased she's the one to say it. 'To be honest, I was a little surprised myself when you rang. Social media has pretty much mopped up this kind of thing – chasing up old mates, I mean. You said on the phone you'd tried all the usual routes?'

'Yes – and then some. I'm a television researcher, so we're pretty experienced at tracking people down. I've tried everything I know, every trick in the book. I'm assuming you're ex-police? Your website suggested that. So I'm hoping you have contacts . . .'

'You think she may have a *police record*, your friend?'

'No, no, no. I didn't mean that. Goodness, no. I just meant you'd be very experienced about what to do next. When you hit a brick wall like this over trying to find someone.'

Matthew watches her sip again at her coffee.

'So, the police force? Do you mind me asking why you left, Mr Hill?'

'Matthew – please. It just didn't work out for me. Now, did you bring the photographs and notes I asked for?' Matthew brushes imagined fluff from his jeans. People always ask but he can play the game of changing the subject as easily as Beth Carter.

She holds his gaze for a second then hands over a sequence of photographs and notes.

Carol Winters. Age 38. Only child. Tall, natural blonde. Striking. Freelance artist. Mother Deborah lived in Brighton (address below). Moved years back, no forwarding address. Father Simon died when she was a child. Car accident. Boyfriend Ned (sorry – no surname) has international property business (company name not known). Was living in France. Lots of travelling. Hotels and rented places mostly. Last we know – well off. Happy. Smart cars, holidays, etc. . . .

Matthew sifts through the photos – he always asks for several across different time periods and Beth Carter had warned on the phone that the early prints weren't digital. He can't help his response.

'Yes, she's stunning, isn't she?' Beth's tone is teasing.

Matthew feels the embarrassment of a blush as he looks through the more recent photographs – from around a decade back – and then more carefully at the older pictures from schooldays.

'And remind me. You want to find her because . . .'

'Our old school's closing. It's going to be demolished. There's a final bash for old girls but it's not just some standard reunion. More the end of an era. This is the very last chance to see the place before it's all gone.'

'And that's really it? That's the only reason?'

Matthew again sifts through the sequence of images from the girls' schooldays and places three flat on the desk for comparison, before picking up the middle one to hold out to Beth Carter. He can't always explain the way that his brain works but he's spotted something and he always goes with his gut.

'Here. I'd say *this* is where she changed. Something happened. Yes?'

Beth looks shocked. She places her coffee on the desk and breathes in through her nose as if offended or worried or both.

'Drugs? Something like that?' he says. 'Look, I absolutely don't want to cause offence here, but it really helps for me to know everything.' Matthew puts the photograph into the sequence on the desk and taps

Carol's face. 'Her eyes, her whole posture, everything about her changes from here. In all the other pictures afterwards, she looks different. In her eyes. So, was it drugs? Self-harm? Anorexia – something like that?'

'No, absolutely not.'

'And you were close enough to know that?'

'Yes, we were very close.'

'But not close enough to stay in touch.' Matthew watches Beth Carter intently, worried he may have overstepped the mark but keen to signal he's no pushover. The last couple of weeks have been especially quiet, business-wise. He can't afford *not* to take this case but this woman isn't telling him the whole story – he knew that even from their telephone conversation yesterday. It's important she at least knows that he knows.

He carries on shuffling through the pictures and suddenly comes across a postcard. It looks like something from a museum gift shop – a small print of a strange and rather haunting painting. Three young women in almost ghostly translucent gowns, tending some kind of flowering plant.

'Oh goodness. Sorry – my bookmark.' Beth Carter almost snatches the postcard back, her face flushing deeply. 'Must have got muddled with the pictures. Sorry.'

Matthew watches her put it into her handbag and notices that she zips it very carefully into an inside pocket. So it's precious, this picture. Significant?

'Right then.' Matthew sweeps up the photographs and taps them against the desk to straighten them into a neat pile. 'I've got the digital photos you sent me. I'll just need to quickly copy these older ones on to my computer and jot some more notes.'

He asks the usual run of questions, concentrating on Carol's mother, Deborah. This Brighton lead is clearly the best bet, given the work Beth has already done herself. Matthew feels his head tilt involuntarily as she shares Carol's mother's obsession with bingo. Beth says it always amused the young friends.

Next, the tricky part, which he still finds awkward. Matthew moves over to the desk drawer to take out the sheet setting out his terms, and hands it to her. 'OK, so the mother is the best lead. I'll put in some calls but as you've pretty much covered all the usual first bases, my gut says I go to Brighton. If I can find the mother, I can find your friend. If you're right and both mum and daughter are entirely invisible on the web, it's pretty much our only option unless you have more on the boyfriend?' Beth looks through the list of fees. 'As you see, I work on a day rate. I clock my hours and set everything out for you very clearly. Travel expenses and so on will be fully itemised. So – do you want to go ahead?' Matthew has had so many time-wasters that he's learned to push for confirmation at this crucial stage, as the client properly confronts the cost. He has a new living to earn now. Beth looks a little shaken suddenly. 'More expensive than you were expecting? I can assure you my rate's very competitive.'

'No, it's not that.' She looks at her watch. 'We'll pay for one trip to Brighton and then regroup.'

'We?'

'Me and my friend Sally. I mentioned her on the phone – the other girl in some of the pictures.' She looks at her watch yet again as if she didn't take in the time properly before. 'Goodness. Sorry, I really have to dash to pick up my boys from school. It's later than I realised.'

Matthew can't help himself. The familiar punch deep inside.

Mothers. Sons.

'*Boys*, you say?'

'Yes, two. Eleven and eight – well, nearly nine, actually. I have a birthday party to organise.' In proud mother mode, Beth pulls her phone from the side pocket of her handbag to share the screensaver of her two boys, each of them poking out their tongue. 'A handful. Monkeys, the pair of them.'

Matthew looks at the phone screen and then suddenly at the floor. The familiarity of the face and the freckles is a shock. He closes his eyes and concentrates, trying very hard to spare himself embarrassment in front of this new client but he gets it wrong and keeps his eyes closed just a tad too long. Despite his best efforts, that other boy's face is suddenly right in front of him.

The mother's too – her voice echoing across the court and deep inside his head . . . *I hope you never sleep again* . . .

'Sorry, are you all right, Mr Hill? Matthew, I mean . . .'

'Yes, of course.' But by the time he opens his eyes he's let his coffee cup tip to the wrong angle and the dregs of his drink drip on to the wooden floor. *Damn.*

'Goodness. Look at me. Clumsy oaf.' He darts across to the bookcase for a tissue to mop up the mess, conscious that Beth is watching him closely, her expression now all puzzlement.

Next he lays out the older school photos on his desk for the excuse to turn his back on Beth to photograph them with his phone. He does this slowly and carefully, trying to buy time to calm himself before returning the snaps and promising to be in touch soon. But he's still feeling unsteady, wrong-footed. *That picture of her son* . . . And so he lies. He stands and says he has to leave for a meeting – a new wave of guilt as she gathers her things, their parting hurried and uncomfortable. His heart still pounding.

CHAPTER 9

BETH - NOW

In my car parked around the corner from Matthew Hill's office, I sit for a time in a state of stunned disconnection. I keep looking at the people walking by and trying to anchor myself back in the normality of this day. I watch a woman with a small tan-and-white Jack Russell which is refusing to budge – pulling back on the lead as if on strike. Finally it sits right down. *Nope, I've had enough walkies. I'm done.*

I check my watch. Matthew's office is on the outskirts of Exeter. I have an hour before school finishes. It's enough time in theory but I always worry about traffic. I look back at the dog, still rigid – its owner at a loss. I realise that I need to shake myself out of this daze, to get going, but also find I very badly need this little pause, a quiet moment to process what on earth just happened. It's not only the surreal fact that I, Beth Carter, have just engaged a private investigator, for heaven's sake, but the surprise of that final and very odd little impasse. The spilled coffee. The unexpected reaction when I showed Matthew Hill the picture of my boys. The rush to get me out of the office. *So what the hell was all that about?*

Finally the woman picks up the Jack Russell and I blink – only just acknowledging that I've been staring. I turn away to reach into my bag to retrieve the postcard. I feel the sigh leave my body as I examine it more closely.

It's a little faded and creased now – my copy of the Whistler painting, though I still take it everywhere with me, tucked in a bag or in a book, unlike Sally who has her copy framed, pristine, on her dressing table.

I stare at the image and I think of her: *Carol.* That other version of her.

It was Carol who spotted the Whistler first, in the last half-hour before we were due to leave the Tate Gallery. A school visit in second form. I remember the nun in charge getting in a flap. *Now don't dawdle, girls – the coach won't wait. Outside. Ten minutes max.* Some of us were in the gift shop and others were queuing for the toilets. The usual chaos of a school trip winding down.

Carol was ahead of us when she saw it and just stood mesmerised as we joined her. *Good grief – look at this picture, Beth. It's us.* Her voice was hushed as if she were standing in a church or space that commanded whispering and respect and that's how I remember the first time we saw the Whistler. That exposed feeling of being a small person in a larger space. Echoes all around as if something bigger was at play. It honestly felt as if the picture had been waiting for us – suspended there in time. *Three Figures: Pink and Grey.* A painting of three beautiful young women in a garden – the colours all tones of grey and pink.

Just like our blankets, Beth. Good grief. Look – it's our colours. Pink and grey. It's us . . .

It was on a stand with notices confirming prints available as postcards and larger posters too. For a time the three of us just stood there together, quite speechless, as if Whistler truly had all those years ago painted the picture especially for us. For our dreams. They looked so happy, the women – so graceful and serene.

The shop assistant told us the painting wasn't always on display at the gallery but that prints were normally in stock. We couldn't afford the larger versions but she found us three matching glossy postcards out the back and so we held on to our little souvenir bags, rushing for the coach, as if we had found treasure.

Our very own painting. Beth, Sally and Carol. *The three figures . . . pink and grey.*

I glance one final time at the street housing Matthew Hill's office, wondering what on earth I have done. I turn on the ignition, put the Whistler postcard carefully back into my bag and take out my phone to dial Sally.

As she picks up there's an odd rumbling sound in the background, like thunder.

'Beth? Sorry. I'm at the cottages and I've got builders unloading stone here. Nightmare. Can I ring you back?'

'Sure. I've not got long myself. Need to hurry for the school run. I just wanted to say that I've hired him. The private investigator.'

There's more rumbling before she responds.

'Right, OK. Goodness. So did he ask a lot of questions?'

'Yes, he did – of course he did. He's sharp. But I think that just means he's good.'

'But he wasn't *suspicious*? Difficult or anything?'

'I don't know. I don't think so.'

'You don't think so? You mean you're not sure?' Her tone is more nervous now.

'It's fine, Sally. Honestly. He's good, I think – nice too. He'll help us. We're paying him so he'll do what we ask him to do. I'll ring you again later.' I almost add that he's surprisingly attractive. Very striking eyes. No – *why would I say that?*

She rings off and I put on my seat belt, turning over a whole sequence of questions in my mind. I'm wondering why a man as apparently sharp and competent as Matthew Hill would leave the force.

Wondering again why he reacted so strangely to the picture of my two boys. And wondering most of all when I'll find the courage to tell Sally that our new private investigator spotted it straight away. The change in Carol's eyes.

The change that Sally and I like to believe is obvious only to us.

CHAPTER 10

BETH - BEFORE

I was right about missing my mother at boarding school. At first I missed her so badly, it physically hurt. I would wrap my arms around myself in bed, pretending that she was hugging me like she did when I was very little, and some nights after lights out I'd take out the little blue torch from my bedside locker and reread her letters in the dark of the dormitory until I could recite them in my head and imagine her voice reading them to me, to soothe me to sleep.

The shock for me was to realise not how much I *loved* her (that I knew) but how much I still *needed* her. I guess at twelve and thirteen, mothers are like thick, itchy blankets – essential to keep warm but prone to smother and irritate. Take the blanket away though? It's a shock how cold those nights become . . .

We learned this the hard way at school, taking it for granted – Carol, Sally and me – to be mothered and smothered as we were, so that it was a shock to see other girls driven to school at the beginning of term not by their parents but by the nanny, the housekeeper or in some rare cases the chauffeur.

We were impressed at first but not for long, for the same girls often had to stay at school over half-terms because their parents were too busy. Exotic jobs in exotic lives. The nuns did their best to make a fuss. Sister Veronica, we were told, was especially kind, organising long walks across the Downs and indoor treasure hunts on wet days. The girls were taken to the cinema and the theatre, allowed to watch *Top of the Pops* and to stay up for the late film, not in the common rooms but in the nuns' private sitting room with its high-backed chairs and embroidered footstools.

But the treats and the privileges did not help the sadness in their eyes when they watched us all return from time with our families – our mothers blubbing their goodbyes.

Jacqueline Preer would always watch, I remember, like a ghost at one of the windows of the middle dormitory at the front of the house. She would never turn on the light, just stand at the window in the shadows of the early evening – no expression on her face. Rumour had it that Jacqueline was the richest girl in the school. She had everything we coveted – a pony, a clothes allowance and an account at the local hair salon. She wore the latest fashions, real diamond stud earrings and the saddest eyes I have ever seen.

In the third year she was assigned to our dormitory and one night we heard her crying. We tried to comfort her, but she raged at us, pulling our hair and lashing out so wildly that all the brushes and toiletries flew from her bedside locker, smashing a perfume bottle so that shards of glass were strewn across the floor. I moved to help her but Jacqueline glared at me, then stamped quite deliberately on the broken glass until she was eventually led away by one of the nuns, sobbing and still flailing her arms, with blood trailing from her foot. We did not see her until the morning, when she joined us at breakfast, limping with her bandaged foot in an outsized sandal but still scowl-ing and defiant – her eyes tired and red.

Jacqueline went on every school holiday the nuns organised – skiing in the Christmas break and the 'art tour' of Italy at Easter. Her father, we were told, was some kind of ambassador – very influential and *very* generous. There were plaques all over the school with sombre engravings *sponsored by Lord Preer* or *donated by Lord Preer*. Jacqueline's mother, from the framed photo by her bed, was exceptionally beautiful – wearing a pale pink ballgown like a film star. But we never met her.

We tried to be kind to Jacqueline but in the end learned to keep our distance. To *mind our own business* – her favourite phrase.

Until one night in the middle of the summer term of our third year when I came to see the terrible truth about Jacqueline. It was a hot and stuffy night and unusually I just couldn't sleep. I tossed and turned and tried all the usual tricks: counting sheep, relaxing each muscle in turn as we were taught at the end of dance classes. But nothing worked.

In the end, around midnight, I decided to fetch a drink of water from the main bathroom, taking a plastic cup from my bedside locker.

I threw on my dressing gown and crept from the dormitory, careful not to disturb anyone. All was quiet on the long landing with just the night light glowing.

There was a large pane of glass above the door of the bathroom and still keen not to wake anyone, I decided not to bother with the main light as the glow from the landing was good enough. The communal bathroom had a set of three toilet cubicles, a line of sinks along one wall and a bath in the rear corner with a shower curtain on a rail. The curtain was meant for privacy but was in fact redundant as most girls locked the main door when it was their turn on the shower and bath rota.

I decided to use the loo before fetching my drink and was just about to press the flush when suddenly I heard a noise.

In the semi-darkness a shiver ran right through me. For a moment I was simply frozen. The noise came again. *Oh please, no. An intruder?* My mind was racing with options. Run? Or stay behind the locked cubicle door and shout out? Which would be the more dangerous? I waited, trying to choose – my heartbeat increasing. But then came another wave of the sound and I felt a change in my stomach as I realised that – *no.*

This was no intruder. This was more like the sound of pain. Of someone in pain.

Very slowly I edged out of the cubicle and moved towards the bath in the corner, from where there was a shadow behind the shower curtain. I could now see from the shape of the shadow that it was a girl or woman. Long hair. Very slowly I pulled back the curtain and there she was – Jacqueline Preer in the bath. Covered in blood. It was everywhere. Down her arms. All over her nightdress. Her hair. And splattered on to the rear wall.

What happened next is hazy. I must have screamed before I fainted, for suddenly I was on the floor looking up at two nuns crouched over me. I remember thinking then not of Jacqueline but how strange it was to see their hair – long and grey in a thick plait down their backs. I had always believed the myths that the older nuns who wore the most formal habits had their heads shaved beneath them. But no.

I was taken from the room, trembling and unsteady on my feet, and given sweet tea in the nuns' parlour from where my parents were called. I was encouraged to rest on the sofa there as we waited for my father to collect me but I couldn't keep still, let alone rest. I could hear the distant commotion of an ambulance and the nuns reassuring all the girls that everything was all right when very clearly it was not.

My father arrived, ashen-faced, in the early hours and I was told to spend as much time at home as I needed to get over the shock. My mother clucked and baked and soothed and supported but in the end I begged to be allowed back to school after just a week, feeling worse away from the place. Away from my friends. Away from the scene in the bathroom that was so terrible that somehow it frightened me more the longer I failed to confront it. I had already been told that Jacqueline had been saved, thanks to me. Much longer and she would have bled to death. We were never given full details. In prayers it was always referred to as *Jacqueline's accident*, though we all knew she'd slit her wrists. And she never came back to school.

Instead workmen appeared, to carry out the only major renovation work during our time at the school. They ripped out the bath and replaced it with two shower cubicles with sliding doors.

It was a nice try. But still I always chose the other bathrooms, preferring to queue than to think of what had happened in there to Jacqueline. I thought it was the worst thing anyone could have to face. Finding Jacqueline like that. All that blood. But I was young. And I was wrong.

For there was to be another room full of blood and sorrow. Another girl with blue lips who, this time, would not make it.

CHAPTER 11

BETH - NOW

A week passes and I'm behind with everything at work – sick of bullying texts buzzing in hourly from Cruella – when suddenly there is the welcome contrast of Matthew Hill on the phone with news of Carol's mum.

'You're kidding me. You think you've found her already?'

'Yup – bingo.'

'Excuse me?' I swing my chair away from my desk.

'I mean bingo literally. You were right. Carol's mum left Brighton a few years ago. No forwarding address. And like her daughter, no social media presence – unusual these days. But I went to Brighton and checked out the bingo lead. I tried two halls and got lucky on the second. Wednesday night regular, apparently. Never missed and told everyone she didn't play online. So get this. The girl at the front desk remembered her asking for the address of the company's bingo hall in Medford.'

'So that's where she's gone?'

'Well, I don't know for sure. There's nothing showing on the electoral register or phone listings in Kent. Thought I'd check in with you first to see if you want to take it further. I'd put money on her keeping up the same routine. Wednesday night bingo. If she's not the online type, it's definitely worth a try. People are creatures of habit. I've phoned the Medford branch with a story but they're playing it by the book so I can't get anything over the phone. So, then. I'm feeling quite hopeful. Do you want me to go to Kent? And do you have a maiden name for her? She may be using that now.'

I can hear him sipping a drink as I sit back in my seat. *Kent.*

'No, sorry. No idea on the maiden name. But listen – I'll need to call you back.'

I get straight on the phone to Sally, who tries at first to distract me with the horrors of the new stone wall (intended to keep out the sheep), which has apparently been partially constructed in the wrong part of the cottages' rear gardens. The cement isn't dry and like a madwoman, she's taking down the wall herself, stone by stone, because the builder isn't answering his phone and all his workmen have disappeared.

I can hear the thud of a stone being hurled before Sally continues. 'Oh no, Beth. I'm not going to Kent. No way. Too near Sussex. You'll get it into your head that we should go on to the school and there's absolutely no way I'm ready to face that. I honestly can't—'

'Please, Sally. Not to the school. Not this trip, I promise. Just Kent. One night away. Please?'

'But aren't we paying this Matthew whatshisface to do this? Why on earth do we need to go too? It could be a dead end.'

'He sounds pretty hopeful and I just can't bear to wait. Please, Sally. I know it sounds a bit odd, going along too. But all this waiting and worrying is doing my head in. If he finds her, we can talk to her straight away.'

'And he really thinks Deborah's there?'

'It's sounding likely.'

There's a long sigh followed by the thud of a second stone. 'Oh, all right. But one night, tops. Phone me back this evening and we'll sort it out. Meantime – I don't suppose you could give me a hand with this wall?'

'Sorry.'

Back on the phone to Matthew and he's disorientated. 'You want to *come with me*? Why would you want to come with me?' A pause. 'Look, no, no, no. That's not the way I work. You could be wasting your time and you do realise there's still a charge.'

I lie about wanting to look someone else up who happens to live in the area. I say we want him to do his bit and take the lead but that if he's right and he finds Carol's mum, we can speak to her immediately. *Kill two birds in the same trip. Worth the gamble.* Matthew is clearly not at all keen, explaining that it's not the way he operates and would strongly advise against it. We have a long discussion but I remain determined. In the end, he caves in, expecting us to travel together by train but I push it even further, offering to drive us all to keep the costs down. I pick the hotel and negotiate a rooms upgrade through the chain we regularly use for guests appearing on *The Meeting of Minds*. I reassure him that he'll be paid his agreed rate plus all the expenses. Good news or bad, we will pay. Finally, if still reluctantly, he gives in.

Over the next few days, I turf out all the boxes of old photographs not copied digitally and which I've never found the time to put into albums. Matthew insists he must take the lead at the bingo hall and he needs a better picture of Carol's mum to show to staff and regulars. Most of my snaps are from visits to the school by parents – concerts and so on – but there are also a few from half-terms when, by the third year, we began to visit each other's homes. I remember how our families resisted at first – *don't you girls spend enough time together?* – and how we wore them down, then how proud I was of the fuss my parents made when it was our turn to play host; Mum with her best Victoria sandwich sponge cakes and Dad researching local outings, when we would all pile into his estate car. Michael, my brother, would sulk about being surrounded by so many girls and beg to be allowed back early to his own boarding school.

There are a couple of snaps too from Sally's – those trips less predictable, the atmosphere dictated entirely by her father, who could be either charm personified or frighteningly loud. Sally was understandably loyal and defensive, used to his moods, and explained once that he was a workaholic and under a lot of pressure, but Carol and I felt embarrassed and uncomfortable around him and would wince when he poured large whiskies early in the evening, knowing her parents' voices would be raised later in their bedroom next door to ours. To be frank, we liked it best when he was away – the whole household more relaxed, with the delicious bonus of Sal's two older brothers whom Carol and I pretended to detest but of course secretly fancied.

And then the girlfest at Carol's home. Her father had died in a car crash when she was very young and she remained an only child. Deborah clearly missed her daughter badly during the terms and was happy to indulge us all spectacularly. She had perfectly manicured nails and would buy in nail polish in a wide variety of colours for our visits and make home-made face packs of egg whites whipped with honey.

I find a range of pictures of us in the box – pavlova faces with cucumbers over our eyes – my hand drawn to my cheek as I remember it. The tingling from the face pack.

I pick the best three pictures of Deborah – striking like her daughter, although dark with strong cheekbones, large bright blue eyes and distinctive eyebrows set in a permanent quizzical arch, as if awaiting the answer to a question.

Through all this Adam watches me, baffled and unnerved. I haven't told him about hiring Matthew and have just mentioned casually that we're trying to find Carol. I've been dodging all his questions and feel guilty as he watches me watching the news every evening with this new ache in my stomach. It's not just that I'm afraid of being found out.

I'm afraid of what Adam will think of me when he knows the truth about me.

'Seriously, Beth. Are you OK? You look tired. Don't seem yourself at all.' He puts a coffee down in front of me as I finish packing my small case. I've lied. I've told him that I'm off on a girly shopping trip with Sally to a big discount store in Kent.

Last night Adam was pressing me about the convent party and I had to turn away from him, a tightening in my chest. I keep thinking how close we used to be. How I told him everything. Everything, that is, bar my one big secret – this darkness so deep in my past that I'd stupidly assumed it would never come between us like this.

'So why don't you just drive on to the school after your shopping trip?'

'I'm sorry?'

'This trip. It's only an extra hour or so to Rye.'

'No, that wouldn't work – it would spoil the whole thing. We don't want to go there beforehand. And we don't want to go without finding Carol.'

'So why do you want to go to this school thing at all? I don't get it, Beth. All these years you've never shown the remotest interest in reunions. Always been so odd about the place and now – look at you.' He follows me into the hallway with his own mug of coffee in his hand, and I deliberately keep moving ahead of him.

'Look, this party isn't a reunion. It's goodbye. The place is being pulled down and the whole site redeveloped – student accommodation as far as we know. Anyway, this is just a girls' trip. Shopping. We're not going to the school.'

Eventually Adam gives up and we part uneasily – just pecking each other on the cheek. One of those horrid kisses where the flesh meets but the eyes don't.

And then comes the unexpected complication as I pick up Sal and then Matthew – so that when I watch them hold each other's stare for just a little longer than is comfortable (for me) as Matthew climbs into my car, I am shocked by the ripple of irritation I feel.

He has only a small black rucksack, which he puts in the boot before climbing into the back of the car – at first behind Sal, but then shuffling across to the seat behind me, apparently to get a better view of her.

I try not to prickle. I try to be pleasant. I try to steer the conversation to the job in hand, but I might as well paint myself green and stick little sharp hairs all over myself.

'Don't be ridiculous.' Sally's tone is defensive as we unpack in the hotel later. Matthew has a single room on the floor below us. We're sharing a twin. 'You were not a gooseberry. I was just getting to know him. Jeez, Beth. This whole thing was your idea, remember. I didn't even want to do this.'

◆ ◆ ◆

Finally comes the shock of the bingo hall itself – sitting in the stench of a room paying lip service to the smoking ban with a cloud of cancer wafting in through double doors to the adjoining 'smoking shelter'. It's Elvis night and onstage there's a man in a studded white jumpsuit wondering if we are *lonesome tonight* before a number caller appears in a silver sequinned jacket. It's surprisingly stressful, trying to keep up. The players all around us seem to be taking it all terribly seriously and so while Matthew talks to some of the staff, we just pretend to play, feeling pathetic and self-conscious, while occasionally scanning the room for any sign of Deborah.

I can see why online bingo is taking off as we watch Matthew finally return from a long spell at the front desk.

'Success,' he whispers, smiling at Sally. 'The new girl just on shift recognised the picture straight away. Deborah's a Wednesday night regular, apparently.'

'So why's she not here?'

'Well, it's early still. Do you want me to wait with you or show the picture around elsewhere in case she doesn't show? Someone might know where she lives?' He's in a good mood. Having a good time. *On our money*, I think cruelly. Not liking him now – punishment for him liking Sally.

I endure about ten minutes of the fug, of Elvis crooning between games and of Sally and Matthew exchanging shy smiles. I excuse myself to the toilets where I ask the woman in the mirror what the hell this is all about.

Jealous? Of Sally and Matthew taking an unexpected shine to each other? What kind of new madness is this? I'm a happily married woman. Lucky. And sure – Matthew's an attractive man. Nice eyes. Nice voice. But it simply hadn't occurred to me that he and Sally would start behaving like kids.

For some reason it makes me feel uncomfortably lonely and I want to ring Adam, to say sorry for the horrible kiss. I hate that I'm letting all this stress come between us. But I'm afraid he'll be in the middle of football and a takeaway with the boys and will use that tone I so hate, trying to disguise his eagerness for me to get off the phone, which will run the risk of making me feel even more upset. I'm cross with myself. And feel stupid – like a sulky teenager whose best friend is getting all the attention. I linger in the ladies' room, ashamed of myself, pretending to touch up my make-up, but in reality amazed by all the women who rush in and out, continuing their conversations loudly across cubicles, not even noticing me.

What astonishes me most is that they're clearly all having such a good time. A laugh. In this awful place. With their cheap Elvis and their greasy sausage and chips. Smoking themselves into early graves in the adjoining shelter. And in the end I'm jealous not just of Sally and Matthew but of all these smiling faces. Friends having a laugh together. For some reason it makes me feel stuck-up. Sour. Also desperately sad. I keep thinking of what Carol and Sally and I used to be, what the three of us should have become together. If . . .

I close my eyes to the memory of *that room*. The blue-painted shelf and the little row of shells. The blood and the dread . . .

And then as I emerge from the toilets, hot and disorientated, I spy her suddenly across the room. Such a complete shock. I'd forgotten for a moment why we're here.

She looks as if she's only just arrived, a beige coat with a chocolate silk lining folded over her arm. She's queuing for a drink and turns away much of the time but every now and then she glances across to the stage and there is no mistake. She's still dark – the hair dyed a warmer brown which suits her. She's aged well – still striking, with the same eyebrows asking me with their quizzical arch from across the room what the devil I want before she's even seen me. Her fingernails – clasped around the purse she has ready in her hand to pay for her drink – are as long and elegant as ever, glinting scarlet in the gloom of the low-level lighting.

I watch her adjust the coat as she queues rather self-consciously and realise I have not the foggiest idea how to approach her. What to say. How to explain what we're doing here – me and Sal after all these years with a private detective in tow. I look over towards Sally and Matthew, leaning in towards each other. I try to focus, like a drunk sobering up, and edge my way back to their table.

'She's here,' I whisper, nodding my head in her direction. 'Deborah – over there, by the bar.'

They both turn their heads.

'Are you sure it's her?' Matthew narrows his eyes.

'No, no. Please don't stare. I'm sure it's her but we've got to think what on earth to say. I mean, what will she think? With Matthew here, I mean.' I'm worried it'll seem over the top to Deborah. To pay someone to track her down like this.

To his credit, Matthew takes the hint. 'OK, how about I hang back while you go across. I'll watch how things go. Once you're happy, text me and I'll head back to the hotel. See you both later?' He smiles at Sally as he stands, crunching an ice cube from his glass of Coke. 'Good luck.'

Sally blushes and I watch her watching him move across the room to an area displaying tourist leaflets, which he pretends to read. We wait a bit and then head for the bar to approach Deborah from behind, Sally speaking first. 'Hello. It's Deborah, isn't it?'

She turns through 180 degrees – at first merely puzzled and then alarmed.

'It's Sal and Beth,' I say. 'Carol's friends from school. It's been a very long time but you remember us?'

Now Deborah is unsteady, one leg seeming to buckle. She drops her purse so that we all end up grappling around on the floor, picking up the silver and coppers from the sticky carpet.

'Sorry, we've given you a fright. Here – I think that's most of it.' I pass Deborah a handful of damp money and we guide her by the arm to the back of the room, away from the noise of the queue at the bar.

'Good grief. But what on earth are you two doing *here*?' She is gasping for air and reaching out for a chair. I take in the look in her eyes, which goes beyond surprise – something like worry, or guilt, or maybe even fear. So that I realise almost immediately that something is not right here.

Not right at all.

CHAPTER 12

MATTHEW - NOW

Matthew is for some reason struggling to keep still. He tries the TV, flicking between channels. *Nope.* He throws the remote on to the bed and paces the hotel room, staring at the blue carpet.

He's thinking about Sally and how it's going with Deborah. But mostly he's just thinking about Sally. Still, he can't believe anyone could be *that* unphotogenic. Sitting back on the bed finally, he jiggles his left leg up and down.

He checks his phone. Just the one text from Sally to say they have taken Deborah to a little bar-cum-restaurant for food. She's still shaken.

The truth is, he knows this already. When Deborah nearly collapsed in the bingo hall, he came close to intervening. Beth and Sally revived her with a glass of water but Matthew was unnerved. Shock can be a tricky thing. But there was something about Deborah's reaction that went beyond that. It worried him.

He followed them down the street and watched through the restaurant window as they settled at a table.

He uncrosses his legs and tries harder for calm, reaching for his iPad to look back over the pictures from this case. He feels wrong-footed and cross with himself, sort of guilty and disorientated for failing to notice Sally properly from the off. He scrolls again through the pictures. Extraordinary. Turns out the camera *does* lie.

In the car he had wanted to say this out loud, the very minute he saw her. The perfect, small nose and sculpted cheekbones. The translucent quality of her skin. He couldn't quite believe it – that first glimpse of her profile as he climbed into the car. *Crikey.* He had shuffled across the back seat to check her face from a different angle and still it was extraordinary. The skin. The cheekbones. The way her skin seemed to reflect the light. He was thinking – how the hell could he not have noticed from the photographs? The ex-copper. Him supposed to be observant for a living.

He's only glad now, in the safety of the hotel room, that he didn't blurt it out. *Has anyone ever told you how much prettier you are in real life?*

Matthew's embarrassed. He rakes his fingers through his hair and stands up to pace again. This, of course, is inappropriate on every level, especially given this is a *client.* But here's the truth. In all the photographs he had been shown for this case, through school and the birthday get-together nearly a decade back, the elusive Carol was the one who caught your eye. Carol, who was so obviously and classically beautiful with her long straight hair. Matthew remembered his blush as Beth had caught him out that first meeting in his office. *Yes, she's stunning, isn't she?*

He'd noticed Sally only in the abstract, out of the corner of his eye. The third friend in the photographs. Long brown hair, which back then was quite bouffant, borderline frizzy. He looks now again at that most recent photograph taken in an Italian restaurant for Beth's thirtieth. Carol – stunning as ever. Beth, busy and beaming. Sally, more ordinary. No. *Not . . . ordinary.* That stab of guilt again. He uses his fingers to zoom in on her face. Her smile. Those perfect teeth . . .

As he looks at the photograph, he can hear her laugh in the car. Loud and warm and real, sending this extraordinary sparkle to her eyes as she teased Beth about her driving.

You don't have to indicate when there's no other traffic, Beth. We have a policeman in the back.

Ex-policeman.

Matthew realises this case is somehow changing direction for him. He had at first been a bit embarrassed to even take it on. Now? There's something in the shadows that he doesn't understand and doesn't like. And he also doesn't understand why he simply can't put Sally out of his mind. He needs to get a grip. *For heaven's sake, man. What are you – twelve?*

He puts the iPad on the bed and crosses the room to examine the tea tray. He rejects the instant coffee and checks through the tea options. Earl Grey. Breakfast. Peppermint . . .

Now he pauses yet again, staring at the peppermint sachet and thinking once more of Sally on the journey here, turning around in the car to offer him a mint – their hands brushing for the first time accidentally as she struggled to peel back the foil of the packet. He recognises the cliché, and yet? There really is that ridiculous boyish excitement at the memory of the first physical touch – that tingling through his hand and right up his arm as she laughed, mints spilling on to the handbrake and the floor of the car. *Sorry, sorry.* The flip to his stomach as she tried again, their hands brushing for the second time.

She told him this sweet story about Beth's late father who used to challenge himself to tear back the paper and foil on his mint packet in one single piece. No tears. A single, unbroken spiral of paper and foil.

Matthew flicks the switch on the kettle, decides on the breakfast tea and does some more pacing, pinching his bottom lip over and over. No, no, no. He needs to be careful, can't be doing with this. He has ticked the box, he has found the mother and he needs to put this in its place. Job done, invoice to be served. He needs to get home and look into some more advertising to try to bring in new work. He needs to think about his alarming new business loan and *stop* thinking about whether it would be unethical or simply out and out embarrassing to ask the lovely Sally if she'd like to go on a picnic. Matthew closes his eyes for a moment and winces. *Picnic.*

He will not, of course, extend this somewhat childish invitation for real, but in his imagination now he's picturing them at his favourite little spot on Dartmoor – the clear, flat patch of rough grass with stones for seats and a deep little pool to cool wine or beer. Or maybe Stover Country Park with the lake and the birds and the wooden tables amid the trees? On the drive, he had in passing mentioned his love of walking. And picnics.

Beth had practically choked. *Heaven help us. Not another one.*

Very soon he'd learned that Sally – by coincidence, cliché or just maybe a sign from the gods – was a picnic enthusiast also. She too had been gifted a proper wicker basket with plates and cutlery and liked very much to use it.

Beth, who confessed she was more inclined to stuff rolls in foil in a rucksack, roared with laughter at the pair of them, announcing they clearly had more spare time than sense. *You want to try picnics with plates and cutlery with two boys in tow. Dear Lord, you'd soon learn.*

Matthew stares at the alarmingly dark colour of his tea, fishes out the teabag and opens a second little carton of milk. He wonders again if it really is a sign. This shared penchant for picnics. Matching wicker baskets. In the car he had babbled about his mother who'd given him the picnic set one Christmas. She liked things to be nice, his mother – hated paper plates and plastic cups. Taught him to shop at the deli for proper pork pies, pâté and freshly baked bread.

Beth had scoffed some more. *Pâté on a picnic? What is this – Downton Abbey . . . ?*

Matthew sips his tea and checks his watch. He finds that picturing food – the pork pie and the pâté – is making him feel hungry suddenly and he decides he'll watch the football, then maybe grab a drink and snack down in the bar. He taps his foot up and down some more and worries again how his two new clients are getting on with Carol's mother.

More and more he's concerned about what it is Sally and Beth are hiding from him. They're not telling him the truth about Carol, he knows that. No one pays a private investigator to track down a friend simply for a reunion – end of an era, or no end of an era.

Matthew narrows his eyes and wonders at the truth. Drugs? Anorexia? Bullying? He feels a frisson of something uncomfortable.

So why did you leave the police force?

He takes in a deep breath, thinking of his own lies and again of that courtroom.

The mother's eyes. *I hope you never sleep again . . .*

He pushes the image away, sips his drink once more and chews his lip. He thinks next of his two most recent and equally disastrous relationships. Laura, who said that life was too short to waste time on *men with baggage*. And then Elaine, who said he had 'commitment issues' and should see a shrink.

Senior officers said the same thing after the inquest. But no, Matthew was not up for talking. What was the point of *talking . . .*

So relationship-wise, he is not a good bet. Not a good boyfriend. Not even a good person really.

So that's decided then. He one hundred per cent will not be asking the lovely if mysterious Sally on a picnic. Matthew takes a very long and very deep breath and feels a mixture of both sadness and relief just as another text buzzes in from her. He opens it and sucks in a breath. He reads it again:

There's something not right here, Matthew.

CHAPTER 13

BETH - NOW

I stare at Deborah's flushed face and wonder what the hell I was thinking, what I expected to happen. Closure? A neat tearful phone call to Carol in which we would decide to go to the police? Face our past? Our demons? Wipe our bloody slate clean?

We are now in a tatty bistro just off the High Street. Deborah has had a strong coffee and we've ordered food. But she's still breathless and disorientated – her skin worryingly pale.

Nothing has been said to suggest there is any immediately bad news on Carol but that's the problem. Nothing has been said about Carol. It's beyond odd – borderline sinister. Deborah has volunteered no information at all, countering my every inquiry with questions about our own lives.

Watching her fidget, I see just how badly I've blundered into this – dragging a reluctant Sally with me. Selfishly, I gave no thought to the impact on Deborah.

To see her this wretched is terrible. At the bingo hall I was so completely thrown by Deborah's initial shock that in the end it was Sally who stepped up to suggest food. A restaurant? A bar? Anything to help us catch Deborah's breath for her.

I think of Matthew back at the hotel. I should have listened to him from the off. *My advice is to let me find her, then reach out by letter or telephone. Tread carefully – it's been a long time.*

'Do you think it's asthma?' Sal whispers as Deborah leaves our table, looking for the ladies' room.

'I don't know. I have no idea what's going on. She won't answer a single question about Carol . . .' I look at Sally's phone, resting on the table. 'Who were you texting?'

'Just updating Matthew.' She blushes.

'You need to be very careful what you tell him, Sally.'

'You think I don't know that?' She looks stressed. Tucks her hair behind her ear. 'I just said I was worried. That Deborah is being very odd.'

'Oh, great. So you've made him suspicious?'

'Don't be like that, Beth. I didn't want to come, remember. This whole trip was *your* idea.'

And then, much too quickly, Deborah is back, ordering a large gin and tonic, which she drinks very quickly. I repeat how sorry I am that we lost touch with Carol, how we got lucky with a lead while in Brighton. I tell lies about visiting an exhibition in the museum next to the Royal Pavilion that I read about online.

'But who told you I moved *here*?'

'Oh. I can't remember now.' *Pants on fire.* 'Someone in one of the post offices near where you lived, I think. Can't remember.' There are crumbs on the table, which has not been properly wiped, and I press them into the fleshy underpart of my fingers. 'So how is she doing then, Carol? Still abroad?'

There's a very long pause and Deborah glances from me to Sally and back again, tapping her nails against her gin glass. 'Oh, she's fine. Fine. And what about you both – Devon did you say, Beth?'

Sally catches my eye. 'The thing is, Deborah, St Colman's is closing. They're selling the land for redevelopment and there's to be this big final bash. Not our cup of tea, actually, the whole reunion vibe, but this is a last chance, so it made us think it was high time we got back in touch. With Carol. We think she'd like to know.'

'The convent? Closing?' Deborah reaches for her handbag – an old-fashioned tapestry affair with a proper metal clasp, like a giant purse. She twists it with a distinct click, takes out a tissue and blows her nose. 'Goodness me.' Click. 'I haven't thought of the place in years. Carol never really talked about it after she left.'

The waiter arrives with our first course and I lean to the side as he places my smoked salmon down – dry and unappetising with a slice of shrivelled lemon. There is a puddle of salad garnish – the leaves wilted and unpleasant as if they've been sitting in the dressing a while. For a beat, I consider complaining but change my mind.

'So, the thing is, Deborah, this party isn't far off so we need to get the details to Carol as soon as possible?'

A different waiter appears then with the rest of our order and we pause until he's left the table.

Deborah shakes her napkin, spreads it over her lap and starts to spread pâté on to her toast. 'She's still abroad mostly. Find it difficult to keep track, to be honest. So what part of Devon did you say, Beth? We used to holiday near Torquay when I was young – palm trees they had, very exotic. It's where Agatha Christie used to write. I always liked Agatha Christie. In fact, didn't I read somewhere that the National Trust have taken over her old house? Have you been? Is it lovely?' She crunches into her toast, which is over-crisp and breaks instantly into several small pieces.

'Do you want me to say something? Your toast looks burned, Deborah?'

'It's fine. Honestly. Fine.'

Again we exchange awkward glances and small, false smiles.

'So, is she still in France – Carol?' I have taken a pen from my bag, hoping to write down an address or phone number. Anything. But I give up for now, put the pen aside and instead push the dry slivers of salmon around my plate.

'Some of the time.'

Sally and I are now careful *not* to look at each other. Carol and her mum had only each other after her father's accident. She had been so young, no more than five or six when he died, and there were no other relatives that we knew of.

Across the room I notice a customer remonstrating over his bill and try discreetly to push my fish under the lettuce.

'So, how are your families? Do tell me about your boys, Beth.' Still she does not look us in the face and so I take out my phone to share the latest snaps, speaking too quickly of the family chaos, also of my mother, living alone since my father's death. Deborah is kind and surprisingly comfortable with this topic – the cancer – making me promise that I'll pass on her best.

I think for a moment of Deborah widowed so much younger. Back in school, we saw all adults as old – just this single category. *Grown-ups.* But I realise only now just how hard and lonely it must have been for Deborah. She was probably near our age when I met Sally and Carol.

'So, Carol then. We were surprised not to find her on social media. Is she still with Ned? Married? Children?'

'No, not married. But she's still with Ned, thank goodness. Lovely man.' For the first time she looks right at me but then turns almost immediately to Sally. 'You have children, Sal?'

'No, divorced, actually. Long time ago. I'm better off rid but it wasn't pretty – the divorce, I mean.'

'Oh, I'm sorry.' Deborah's voice is gentler as she shakes the scorched toast crumbs carefully from her napkin on to her plate then pats the cloth back into place on her knee. 'Carol and Ned, they've been unlucky in the parent department. They've been trying to adopt – very stressful, very difficult.'

Deliberately I do not look at Sally.

'So, is it all right for us to take Carol's number and address?' I have again picked up my pen.

A longer pause.

'She's so busy – Ned's business and everything. And the stress with this adoption. It's been a trial.' Deborah begins shaking more imagined crumbs from her napkin, then fidgets with her bag so that I have to fight the urge to reach out. To still her hand.

The argument over the bill across the room has become more heated but we each pretend not to notice – me in a high-pitched voice telling jokes about my work and my boys, our laughter ringing false.

Until over stale cheesecake, which sticks to the roof of my mouth, Deborah finally comes clean. 'This'll probably sound a bit odd but I don't actually have a current address for Carol. Or a landline number.' She blushes and then stares at me as if challenging for a reaction. I'm so shocked, I have no idea what to say.

Finally Deborah tilts her head. 'The thing is, they rent and she moves a lot and you know what you young people are like – all mobile phones and laptops. I don't understand online myself. I worry about scams. But I have a mobile telephone number for Carol back at the house, I think. For *emergencies*. Mostly she prefers me to leave it to her to get in touch. We tend to find it's the best way. And she always turns up. You can come back for coffee, if you like. I'll see if I can find it – her mobile number.'

We take a taxi. More terrible small talk. The weather. The bingo.

And then? It's just as I fear at the house. If loneliness can have a smell, it hangs in the air here – a neat modern semi that smells of polish and room freshener and the ache for company. Pictures of a young Carol smile from every surface. On a beach. Up a mountain. A cable car. A ski slope.

I look around the room as Deborah appears with a tray immaculately set with a crisp linen cloth, three cups and saucers and a pot of coffee. She has an address book with a frayed spine tucked under her arm and I notice that the corner of the tray's cloth is yellowed from the sun as if it has been set for some time by a window. Waiting.

'Now then. She only ever gives me a mobile number because she moves around such a lot. Ned's work, you know. Sorry – I said that already. Anyway, he's always developing this or that. All over the world. I think that's why they rent, to keep things flexible. So – ah. Yes, here it is. But the thing is, it may not be the current number. She's always changing it.' She coughs. 'She prefers me only to ring her in emergencies. Otherwise I always catch her at a busy time. You know how it is – running a company.'

Deborah reminds me suddenly of my own mother with her tray and her best china.

'Let's try it *now*.'

'Oh no, no, Beth. That's not a good idea at all. It's late. And, as I say, she normally likes to ring *me*. It works better that way. Really. It's an understanding. You can try it tomorrow. Let's have our coffee – white?'

'Come on, give me the number. I'll pay for the call. She won't mind – it's a sort of emergency. *Please, Deborah.*'

Coffee pot in hand, her expression kills me. So torn – glancing between the address book and the tray. She puts down the jug and I can hardly bear it. The nervous smile. A mother who seems to need an excuse to ring her daughter.

'Oh, go on then. She won't believe you two being here.'

She leafs through the book for the number and stretching the phone to the arm of her chair dials, lifting up her shoulders like a nervous child playing a prank. As we wait for the line to ring, she signals at the coffee and Sally kneels forward to pour.

'Hello. Hello, Carol? It's Mum.'

I'm holding my breath again, staring at the phone. Deborah's hand is actually trembling.

'No, no, I'm *fine*, darling. Nothing wrong. I know it's late, love. Yes. I'm sorry, dear. I didn't want to worry you. Yes. Yes. But – listen, I have a surprise for you. You'll never guess who's here? Right in the room with me.' Deborah pulls a face for our benefit. 'No, nothing like that. It's Sally and Beth. From school.'

And then there's complete silence. A chilling, awful silence which each of us sucks in as we glance – Deborah to me, me to Sal. A void suddenly in the room as Deborah's eyes change.

'Are you still there? Carol? Hello? Can you hear me, love? Yes, Sally and Beth. No. They came looking for me – to give you a surprise, darling. Wait. There's news. I'll put them on, shall I?'

Deborah hands me the receiver.

'Hello, Carol.' I can hear only her breath for a moment, heavy and loud, but in my head can picture her perfectly – the little beauty spot beneath her eyebrow moving as she frowns. I wait and at last there is her voice – regrouping, doing her best to feign delight but her voice unnaturally quiet so that I can feel her turn away from me almost immediately.

'Beth. Goodness. What a shock.'

Look at me, Carol. Please?

'What on earth are you doing at my mother's?'

'St Colman's – it's closing down, Carol. The site is being sold. It made us think of you. And so we came looking. There's a big farewell party.'

'Closing down?' She sounds disorientated. I guess that she'll be thinking now exactly what I'm thinking.

Of that awful room. The shells on the shelf. The blood . . .

'I'm really sorry to just ring you out of the blue. This must be a shock.'

'Look, I'm sorry too but this is not really a good time. Let me get a pen. For your number.'

And I know this tone. This pretence.

'Hang on while I get a pen, will you?'

Oh Lord, I hate this tone. It's the tone from Paris. Years back. Me just pregnant with Sam. Carol's idea to cheer me up, her treat. It was just a few years before that disastrous party for my thirtieth. We were supposed to have three glorious girly days together. I had even thought that we might talk properly about the past. *The promise.* But no, it didn't turn out like that at all. Instead she turned away from us, just as she's turning away right now . . .

'I'm so sorry. Hang on, Beth. But I really can't talk now.'

Yes. The tone from Paris where we both know she's making excuses, lying, and she won't look me in the eye, yet each of us knowing also that I won't challenge her.

Deborah's phone feels warm and sticky in my hand now. Carol is talking to someone else in the room at her end. I hope it's Ned, that he'll speak up for us as he tried to in Paris. But then she's back and very quickly we're exchanging numbers, or rather she's taking ours – mine and then Sal's, who is soon crowding me on the phone, butting in.

In my head I'm begging her to *wait*. But Carol is asking to speak to her mother again, apologising that she'll have to ring off. *So sorry. But like I say, it's not a good time.* Deborah looks more serious this time, just listening and nodding. Guilty. And apologising.

Finally she hands the phone back to me and Carol is promising to ring us soon when there's more time. That she'll have a think and will be in touch about the school event. *Yes, I'm writing down the date. I'll think. I'll ring. Yes.*

Carol's voice is trembling and I dare not say any more in front of Deborah and so we just mumble hurried goodbyes.

I hand the phone back to Deborah who puts it back down very carefully as if it's made of glass.

'Well. Drink your coffee, girls. It's getting cold.'

Three matching smiles. Muscle-ache smiles. Pretend-it's-not-cold smiles for the wedding photographer. *Just one more. That's it. Hold it like that.*

It stays false and fidgety and borderline farcical – none of us know-ing what to say – until at last Deborah disappears into the kitchen to make fresh coffee, and Sally leans forward. 'Damn it, Beth. I told you we should have left it.'

We wait in silence for Deborah for what seems like an age until eventually I decide to follow her into the kitchen to see if I can help.

She doesn't hear me approach and as I stand just inside the door, she has her back to me as she pours vodka into a pink coffee mug and swigs it straight back. Embarrassed, I watch her wipe her lips with the back of her hand and repeat the process. Then she carefully replaces the screw top on the bottle and I hear the click of the cupboard door as I step back into the lounge, signalling with my hand to Sally to stay back.

A few more minutes pass. It's now so desperately awkward that I cough loudly before stepping back into the kitchen to find Deborah at the sink, dabbing her eyes with a tissue.

'Hey, hey, *Deborah*. What's this?' I move forward to put an arm around her shoulder as she blows her nose. 'I'm sorry. This is all our fault. I'm so sorry.'

She pulls away to wipe her nose with the tissue and her eyes with the back of her hands. 'She won't come—' More nose-wiping. '—to the school thing. I can't let you think Carol will come, or ring, because she won't.' Sally joins us to listen, eyes wide. 'The truth? I haven't seen her in three, maybe four years. She makes promises but always cries off. Excuses. Lies. Ned tries his best to intervene. He's lovely and he does what he can. But she's . . .'

'I expect she's busy. Like you said—'

'And are you too busy to see your mothers?' The first time she's looked at us properly. I can think of nothing helpful to say. Sally tucks her hair behind her ear. 'Anyway, I thought you should know. Having gone to all this trouble. She'll change her number now. That's what she does when I push, rock the boat.'

'I'm so sorry, Deborah.'

'Look, I don't want you to think badly of her. I don't really think badly of her. She's my daughter and she's been through a lot – losing her dad so young, I mean. This nomadic life they have. The adoption business. But I don't know – she says she loses her phone, the number changes. I don't hear for a while – years sometimes, and then she just turns up out of the blue. Completely weird. Don't you think that's *weird*?'

'And Ned? How does he handle it?'

'Like I say, he's lovely. He tries, does his best to intervene. One time he tried to organise this special trip for my birthday. All of us in Bruges for a long weekend, but at the very last minute Carol claimed she was ill. Bailed. So it's *her*. It's always Carol who's the problem. She just resists seeing me, pulls away from me and I have no idea what I've done . . .' Deborah's head twitches and her eyes are dark.

'She's very skinny and I comment on that. I probably shouldn't.' She's talking faster now as if needing to turn over all the pages, trying to understand. 'I think there may be some financial issues at play too. Carol said once that they had to move around so much to avoid tax. Or something. They found this place for me and bought it in my maiden name. Cash. All a bit hush-hush. Told me not to tell anyone – a complete secret. Some tax dodge, I supposed at the time. I don't understand these things. She and Ned send money, straight into my bank sometimes, so I can't ask, can I?'

Deborah takes in a long, loud breath. 'So there we have it – we're estranged. A great shame but there it is.' Her tone is embarrassed suddenly and she starts clattering with plates and cups and spoons from the draining board, announcing that she's very tired and really needs to get to bed. I offer to help wash up but it's as if she's regretting saying so much to us. 'Look, I'm sorry but you need to go. You really shouldn't have come. You should have left this alone.'

Our parting is in the end hurried and awkward. And in the taxi back to the hotel, Sally and I sit in absolute silence until the driver sweeps into the little waiting bay just outside the hotel entrance.

'So – Carol is not all right, not at all.' Sal's words are barely audible and I just shake my head in agreement – feeling both helpless and angry with myself too for forcing everyone's hand. Intruding on Deborah's hurt.

So that when Sally decides to stay up for a drink with Matthew in the bar, I don't have the energy to feel anything and am not surprised when she doesn't come back to our room until very late that night.

I pretend to be asleep as she enters the room, but to my surprise she turns on the light.

'You need to see this, Beth. *Now.*' She's holding out her phone.

My eyes are tired and blurred. I can make out her Facebook page but it's difficult to read. A message. Yes, it looks like a direct message to her page but the print is too small for my tired eyes.

'I can't read it.'

Sal taps to zoom and holds it up to my face again, her own expression all alarm, her skin pale. The profile picture is a single bluebell.

I'm warning you. Leave it alone . . .

I stare and stare, hand up to my mouth. It's not just the message. It's the picture. I look up to Sally to ask the question with my eyes.

Who the hell knows about the bluebells?

CHAPTER 14

BETH - BEFORE

It was in Paris we first realised about Carol's eating. We were in our late twenties and I was just pregnant with Sam. The trip was a girls' treat for the three of us, supposedly to celebrate.

In school Carol had always been naturally slim but had loved her food too. *Lucky metabolism*, she said, tucking into cake and chocolate.

In France, we didn't notice the food thing to start with. It was Ned actually who let it slip that he was worried and made us realise that we should be worried too. The baggy clothes, the bony frame.

Just a coffee for me, girls. I'm stuffed. I ate all the fruit and biscuits in my room . . .

Another thing that was our fault.

At first it really was fun in Paris. The three of us having a lark, as if all the bad stuff between us had happened in another life. We were lucky with the weather for the time of year and from the photographs we took you would honestly think it was summer and that we were totally carefree. I can see her now: Carol, laughing at me from the steps of the Sacré-Coeur with her golden hair shining in the sun against a clear blue canvas, only our coats betraying the October truth.

'But you can't possibly need the toilet *again*. For Christ's sake, Beth. Again?' She was standing about ten steps above me and with her hair blowing across her face was attracting admiring glances from a stream of passers-by. One man, I remember, stared for so long, he tripped on the steps – dropping his briefcase, which slid away from him like a sledge on snow. I took the picture as Carol laughed.

I remember too cradling my small bump and feeling this sense of relief, as though a new era was beginning. Pandora's box forgotten? The trip was Ned's idea. He felt Carol was too isolated in southern France and needed to keep in touch with her 'old life' more. Her friends. Her family. So the whole thing was on him and Carol – a treat. Sally and I protested, wanting to pay our way, but Carol insisted it went on the company account. Ned had done some big deal and so Carol booked us all into a swanky hotel in one of the smarter districts.

And so when we finally gave up on the sightseeing (our feet and my bladder defeated), Carol fixed treatments in the hotel spa. Manicures and pedicures – with Carol picking purple varnish for her feet to match a bruise on her leg from a black run, skiing in some glitzy resort the previous week with business pals. Sal and I marvelled at the story of the chalet party – six couples with their own chef in tow. Carol's amazing new life.

We weren't jealous though, me and Sal. We were pleased for her. And yes – relieved. It was what she needed . . .

I remember watching her face shine as she talked about Ned and all the travelling and the holidays and how proud she was of the business he was building – property development. All over the world. I was holding my bump and just wished I didn't feel quite so tired. I had this picture in my head of a future that might finally block out the past entirely. That maybe she and Ned would have a child too? Give up the globetrotting. Come back to England so that our children could become friends. Christenings. Parties. Bouncy castles on the lawn.

Until in the end I had to admit that *sorry, but I was just absolutely done in – exhausted – and would they forgive me?* And when I finally lay down on my bed, the curtains drawn and window open so that I could just hear the hubbub from the pavement below, I fought and fought and squeezed my eyes tight but still found myself drifting back to the place I can never shake. To school. To what we did. *Do not cry, Beth. Do not cry.*

We ate that first night in a tiny side-street restaurant not far from the hotel – unpretentious, just eight tables in dark wood with chairs to match, their backs and seats in contrasting, paler cane. No tablecloths or menus. Just a blackboard with the plat du jour and the most delicious smells and loud conversation bursting from the kitchen with the swing of the door every time a waiter moved in or out.

Carol had fussed at first about the cigarette smoke – *with you in your condition* – but somehow I did not mind. Did not care. What mattered more was that we should maybe find a moment to talk. *Properly.* Only we did not.

Instead I sat staring into the candle in the middle of the table, thinking – don't they see it any more, Carol and Sally? *Don't they?* Have they really blocked it so deeply and completely that it's gone? Blowing my nose on Sally's napkin, wondering if I was going mad or if perhaps somewhere along the way we had all gone a little mad.

We walked by the river after our meal and had our picture drawn in charcoal. There was a queue for the best of the artists available but ours – a tall, skinny young man in a worn grey overcoat – did a reasonable job. While we sat on a low bench as he sketched away, I watched a mime artist further along the pavement.

He was covered in white make-up, wearing a large white sheet to give the appearance of an alabaster statue. The effect was eerie, making his eyes appear yellow – the veins standing out like miniature bolts of lightning as he stared ahead, motionless, watched by a small crowd. I guessed, of course, that at some point he would move to startle the onlookers, and found myself holding my breath with anticipation. He waited and waited until the crowd was quite large and then suddenly lurched forward into a new pose. Two young children at the front of the crowd screamed and I found myself jumping and then laughing – annoyed that he had outmanoeuvred me. One of the children had been holding a bright red balloon and in her panic let go, then cried – distraught as the balloon floated higher and higher and we all watched it disappear. A tiny dot against the darkening sky.

And then suddenly our picture was finished. Not perfect – he got Sal's nose wrong, just a tad too long, and my eyes looked strange, but the likeness overall was pretty good and Carol promised to have copies made and send them on so we could all have one framed. We strolled back to the hotel, arms linked together – to passers-by looking relaxed and happy.

The next morning I soaked for a full thirty minutes in the large bath – shocked at how easily I was adapting to this five-star luxury. We had arranged to meet early for breakfast and Carol was already finishing as Sally and I settled opposite her, the remains of a bowl of fruit and yoghurt to one side.

'Sleep well?' She did not look up.

Sally and I spoke over each other – gabbling yet again about how fab the rooms were and how delicious the chocolates left on our pillows and how decadent it felt to have a whole room each instead of the triple rooms we shared in the old days.

'Do you remember that hostel in Austria when we had to top and tail? And one of the beds was supported on apple boxes!' I was feeling better, more relaxed after sleeping well and so looking forward to our day, but Carol fell silent as the waiter appeared with coffee.

She cleared her throat. 'OK, so you're not to be cross with me but the thing is, Ned's here. He turned up late last night with some papers I need to sign for the next big deal. I'm a director for one of his property companies so there was no way round it; they needed my signature. Fax isn't allowed on this one. Anyway, he flew all the way to make it simple – spare me sorting out a lawyer's office and all that nonsense. He's going straight on to Lyon this morning and, of course, he wants me to stay . . .'

At that very moment Ned walked into the room, beaming and with his hands held up in mock surrender. He looked really well. Handsome, in an expensive suit. I had forgotten just how striking he was.

'Hello, you guys. So sorry about this – you're to pretend I'm not here and to forgive me for intruding. Has she explained? The wretched papers. Sometimes business is such a pain. Anyway, I'm off now to Lyon so it's hello and goodbye. Literally a flying visit. I'll hear all about your escapades when Carol gets back.'

He moved forward to kiss me and Sal on both cheeks and then gave Carol a big goodbye hug, touching her cheek really tenderly. 'I'll see you when you get home, darling. I'll only be in Lyon a couple of days max. Now, you all have a wonderful time.'

Carol smiled as he left the breakfast room, arm raised to blow her a farewell kiss, and then, after a pause, she suddenly stood – 'Give me a minute, girls' – before rushing from the room.

Sally and I didn't know quite what to think but we could hear them in the corridor. Carol was suddenly saying that she wanted to go back with him, that she wasn't feeling very well, actually. A terrible headache. That she was feeling a bit panicky, not herself. Ned was resisting.

No, no, no, Carol. We talked about this last night. You're going to be OK. I came all this way to help. Come on, darling. You never get to see people from England, not even your mother. This will be so good for you. More time with your friends. Please . . .

There followed whispering we could just make out, with Ned pleading for her to reconsider. Next there were questions about whether she was taking her vitamins. Was she feeling faint? Had she been eating? Was that the real problem?

Eventually Carol came back into the restaurant, all apologies. She didn't seem to realise that we'd overheard and said that she'd decided to go on to Lyon with Ned after all, to help with tying up the deal. Also she was actually feeling quite tired so wasn't up to any more sightseeing.

'Oh goodness, but do you really have to, Carol? I thought Ned said . . .'

'Forgive me. We'll do this again sometime. The bill's all sorted – don't worry about that. And I'll make it up to you. I'm just going to quickly pack.'

She rushed from the restaurant, there was more whispering with Ned and then nothing.

After a couple of minutes Ned came through to our table again, his face ashen. He said that Carol had gone upstairs to fetch her things. He would have one final attempt to persuade her to stay on. 'I am so very, very sorry. This is the last thing I wanted. I came so she wouldn't have to cut the trip short. I'd never have come at all if I'd thought—'

'It's OK, Ned. Not your fault.' I glanced at Sally, who was staring at the tablecloth.

It wasn't the first time Carol had fled from us suddenly – as if being around us too long was too much. It reminded me of magnets. An experiment I was shown in primary school. Facing the right way, two magnets pull together. But if you put the same poles close together, they push in opposite directions. Yes, it was just like that with Carol. As if she wanted to see us in theory but couldn't cope with the reality. Push, pushing away. And only Sally and I truly understood why. We felt guilty watching Ned in Paris because the poor man had no idea at all. Looked entirely baffled.

We sat for a while in silence and then Ned leaned forward. 'Look, I don't want to say the wrong thing here. But has Carol seemed OK to you? Has she been eating OK on this trip?'

'*Eating OK?*' I tilted my head.

Ned glanced to the door and then shook his head. 'Sorry, sorry. I shouldn't have said anything. Forget I said that. Please don't tell her I mentioned it. The truth is, there are no business papers. She phoned me yesterday saying she wanted an excuse to come home – wasn't feeling well. I came to try to buoy her up, persuade her to stay. I've done my best. But she's not herself and I'm quite worried about her. She thinks I worry too much, but with you two knowing her so well, I wondered if you'd *noticed* anything? How skinny she is.'

I didn't know what to say but I suddenly started to think over the meals and snacks with Carol during our time in Paris. And come to think of it, she was always at the breakfast table ahead of us, claiming to have just finished. Later, as Sal and I ordered patisseries, she would claim that she had just scoffed all the biscuits and fruit in her room. *Wasn't hungry . . .*

Dear Lord. Another problem. Another change. Another insidious thing that was secretly but most definitely *our fault.*

CHAPTER 15

BETH – BEFORE

We were just fourteen when it all began. The fourth form. It was the year we were all to leave our childhoods behind – stepping into a much darker place.

It was just a small thing that started it, really – or rather it seemed so at the time. Only much later, with the school to close, will I realise that the first proper trigger was never small.

Not to Carol.

It was the autumn term – two weeks short of the half-term break – and the weather was dreadful. Rain – day after day. Walks were impossible. The tennis courts were sodden and out of bounds and Sal, Carol and I were bored rigid.

Which is why Melody Sage's arrival caused such a timely stir. Ironic, really, but it was the kindness of Sister Veronica that set us on the path to disaster. I suppose she hoped we'd be a good influence on Melody – not foreseeing the exact opposite. Melody Sage joined us very suddenly, moving from a grander and more expensive boarding school in Scotland with the unconvincing explanation that she needed to be nearer relatives.

Everything about Melody smelled of rebellion and we could only assume our nuns were desperate enough for her fees to offer her family one final chance. Breasts were the first thing you noticed. A glorious chest, celebrated by a school blouse deliberately selected just a tad too small so that the material strained between the buttons, revealing spectacular cleavage, maximised by that most glorious of fruit – forbidden to the rest of us. A Wonderbra.

At first Melody kept a lower profile than her chest but the honeymoon period was short. Simple mathematics brought her into our own circle, our odd number being the problem. By the fourth year the dormitory dynamics changed. Instead of a large open-plan dormitory with eight to ten girls, the fourth years were allocated smaller, four-bedded rooms with double sinks and built-in sliding wardrobes. These suites of smaller rooms were in a side wing patrolled less regularly by staff, which gave the opportunity for midnight feasts and misbehaving. School rules demanded lights out at 9 p.m., after which Carol, Sal and I would huddle on one bed to shave our legs, listen to late-night radio and read magazines by torchlight.

The challenge was the spare bed. After the horrible experience with Jacqueline's suicide attempt, our trio had been left alone. Allowances made. But Sister Veronica now selected Melody to join us, hoping no doubt that we might calm her down.

At first Melody – in regular detention already for smoking or swearing – spent little spare time with us. For a few days, she rebuffed all overtures of friendliness and turned up in our room just in time for lights out. But then suddenly Melody spiced things up.

It began with one of Mother Superior's legendary announcements in assembly. It was most important, we were told during these frequent and dramatic soliloquies, that we took it on board that Mother Superior was thinking *not of myself, you understand,* but only of the girls. The school. The truth? She was hurt. Wounded on this particular occasion – pounding her chest by way of emphasis and rolling her eyes to her good Lord – because reports had reached her that some of her girls had been letting themselves down. *Letting us all down.* She could hardly bear to say it out loud but the reports seemed to suggest some foolish and unseemly behaviour in the very grounds of the school . . . *with boys from the comprehensive.*

There followed the fluttering of nuns' handkerchiefs along with warnings of dire and ungodly consequences so that as Sal, Carol and I blushed with immediate false guilt, all other eyes flickered momentarily towards the most likely suspect.

By lunchtime Melody was a celebrity – gangs of girls snapping at her heels for details with the buzz around school by the end of the day that Melody had actually done it *standing up* by the gymnasium with one of the comp's sixth formers.

Sal, Carol and I were in shock and awe.

As soon as lights were out that first evening, we were around her bed, tongues lolling for the dirt. At first Melody merely looked bored, rolling her eyes, but then she appeared to re-evaluate our interest with distinct amusement. Very quickly she conceded there was nothing exciting to report at all. No sex – she'd simply been getting some boys to buy cigarettes for her and someone had spotted her from a distance doing the trade at the school boundary. Luckily for Melody it was a nun whose glasses were so poorly prescribed she could barely recognise her own reflection in a mirror, let alone a pupil at three hundred yards.

The disappointment must have shown on our faces. Melody laughed out loud. Over the next few days she teased us mercilessly for our naivety but then slowly the mocking subsided until finally, out of pity, boredom or maybe a little bit of both, Melody took it upon herself to contribute to our education. This was when we learned that she'd been expelled from her previous school following a string of misdemeanours culminating in her being caught half naked with a tattooed builder in a bus shelter close to the school's hockey pitch.

'Real bitch is, we were caught before we could do anything,' Melody complained.

Carol, Sally and I, who – knocking on the door of fourteen – still hadn't even kissed a boy, were seriously impressed. Whereupon Melody enrolled us in classes distinctly outside the curriculum. Although technically still a virgin, she shared in graphic detail her experience of heavy petting and regularly at night would disappear to one of the bathrooms to masturbate, returning red-faced and triumphant, apologising that *sorry, girls, but some nights I just can't get to sleep without it.* Best of all, she knew the names of *everything.* At last we were to learn that fellatio and cunnilingus were not Greek gods and while still awaiting our first French kiss, we at least now knew what a French letter was.

So grateful were we to Melody for this previously missing link in our education that we completely dropped our guard. We tried to include her more in our dormitory get-togethers and although we were wise enough to decline her offer to teach us to smoke, we couldn't see the harm when she suggested a dormitory seance. She'd been offered the loan of a Ouija board and I remember thinking it would be a laugh – something for our street cred. Knowing absolutely nothing about Ouija boards, I imagined some kind of spirit Scrabble. A bit of harmless fun.

Melody had arranged to borrow the board from one of the boys who ran errands for her. She explained that he had a soft spot for her, but that she was merely stringing him along. *Not a looker.* The board belonged to the boy's mother, who was obsessed with the occult – visiting clairvoyants regularly in a bid to make contact with her own mother, who had died when she was young.

I will realise in later years that I should have read the warning signs from the very beginning – the way the colour drained from Carol's face when Melody said that the board had made definite contact with the grandmother. A true message from beyond the grave. But it was too late. We'd promised Melody we would give it a go and, given all she'd done for us, it was way too late to play chicken.

We picked a Thursday night when Sister Veronica was on duty – knowing that she would check our dormitory only once. Lights were turned out at 9 p.m. and soon after that we assembled alongside Melody's bed with our torches.

Earlier in the evening Carol had quietly confessed her anxiety to me but in my teenage selfishness I did not take her reticence seriously. *It's just a game, Carol. A charade. Nothing to worry about. It's not real. You know it's not real, yes?* It never occurred to me there was any personal foundation for her misgivings.

We sat on the floor, the board between us. It was a golden colour with the alphabet in capital letters in two arched lines. Below this there was a line of numbers. In the top of the left-hand corner the word Yes was set beside a face on the sun and on the opposite corner No was written beside a half moon. There were a few other random symbols – stars and the like – around the board.

Melody then produced the wooden, heart-shaped pointer. 'It works best in twos. Come on, Beth. We'll go first.'

'Don't we have to ask questions? To get it started?' Sally was whispering. 'I've seen that in films. You have to ask something straight away.'

'Is there anyone there?' Melody's own ridiculously ghostly tone was all cliché yet Carol seemed genuinely upset, pushing at her shoulder.

'I'm not doing this if you're all going to be stupid.'

'Is there anyone there?' Melody repeated. And then the pointer under my hand moved across the board, circling first then pointing to the *yes.*

'*You* did that!' I snatched my hand away from the pointer – embarrassed to be caught off guard. Also I could see Carol's eyes widen with real fear and was beginning to regret getting drawn into the stupid game. For some reason I was thinking of Jacqueline in that bathroom, months earlier. All the blood. Me passing out. I had honestly expected this to be a joke, to give it up as a bad job. I'd not expected to feel afraid.

'Don't be a sissy,' Melody teased. 'Come on, Carol. You have a go.'

'No, I don't want to.'

And that's when I saw Melody's true colours. The glint of pleasure in her eyes. Enjoying Carol's weakness, her reticence. Looking back later, I will see very clearly that I should have stepped in, for Carol's sake, and made Melody put the stupid board away. But I'm ashamed to say that I did not.

The truth is, I was trying to push the picture of Jacqueline out of my mind and I was afraid of looking stupid myself. It suddenly occurred to me that no one had heard anything about Jacqueline since she left. What if she'd tried it again? Succeeded?

Did any of us even believe in any kind of afterlife?

While all these thoughts were racing through my mind, Carol shifted to sit alongside Melody. She went visibly paler, her hand trembling, as the pointer answered Melody's questions. *Yes*, there was someone there. *Yes*, they had a message. And when Melody asked who for, the pointer moved swiftly.

-P-R-I-N-C-E- . . .

Our jaws were nearly on the floor. I was at least relieved that it wasn't Jacqueline but Carol was completely ashen. I'd never seen her so pale.

'Stop it, Melody. Carol doesn't like it. She's shaking. You're *frightening* her. Stop it right now!' My voice was a hissing whisper but Carol, for all her trembling, would not take her hand from the pointer.

-S-S-

'Princess?' Sally sounded intrigued. 'Princess *who*?'

But then Carol pulled back sharply, crashing against the bedside locker and shaking as if she were having some kind of fit. Too late, Melody tried to hide the board under her bed as Sister Veronica appeared, standing right above us while I put my arms around Carol, trying in vain to stop her body from shaking so violently.

The nuns acted quickly once the board was discovered. You'd think we'd been drinking bats' blood. Our parents were called that very night and all four of us were sent home, instantly suspended.

Over the next few days tearful phone calls were exchanged between Sally and myself as our parents negotiated with the school. We tried meantime to speak to Carol but were told by Deborah that she was unwell and needed to rest. For the best part of a week I believed we'd be expelled and I would never see my beloved friends again but then, out of the blue, we were summoned to a meeting with Mother Superior.

We sat, Sal and me, in the nuns' sitting room, listening only to the ticking of the large clock on the mantelpiece as the Mother Superior told our parents that no dabbling with the occult could be tolerated in such a God-fearing school. People had been known to go mad, she warned. *Tick, tock, tick, tock.*

She confirmed that all the nuns had been praying for us daily, which made my father exchange a very odd look with my mother and she had to seek refuge in a handkerchief. *Tick, tock, tick, tock.* And then thankfully came the *but*. Sister Veronica had spoken up in our defence, blaming herself for putting Melody in our small dormitory. We were told we could return to school after the weekend but Melody had been expelled. It was sad but the decision was final.

Carol and her mother were not present for this meeting and she did not return to school until a week after us – a nasty virus being given as the explanation.

'I don't want to talk about it,' was all she would say when we tried to find out what had been going on. 'I don't ever want to talk about it . . .'

After that, Carol was never quite the same. Introverted suddenly, as if there was some private struggle that was none of our business. She point-blank refused to discuss it with us – a first – and so we had no idea why.

All we knew, from that first change in her eyes, was that something very bad had begun.

Something, we would realise only later, that would lay the true foundations for much darker sadnesses ahead.

CHAPTER 16

BETH - NOW

'But who would want to threaten us? Not Carol herself – you don't seriously think it would be *Carol herself*?' Sally, in the passenger seat, has her hand pressed against her forehead as if her brain is hurting.

'But what about the bluebell, Sal?'

'Lucky guess. Coincidence. Someone from school. Someone trolling us?'

'No, this is someone who *knows*. I feel it.'

'But it can't be, Beth. Be rational. It can't be someone who knows unless it's Carol.'

We are halfway home after the disastrous trip to Kent, parked outside a small café. Matthew is inside, queuing for takeaway coffees.

Neither Sally nor I have really slept and what I hate the most is this atmosphere, everything so strained and awkward between us suddenly. Matthew, who clearly has a serious soft spot for Sally, is being almost too helpful. I badly wish he were not travelling with us so that Sal and I could talk more openly.

At breakfast, Matthew shared his professional take. The message – *I'm warning you. Leave it alone* – was from a brand-new Facebook page.

No friends. No history. Just the picture of a single bluebell as its profile pic. Thankfully Sal took a screenshot because soon after breakfast the message mysteriously disappeared along with the entire new profile, as if frozen or deleted.

Matthew wondered if Deborah was more internet-savvy and upset than she let on. We confided in him that she clearly liked a drink and he wondered if she'd sent the message late at night after having a few too many, then regretted it. But for me, it just didn't fit. Not Deborah.

And what about the bluebell? Matthew asked, of course, about the significance of the flower. He didn't see the message as particularly strong or worrying in itself. But there was no way we could tell him the truth about the flower, how sinister the bluebell felt to us.

How could we?

To test the water with Deborah, I phoned her before we set off for home to apologise for upsetting her and promised to stay in touch. I mentioned we'd had an odd message on social media about Carol but she really didn't seem to understand what I was talking about. It didn't feel like she was acting, more like genuine puzzlement.

'I don't think it was Deborah, Sally. I really don't. I can't believe Carol would ever threaten us. So who else could it be?'

'I don't know. Matthew reckons either Carol herself or it could just be a troll who noticed the appeals I put out over Carol on the school group pages.'

'And the flower?'

'Well, some people at school knew we planted bluebells.'

'No, this is sinister, Sal. This isn't just a lucky guess. So what exactly did you say on the group page?' I'm thinking that I really ought to get back on Facebook myself. I suspended my profile after some trouble with a few guests who appeared on *The Meeting of Minds* and were unhappy with the editing of the programme.

'Look, I was very careful. I just said we were trying to trace Carol Winters for the school event. Nothing more than that.'

'And you didn't mention bluebells?'

Sally turns to look at me as if I've gone completely mad.

'Sorry, sorry. Stupid question. So did you have any response?'

'No, like I told you before – just a few comments from people looking forward to the party. No one in touch with Carol.'

I turn to see, through the window of the café, that Matthew is nearing the front of the queue. We don't have long to ourselves. 'Why does Matthew think it's a troll?'

'Because it's so common, I guess. Some haters just latch on to things for no good reason. Jump in and get a bit nasty, purely for the sake of it. Apparently it's really tough for the police to do anything. It's really easy to set up fake social media accounts and it takes ages to track them and make a case to get stuff taken down. There's been loads posted lately and shared about the school closing, so maybe it's just stirred someone up.'

I still don't buy it. Why would anyone else care? And why use the flower as a profile pic? So I say nothing for a bit as Sally watches Matthew, catching his eye as he turns to look at the car through the café window. In the queue, his height is especially striking. Nearly a head taller than everyone else. He puts his hand up. A sort of shy wave. He smiles too.

'You like him, don't you, Sal?'

She fidgets with her seat belt as Matthew turns away. 'Yeah, I guess. He's nice. Easy to talk to. Why – don't you then?'

'I suppose. Bit funny on the subject of kids though.'

'I beg your pardon?' She has turned again to look me directly in the face. 'Why on earth did you say that?'

'Oh, I don't know.'

'Yes, you do. Spit it out.'

'Look, I didn't like to say anything to you before. It didn't seem relevant. But he was very odd at his office that first meeting when I mentioned my boys. And he gets sort of fidgety whenever I mention the family. So clearly not the family type.' Even as the words come out of my mouth, I regret them.

'So what the hell does that mean? *Not the family type*. What are you saying here, Beth?'

'I don't know really.'

'Look, I've said I'll go on a picnic with him. Maybe. We've not booked a bloody church, Beth.'

'So you're actually going on a *date*. With our private detective.'

'Not a date – a picnic. And he's not our private detective any more. Job done. A complete disaster. Carol wants nothing to do with us, which is no great surprise really, is it? And into the bargain, we've stirred up some troll.'

I hate this. We never argue like this. I hate that I've made things worse with Carol and that the dread and the fear feel so much worse too – not knowing what's going to happen. Stuck once more in the limbo that has haunted our whole adult lives. Pandora's box firmly closed.

'You don't really think Carol could have sent us that message herself, do you, Beth?' Sally has softened her voice. 'Carol wouldn't do that to us. *Would she?*'

It was Matthew who had pressed us on this. He said that people can change. *It's been a long time*. I watch again through the window as Matthew hands over money for our order.

I can't let myself do this. Wonder what Carol is truly capable of. It feels much too dangerous . . .

And so instead I find my mind drifting back, back – thinking of that other version of Carol. *Before*. I think of my favourite picture, stored safely in my bag with the Whistler – a picture of the three of us on a walk back in school. A photo too precious to share with Matthew. In that picture, Sally and I are sitting cross-legged on the grass – Carol alongside, lying on her stomach with her chin propped up on her arms, strands of hair escaping her ponytail and blowing across her mouth. The image is so vivid, I can feel the wind on my own face. Carol is beaming from ear to ear and I can hear her voice too. So happy. So carefree.

You love it up here, Beth, don't you?

And she's so right. This young Carol. This different, innocent and entirely hopeful version of herself. The Carol *before* . . . The Carol she was meant to be.

I hear my answer as an echo on the wind, taking in the view.

Yes, Carol. I do.

CHAPTER 17
CAROL - NOW

Friday

So now this is serious. And I must be careful. Not lose my head and do anything too silly.

I've changed my phone number and burned theirs – Beth and Sally's.

I know exactly what they're thinking and what they're afraid of too, but they're completely wrong if they think that we can go back there. Fix it.

Deluded.

Mad.

No, I must stop this.

It's my mother I worry about now. She'll get herself all wound up and I can't cope with that. What if the drinking gets out of control again? What on earth will I do? She can't come here. I can't go there.

Such a mess. All of it.

And on top of everything, Ned is fussing, fussing, fussing again about the eating. Oh Lord . . . why do people make such a fuss? I eat enough. I like how I am.

I think I'm going to have to give up the meetings for a bit. Yes – I'll help Ned with the business for a while, forget the spiritualist group. All of it. Focus. Focus. Focus.

I'll pace myself and show that I can sit down for a meal. Eat in front of him and other people too. I'll fix another dinner party.

Yes. I'll concentrate on stopping Ned from all this worrying and wait until I'm calm again and am sure that Beth and Sally have stopped this.

And then when Ned stops fretting and has another big deal to distract him, I'll try that woman in Paris. The one who was on the television. The one all the film stars use. She is one hundred per cent for real. She has the gift and she's the one who can help me. I can feel it.

I just know that if I could hear from him properly. If I could find out what exactly it is he wants to say to me . . . Ever since school. Ever since the Ouija board, I wish that I'd been braver when he tried to speak to me that time. I wish I could travel back in time and ask him what he was trying to say. That night in the dormitory. I wonder now if he knew what was ahead for me? Maybe he was trying to warn me of what was going to happen?

I just need to find someone or some place who can do this properly. Reach him for me. My dad, I mean.

Yes.

Ask my father exactly what he wants to say to me . . .

CHAPTER 18

BETH - NOW

The second threat comes just a week after our return from Kent.

My two boys play football every Wednesday after school and so I collect them from a small bus shelter alongside the pitch. It's the agreed pickup point for all parents and a member of staff is always on hand to supervise the handover of the younger children.

I'm at home, just about to leave to collect the boys, when a call comes from the school office.

'We were just checking whether you just telephoned with a message.'

'No, not me. Why?'

'So you're coming to collect the boys as normal?'

'Yes, absolutely. Why?'

There's a long pause and I can sense the unease. I press the office secretary to explain. She says there must be some kind of confusion because her colleague took a call with a message saying that I was unable to collect and that the boys should be told a friend would be coming instead.

'A friend. *What* friend?' I'm thinking of Sally but there's been no arrangement with Sally and she would never call the school herself. Why would she do that? She has never done anything like that.

The secretary asks me to wait while the colleague checks a note on a piece of paper.

'Carol. The caller said your friend Carol would be collecting the boys. So that's not right?'

'No, no, absolutely not . . .' My heart is now beating even faster and I feel so unsteady that I have to sit down.

'So, my boys – where are they now? You haven't let anyone take them?' Fear floods through me.

'No, of course not. That's why we're ringing. Please don't upset yourself, Mrs Carter. We always check these things.'

'So, who rang? Was it someone called Carol who rang?' I try to calm my voice but I have this picture in my head of the boys climbing into someone else's car.

I can hear muffled voices as if the secretary has put her hand over the receiver while consulting her colleague.

'Look, I'm sorry but we don't know who called. A woman. She didn't give her name. Just left that message to say Carol would be picking the boys up instead of you. But please don't worry – we *always* check this kind of thing. We thought it was a little strange, which is why I'm calling. We'll have to log it officially, of course, but it may be our mistake. It's been a bit hectic here and my colleague is saying she may have got the wrong name. Someone may simply have got muddled.'

'Right. Yes, OK. But I feel quite worried now. Should I be worried? Could you check again with your colleague?'

There's a pause. Whispering.

'Look, we do have hiccups occasionally.' She clears her throat as if checking herself, lowering her voice conspiratorially. 'There are sometimes parental disputes – difficult divorces, access arrangements and so on. But as I say, you are absolutely not to worry. The school protocols are watertight. It'll go on the log and we'll let you know if there's any further development.'

'Further development? Do you mean the police will be involved?'

'The *police*? Goodness, not automatically. Not unless there's any specific reason you feel we should report this to the police? Do you want us to, because I'm very happy . . .' Her tone has changed completely.

'No, no, no. There's probably just been some confusion with the names as you say. Look, I'll put some feelers out and try to get to the bottom of it at this end.' My mind is racing now and I realise that I don't want them to involve the police. Or ask too many questions . . .

I seek reassurance that my boys will never be released into anyone's care but mine or my husband's. Once this is confirmed, I put down the phone, grab my car keys and head for the school.

En route, my head's still pounding with all the possibilities. It's starting to rain. Windy, too, with the trees leaning to one side.

I think of Deborah. I think of her switch to anger when she wanted us to leave her home. I deeply regret upsetting her but I struggle to imagine her capable of anything malign. I think back to the visits to Carol's home when we were young, Deborah always so very kind. No. No. She would surely never do something awful like this.

And then, *Carol*?

I feel my hands involuntarily gripping the steering wheel. I think of her on the phone at her mother's. Distant. Lies. Excuses . . .

I remember her split personality in Paris.

The message from the profile picture with the single bluebell.

I realise I will need to run this new school thing past Sally but feel a familiar hollowing to my stomach, the dread of her reaction. I think of how spiky Sally was in the car on the journey home from Kent. She wishes we'd left this all alone.

And next? I can't help myself – I'm thinking of the very thing we have been trying all our adult lives to forget. That terrible room all those years ago. The blood. The tears. The disbelief. I drive faster than I should and find that there are tears on my own cheeks now as I finally turn the last corner towards the sports fields.

I quickly brush my cheeks with the arm of my jumper. I am ridiculously jubilant when I catch sight of Sam and Harry standing with about half a dozen others in the bus shelter. Harry is swinging his kitbag into his brother's legs to wind him up. He swings once, twice and the third time really high and hard so that the teacher has to intervene. I should be annoyed with him but instead feel only a rush of relief to see them standing there. Safe. Waiting.

I wave to the teacher, who recognises me, ticking the names on her list and releasing the boys, who run along the pavement towards the car.

'What's for tea?' Sam asks.

'So did you win?' I say.

'Just practice. Nobody wins. It's not hotpot, is it? We *hate* hotpot.'

I turn to look at them both. I take in their red faces and dirty kit and fight the urge to cry, wishing I could hug them both tight without giving myself away. I'm praying that I have not done something to put these two darling boys in any kind of danger . . .

'So is it *stew*?' Sam stretches the word *stew* into an insult, and for just a moment I'm sucked back into the normality of this nightly tussle.

What to eat is a renewed source of conflict following my recent purchase of a slow cooker. I find it completely marvellous. The answer to my working mother prayers. Everyone else suddenly hates stew.

'Let's get fish and chips.' A superficial and ridiculous bribe to get me through this car ride.

It works.

They launch into a loud debate over whether to go for fish or battered sausages. Meantime I pull away, heart beating fast and warning myself to postpone the lecture on taking lifts from strangers. *Never, never, never.* I will save this for bedtime. Drill it into them yet again.

An hour later, with sausages and chips devoured, I send the boys upstairs to do their homework and move into the conservatory to phone Sally.

She gasps. 'So do you really think Carol called the school? Another way to warn us off?'

'I don't know, Sally. I honestly don't know what to think.'

'But that's really creepy. Properly *threatening* . . .'

'I know, I know.' I'm glad she's said it out loud, that I've not been overreacting. Who the hell would do anything so cruel? 'No, no, no . . . Carol wouldn't do anything like that. I'm sure she wouldn't. So do you think we should phone the police, Sally? I told the school not to but I just don't know now. I mean, this was someone who worked out where my boys go to school. I will at least need to tell Adam, won't I?'

There's a very long pause.

'If you tell Adam, you'll have to tell him everything. Please don't do that. Not after all this time. Please, Beth.'

'But what *else* can we do? I mean . . . this is about my children, Sally.'

'Have you warned the school to be careful?'

'Of course I have.'

'Right. Good. I'll talk to Matthew. Ask his advice. He'll know what to do.'

'So, you're seeing him. You're really going on a date?'

'Not a *date* date. I told you. It's nothing. I'll run this past him. He's ex-police. He'll know what to do.'

CHAPTER 19

MATTHEW - NOW

Matthew checks his watch. Fifteen minutes early. He taps his right hand on the steering wheel then turns the radio on – some kind of music quiz. Snaps it back off.

He hears a car turn the corner into the parking area. Eyes wide, he turns. *No, false alarm.* An elderly couple with a golden retriever in the back of a Volvo estate.

He checks his face in the mirror and runs his hand through his hair. It's quite curly so he has to keep it short; he's never been able to try different styles as all his friends did when they were younger. He tilts his head to the left and then to the right. He's always wished he were darker. The fair colouring is from his mother's side of the family. He wonders if Sally finds him attractive – whatever that means? Matthew honestly has no idea. He turns on the radio, forgetting he's already tried this. Turns it off yet again.

Five minutes later and a silver Polo pulls around the corner. Sally, on spotting him, waves and pulls into the slot alongside Matthew's car.

He gets out and can't help himself, beaming at her. She's dressed down but looks glorious in a dark green waxed jacket and bright striped scarf. The colours seem to make her eyes shine. For just a moment there's an awkward silence. Matthew can't decide if he should kiss her on the cheek? *No.*

'So you found it all right?' His stomach flips. *Damn.* 'Sorry, sorry – some detective, eh?'

She laughs and then takes in a long breath, looking about her and putting her hands in her pockets. 'I can't see the lake.'

'It's through the woods. I'll show you. Shall we walk first and then I'll come back for the picnic?'

'Sure. I'm in your hands. Whatever.'

Matthew had in the end decided against his favourite Dartmoor spot on the grounds it was perhaps too remote and might send the wrong signal. He's pleased to have opted for Stover Country Park, which is quiet midweek this time of year but always lovely. There's a path around a lake populated by all manner of birds, and plenty of picnic tables set among trees with gorgeous views and the bonus of cheeky squirrels darting this way and that.

It takes them just half an hour or so to circle the lake with Matthew pointing out the various highlights and then, all of a sudden, he spies two especially large swans heading for the bank. He wills them to do an about-turn but instead the swans seem to eyeball him. As if smelling his secret, they leave the lake and begin waddling directly towards him.

Matthew steps back and holds out his hand as a signal to Sally to keep still.

'You're not frightened of swans, Matthew?'

'Of course not.' He is. *Terribly.* 'It's just they can be a bit unpredictable. There could be a nest nearby.' Still he has his arm out, hoping to stop Sally in her tracks.

'They're not dangerous,' she says. 'They're not like geese. They're not going to attack us.'

'They've got very large beaks, Sally.'

She laughs. 'You *are* afraid of them . . .' She's still smiling as she moves forward, shooing with both her hands. The swans move to the side, but their eyes are still fixed on Matthew.

'They don't like me. Look at the way they're staring at me.'

'They're just being nosy – here.' Sally links her arm through Matthew's to lead him past the swans.

He can feel his heart still beating a little too quickly and twists his neck to keep his eye on the birds until they're at a safe distance. The truth? He doesn't mind swans as photo opportunities – safely out on the lake. It's the first time here that he's seen them venture on to the path.

'There was an incident with a ham sandwich when I was a child.' He winces at the memory of the swan suddenly lurching towards his lunch. He was a small boy on a park bench and the bird seemed huge, snap snapping towards his hand.

Sally keeps her arm looped through his and squeezes it as she shakes her head in continued amusement, so that Matthew is starting to be grateful for his phobia.

'You are to tell no one,' he says. 'Bad for my image.'

They decide to circle the lake a second time before Matthew selects a picnic table set deep within the trees and leaves Sally to enjoy the view while he fetches their lunch from the car. He returns to throw an old blue and white chequered tablecloth over the picnic table – the easiest way to deal with the inevitable bird droppings.

'Tablecloth? You weren't kidding about doing it properly, were you?'

He's smiling as he takes out the plates, cutlery and plastic containers. Pork pie from the deli. Home-made potato salad. Smoked salmon. Olive bread from his favourite bakery.

'Look, I brought some bubbly, Sally – just a glass each as we're driving – but if you're not keen?' He can feel himself blushing, fearing now that this is too much.

'My goodness – *champagne*! Now you're talking.'

They chat easily throughout their meal about their backgrounds, their families. It's like that night in the bar in the hotel when they both talked about their schooldays. This, that – everything and nothing. Matthew is at last properly relaxing and once the bubbles are gone, pours them water and then coffee from a flask.

It's only after they have finished their drinks that the mood seems inexplicably to change. Sally is suddenly answering his questions much more briefly. She keeps glancing out at the lake and starts to fiddle with her hair and fish around in her pocket.

'Is something the matter? Have I said something?'

'No, no. Lunch was wonderful. Thank you.' She takes a deep breath. 'Well, actually there is something but I feel a bit embarrassed – you going to all this trouble and me wanting to pick your brain.'

'Pick my brain?'

Now she's the one blushing.

'OK. So, what is it, Sally?'

'Look, I don't want you to think I'm being cheeky, Matthew. That I accepted this invitation to get some free advice, because that's not what this is. Not at all.'

He pulls his chin back into his neck, a little baffled now.

'OK, so after we set up this outing, something else happened – to worry Beth.' She pauses as if to check his reaction. 'And I said I'd ask your advice but I feel awkward now because it feels like I'm making you put your work hat back on. And I don't want you to think that's why I came – I mean, I don't want you to think I'm taking advantage.'

Matthew watches her closely and takes in the body language: the fidgeting, the nervousness in her eyes. 'How about you just tell me what's happened, Sally.'

'OK, so Beth's boys are both in the same school. They do football after classes on a Wednesday and Beth always picks them up. Yesterday the school got an odd call, claiming she wouldn't be able to make it and that a friend would be stepping in instead to pick up the boys. *A friend called Carol,* so the message claimed. The school phoned Beth to check if it was all right. She picked the boys up as usual and the school have promised they'll report any more calls. And of course they won't release the children to any stranger so they're perfectly safe . . .'

'Christ.' Matthew rakes his hand through his hair. He can feel his frown deepen as he processes this. 'Did the school report it? Take it further?'

'They logged it officially – protocol – but Beth asked them not to report it to the police or anything. I said I'd ask your advice.'

'OK. Well – with children involved, not good, obviously.'

'No, Beth's quite shaken. She doesn't know how worried she should be. What do you think? Should she be worried?'

'Did the school say how old the caller sounded? Deborah's age? Or Carol's age? I'm assuming that's what we're thinking here – that it was either Deborah or Carol?'

'Beth didn't say anything about the age of the caller. So what do you think, Matthew?'

'I think it's proper harassment, that's what I think. Nasty. First the Facebook message and now this. But precisely how *dangerous*? That's very difficult to say. Now if someone had actually turned up trying to collect the children – that would need to go straight to the police, obviously. But a phone call? Could just be malicious stirring to upset Beth even more. And you.'

Matthew looks at Sally very intently as her whole demeanour changes. 'You said Carol didn't react well at all to your getting in touch. That you regretted intruding. And that Deborah was pretty upset too?' She nods and her face darkens further. 'Look, I don't want to pry, Sally, and I know you don't want to buy into this being Carol herself – the message on Facebook and now this. But I do realise there's something you're not telling me about Carol.' He pauses. 'Could she be . . . unstable? Is that likely, do you think? Could she be dangerous even?'

Sally bites her bottom lip.

Matthew waits again, a punch inside as he acknowledges that her eyes are slowly beginning to glisten. He hates to push this, to upset her. But this phone call to the school raises the bar. The Facebook message wasn't nice but was trivial compared to this. 'Look, I want to help you and I will, Sally, but it's much harder if you're holding out on me.'

She looks at him very intently as if weighing something up, then glances away towards the lake and back at him again.

'Something happened, didn't it? With Carol?'

She says nothing.

'Is it very bad? Is that why you don't want to say?' He watches her fighting tears and remembers the change in Carol's eyes in the school photographs.

Sally pauses, rubbing the back of her hand across each of her eyes in turn and then reaching into her pocket again for a tissue. 'We should go, Matthew. I'm getting a bit cold. Do you mind?' Suddenly she's standing and clattering about, packing up the plates and containers.

Damn it.

'I'm sorry. I didn't mean to upset you.' He's mortified. It is all at once awkward as they sort out the picnic basket and she folds the tablecloth. She will no longer meet his gaze and he doesn't know what worries him most. That he's ruined the end of their first date. Or that this could be even more serious than he feared.

CHAPTER 20

BETH - NOW

It's three weeks since the odd phone call to the boys' school. There have been no more messages and I should feel relieved. But I don't.

Instead I feel truly odd, permanently dazed – sort of detached, not quite in the moment.

It's reached the point where I can't bear to watch the evening news at all so I make excuses every night, which is upsetting Adam. It used to be such a ritual, to sit down together at the end of the day with cups of tea and digestive biscuits. To share a little rant over the politics. Put the world to rights. It's something we have always enjoyed, me and Adam – a mutual obsession with current affairs. He's such a kind and gentle soul and I used to love to see his fury on behalf of the underdog. Now it feels like another loss – another barrier between me and Adam – because even the sound of the news jingle makes me panic and think of school. The dread of what may lie ahead for us. So I avoid the headlines, pottering in the kitchen instead with packed lunches and fake tidying while poor Adam thinks I'm avoiding *him*.

Sally is still seeing Matthew. She likes him and has promised me she won't say too much. Give us away. He's still making inquiries at the boys' school to try to figure out who may have telephoned. But with no more messages – no more phone calls and nothing on social media – we remain in this sort of limbo with no real idea of what the hell is going on.

Sally seems to have changed her tune and now fears it really could be Carol herself behind it – a warning to leave things alone – but I think it's Matthew who's put that into her head. Carol simply wouldn't do anything unpleasant concerning my children. I think of her that day we met, sharing her pink blankets without a moment's thought. *No.* I just know in my bones that she wouldn't want to hurt me.

Work continues to be a chore as I struggle to concentrate. This morning I considered calling in sick but it's a recording day.

Now though, as I sit next to Stella in the studio gallery for another episode of *The Meeting of Minds*, I realise that I should have trusted my first instinct and stayed home.

'Christ, Beth. You look rough.'

'Sorry, Stella. Cold starting.'

'So are they all up for it?' She's leafing through my research notes on the guests – booked by me – who are settling themselves in the studio beyond the glass partition in front of us, aided by our floor manager, Fred.

Today's theme is 'Friends and Reunions'. My fault. I suggested it in a moment of madness when we were brainstorming and I was short of ideas. As soon as the words left my mouth, I wanted to suck them back in. But it was too late.

'And you've warned them not to eat the cakes?'

'Yes, they're up for it. And yes, I've warned them not to eat the cakes.' I check through my own notes, reminding myself of today's players – mainly social networking addicts, featured in the tabloids. There are two middle-aged women, Louise and Sheila, who have renewed contact through Facebook after twenty-odd years. Sharon, a woman of thirty who had the courage to get in touch with a girl who'd once bullied her (theirs is to be the story of reconciliation, of confronting past demons). And the rather sordid story (which Stella inevitably likes best) of David, who traced his childhood sweetheart, Catherine, on Twitter and promptly left his wife and four sons.

'So libel-wise, better just watch David that he doesn't bad-mouth the wife too much.' Stella takes off her glasses. 'Everyone ready?'

The director, Andy, is now taking up his seat, winking at me, then secretly rolling his eyes at Stella. Andy is a talent, a complete pro, but Cruella likes to try to call the shots – not just editorially (which is her right) but visually (which is not). But since she's paying the bills, Andy can do no more than grit his teeth. The *Meeting of Minds* budget allows for only minimal editing; he needs to get the shots right first time so tends to save the row with Stella until later.

Our presenter is Adrienne – an experienced, likeable woman who once fronted daytime shows for the network but fell out of favour for a reason none of us ever understood. There were rumours of drugs and some indiscretion with an ITV executive but we never got to the bottom of it. She was out of work for some time before her agent put out the word that she would consider cable series, corporate videos – pretty much anything. Adrienne is good at *The Meeting of Minds*. She clearly hates the concept as much as I do but also needs the money so never lets it show. At least not on set.

Earpiece now in place, she smiles at her guests as Stella presses the microphone button to speak directly to Adrienne via talkback, the interviewees in blissful ignorance of the conspiracy.

'I'm thinking we start with the happy reunion pair, Louise and Sheila. Bullying second. Then stir it up with David. Try and get them all to have a go at him.' Stella has a tendency to lean into the microphone and I notice Adrienne turning down the volume of her receiver, clipped to the back of her trousers.

'All set?' Stella takes a deep breath.

'OK on the floor?' Andy then runs through instructions with each of the four cameramen and the PA begins counting down.

Ten. Nine. Eight.

I fix my stare on the monitor in front of us, the one with the red lights around to signal selection to recording, and try to concentrate – to push Carol's face away, her troubled eyes.

Seven. Six. Five.

Three candles. The Whistler painting.

Four. Three. Two. One.

◆ ◆ ◆

I widen my eyes to try to stay in the moment, staring and staring at the monitor, but it's futile. Drifting to and fro in time is something I can't stop these days. Flashes of scenes from the past pushing their way into my day.

My eyes are smarting and so I close them – to find myself back in school. Another small space. It's the confessional in the school chapel – a wooden cubicle that smells of polish and matches from the candle stand nearby.

We were forced in school to go to confession every single week before Mass. At first I thought it funny and used to make sins up. But not now. Not in the fourth year, not once our worlds change. Now I sit in the confessional, wondering if there really is a God who is all-knowing. Wondering also if it's true that priests are forbidden to repeat what you tell them.

'Is it a sin, Father, to break a promise?' I'm whispering, searching in my uniform pocket for a tissue, hoping he won't recognise my voice.

'Well, that rather depends. A promise is an issue of trust, I suppose. To break someone's trust is not a good thing. But not all promises are good things. Perhaps if you can tell me what the promise is about?'

'No.' My heart is beating fast. 'And God. Can he really forgive *anything at all*? If you're really, really sorry . . .'

'Of course. But we have to repent.'

There's a spider glistening in the light in the corner of the confessional and I watch it for a time in silence, realising as my mind drifts to a memory of drops of rain on blades of grass with ants marching in a perfect line that there's no point going on with this. And so I stare first at the little wooden grille that divides us and then, without speaking, I push open the door and leave . . .

◆ ◆ ◆

'Beth, are you with us? *Beth?*' Stella's tone is clipped, pulling me back to the studio.

'Yes, of course.' A lie. I feel panicky. I have no idea how much I've missed, what's just been said. Again I wish I'd cried off sick. 'Sorry.' I shuffle my papers and clear my throat as the director warns sound to *standby*.

'And – cue, Adrienne.'

Take any six people and one will always dominate. Dinner party. Train journey. Television programme.

Just five minutes into our recording and Louise is our motormouth. In every way she dominates the set. Bright orange shirt and a determination not to let anyone else get a word in. 'The thing is – you just know when you click with some people, don't you?' Louise tilts her head towards Adrienne, who is leaning away, trying to coax others into the debate. 'It's chemical, picking a friend. Like falling in love.'

'Chemical?' Adrienne raises an eyebrow.

'For Christ's sake, bring Sheila in. Ask her how they lost touch,' Stella bellows into the microphone so that Adrienne's eyes flicker. The gallery feels hot – stifling – and I shift in my seat, sipping at a cup of water. It's technically not allowed near the faders and equipment but I don't care.

'Coming to camera three.' Andy switches away from the orange shirt.

'So how did you two lose touch all those years ago?' Adrienne asks.

'It was sad, really.' Sheila's voice is soft and nervous.

Slow zoom on three.

I can feel my eyes widening, coaxing Sheila to go on, but too late.

'Babies.' Louise jumps back in as if she's hit the buzzer on a quiz show.

Camera four. Lord. Can no one shut that woman up.

'I fell pregnant really easily with my first but Sheila had problems, didn't you, love? Endometriosis. Tried everything. Every position in the book.' And then while Sheila stares at her lap, Louise explains how she'd read in a magazine that if you lay on your back with your legs in the air for fifteen minutes after sex you stood a better chance. And she'd told Sheila. *Fifteen minutes. Time it.* And Sheila had tried it. But *still* no baby.

'Nothing worked and so she was jealous,' Louise says.

'I wasn't jealous.'

'Well, whatever. Anyway, in the end we moved away. My husband got posted and we just drifted. But we always missed each other, didn't we, love?'

Sheila forces a little smile and I watch her eyes, which say something else entirely.

'And do you have a family now, Sheila?' Adrienne's tone is softer.

Camera three. Single shot.

A pause.

Slow zoom.

'Yes, two boys. Adopted.' The first smile in Sheila's eyes.

The debate drifts to adoption with Stella soon tearing her hair out as Adrienne valiantly tries to steer the group back to the agreed theme of 'Friends and Reunions', and then suddenly there's a lull and Louise commits the cardinal sin.

'She's eating the cake. She's eating the bloody cake!' Stella is almost hysterical. I watch Louise bite into the sponge, willing her to choke, good and proper, but suddenly David leans forward.

'I think we turn to the past because the present gets so empty.' His voice is steady, considered. Louise, with her mouth stuffed full of sponge, is temporarily helpless.

'Great. Get him to talk about the day he left his wife.' Stella, finger on the microphone button, looks triumphant but Adrienne has had enough. She discreetly pulls out her earpiece as David takes a deep breath to continue.

'People would say I had a good life. Four sons. A wife. A job. But I just thought – is this it then? Sex and a curry on a Friday night. Put out the rubbish on a Tuesday. My turn to unload the dishwasher Saturday and Sunday morning. Same bloody thing every week. Every bloody week. And I just thought – is this it?'

Everyone in the gallery is staring at the monitor as David pauses.

'Get him to talk about leaving his wife. Are you listening – Adrienne, Beth? Is anyone in this studio even listening to me?' Stella is bellowing into the microphone.

I feel faint. Little black dots appearing on the periphery of my vision.

'Give me camera two on David. Close up.' Andy's voice is uncomfortable.

The pause continues as the camera zooms in on David's face. He glances from one guest to the other. Everyone is desperate for him to go on . . .

'And when I saw Catherine's photograph on Twitter, that was it. I remembered someone very different.'

'Different from your wife, you mean?' Adrienne coaxes.

Wide shot, then back on two.

'No, no, I don't mean *them*. I don't mean Catherine. Or my wife.' David is clearly surprised to have been so misunderstood.

'I meant me. I remembered that different version of *me*.'

It is all at once too much. I stand. For a moment I take in everyone looking at me. I pick up my bag. I walk from the gallery. And I go home.

CHAPTER 21

CAROL - NOW

Monday

What a surprise. Maybe things aren't quite as bad as I feared. Maybe everything will be OK after all. Maybe I'm stronger than I think . . .

And today, best of all – a complete surprise. I met a young girl and I find it difficult to explain, even here, how I feel about it. Such an unexpected distraction, like a turn suddenly in a better direction. She's the most extraordinary child – brash, beautiful, sparky. Cheeky to the point of rudeness but also terribly good fun. She's coming over again tomorrow and I feel ridiculous admitting how much I'm looking forward to it. She's called Emily and is just twelve years old – in that valley between childhood and adolescence – one minute looking so grown up, the next like a very little girl with a pout. I am absolutely intrigued by her.

Ella is behind it all – turned up last night, about 11 p.m. in the most terrible tizzy. Guests due in the barn and the pool filter's failed. The water a disgusting murky mess and no chance of the right part to repair it for at least a week, maybe two.

'Their daughter is a CHAMPION swimmer!' She was almost in tears, fearing they'd want their money back. Worse, sue.

'And I was wondering – I know it's a cheek – I don't like to ask . . .'

And I'm thinking – oh, great. Here we go.

So, they came over mid-morning – Emily and her parents – just after Ned left for work. I was dreading it. Seething inside too when I sussed the set-up. Charm personified, the parents, but not the slightest intention of spending the break with their poor daughter.

Quick cup of coffee, admired the pool, then dumped Emily here and disappeared.

'You don't mind, do you? So good of you.' The mother was UNBELIEVABLE! One of those superior sing-song voices. 'She just swims and swims, like a fish. You'll hardly know she's here.'

Of course I bit my lip – for the poor girl's sake. But I bloody well did mind. My first real peace and quiet in months. Ned AND Pierre away all day. I was hoping to get my head together. Maybe book that medium in Paris . . . But Emily just looked on, deflated. Used to this, no doubt, and I felt really sorry for her. When they'd gone, she didn't say a word, just got into the pool and did lengths. Twenty or so. Backstroke, crawl – even butterfly, which amazed me.

She has a gymnast's shape – long and lean with that S shape from the side that girls carry until they hit their teens and when I brought lemonade down and saw her expression, I felt guilty for resenting the intrusion.

'It's OK.' Her voice all grown-up and deadpan. 'You don't have to be polite. I know you don't really want me here. I'll just finish my training and cycle back. You mustn't mind my parents – I'm used to it. And I've brought loads of books to read.'

Well, I was speechless.

And then she looked at me as if she was weighing me up really carefully before launching into the most extraordinary sequence of questions.

Sat on one of my loungers with her towel wrapped round her, hugging her knees and sipping lemonade. Told me, bold as brass, that I had unhappy eyes. But thought I was very beautiful. And why was I on my own? And why was I living in France? And did I like the food? And didn't I miss England? And why didn't I have any children? And what books did I like to read?

On and on. Questions just pouring out of her mouth – no shame, no blushing. And I couldn't believe her confidence and her nerve – so much so that I found myself answering her out of sheer bloody surprise.

And do you know what? I liked her for it. And it suddenly hit me how worn down I am by all the small talk. Me, Ned, Ella and Jonathan – all of us. And here is this kid, telling it how it is. Asking me stuff no adult would DARE to. Important stuff.

I laughed out loud for the first time in as long as I can remember.

And she's coming over again tomorrow.

And I'm looking forward to it.

Tuesday

So get this – I'm learning butterfly stroke. Thirty-eight years old and I'm being taught butterfly stroke by a county under-thirteen champion! I haven't ached so much in years. Emily is an absolutely bully – so deadly serious about teaching me. And I'm in the pool, thinking how utterly ridiculous it is, being shouted at by a child but having a ball.

She arrived on her bike at about 10 a.m. and didn't leave until much later today – around six. We had lunch by the pool and this afternoon she demanded to see my clothes. Spent two hours going through my wardrobe, trying everything on – hats, shoes, my ballgowns (which, to be frank, nearly fitted her).

'You're so thin,' she kept saying. 'Don't you eat? Are you anorexic?'

And I'm thinking – excuse me?

Thursday

She didn't come over yesterday and I was shocked at how disappointed I was. I'm so good at being on my tod normally – especially when Pierre goes to his mum's (hurrah, no spies in the kitchen) – but after Tuesday, it seemed so quiet around the place. I completely forgot about Paris and in the end just practised my bloody butterfly stroke!

Then she arrived a little late today – and I knew immediately there was something up.

'Dad's been shagging his secretary.'

I told her off for the language but not too convincingly. Poor kid. The trip's apparently the make-or-break deal for the parents and there was a huge scene yesterday. Tears. Suicide threats. Emily trying to referee.

She says it's not the first fling . . . though her mum doesn't like to admit it.

'An ostrich,' she pronounced – and I felt terribly sad for her. No wonder she's like she is. Reckons the lawyers will be called in as soon as they get back home.

Then she did about forty lengths and I made lunch – understanding completely now why she swims so well.

You can't hear the world in the water. I've done it myself often enough. Dipped under the surface until the water fills your ears with echoes from a different place.

CHAPTER 22

MATTHEW - NOW

Matthew has his feet up on his office desk, coffee mug in hand. He's thinking about last night. Fifth date with Sally. They went back to The Anchor – a favourite pub of his and the place he took her to patch things up after the picnic. Log fire. Nice food.

The phone goes.

'Is that the private detective?'

Matthew recognises the voice and his heart sinks.

'The little people are still after me. They're going to kidnap me – I know they are.'

'I'm so sorry but we've talked about this several times, Mr Ellis, and I'm really not able to help you. You need to do what I suggested in the first place – pop in and have a chat with your doctor.'

'One of them has a gun now – a tiny one the size of a peanut but it could still do damage. I have delicate skin . . .'

Matthew hangs up. The phone rings again instantly and so he disconnects the caller and lays the phone on the desk, off the hook. He moves across the room to top up his coffee from a jug on a tray and settles back in his chair to think once more about Sally.

She's still holding out on him about Carol, he knows that, but it's good that there have been no more Facebook messages, no more odd phone calls. His best hope is that the whole hassle will go away on its own if Beth and Sally can be persuaded to let this go and leave Carol be. That said, he has quietly looked into the two other girls from school that Sally mentioned just *might* have reason to upset Beth. It's a long shot, frankly – his money is still definitely on Carol or Deborah – but it's technically possible that someone else with an axe to grind is involved. It seems as if Sally put out quite a few appeals about Carol on social media. Could that have backfired? Put someone's nose out of joint?

There were only two tricky incidents in school that Sally could think of. First – Jacqueline Preer, who tried to top herself and left on the quiet. Matthew has been unable to trace her and wonders privately if she tried again and succeeded. Next there was Melody Sage. She was apparently expelled over some Ouija board prank. She might have seen all the stuff about the school closing and could hold a grudge but would she really give a damn? After all these years?

It proved easy enough to find Melody on social media and to Matthew's surprise, she had indeed been bad-mouthing the school and the upcoming party. *Coincidence?*

He found a number and rang her first thing, just to exclude her, but she sounded spaced out despite it being so early – drugs would be his best guess from her speech pattern. Melody certainly knew about the school gig coming up but gave nothing away. He put out a gentle warning – said that there was some trolling going on around the school's Facebook group and wondered if she knew anything? *Anyone who might have a grudge against the school or any of the old girls?*

She hung up.

Matthew now narrows his eyes, remembering her voice on the phone, and reconsiders. Maybe he should pay Melody a quick visit? He wouldn't bother were it just the Facebook post but the call to the school was more worrying.

He sips his coffee and closes his eyes. Sally has invited him to dinner the next evening – his first visit to her Barbican flat – and so he is, of course, daring to *hope* . . . He feels a flush of both excitement and wariness and then the flip of the familiar contradiction. The punch of guilt. Hell's bells – is he being unfair to her? Should he tell her? Come clean about himself?

Not for the first time he thinks of the picture Beth showed him in his office of her two boys. *Damn.* He wonders if dating a client is even allowed. Against the guidelines for the Society of Private Investigators – an organisation he rather rashly joined so he can put a badge on his website.

Possibly. Probably . . .

He sips his coffee again, glances at his watch, then his diary. Empty. To hell with it. Melody Sage is on the electoral register and, as luck would have it, now lives just a couple of hours away. He didn't like how she sounded on the phone and he has nothing better to do. It will give him something with which to reassure Sally at dinner.

◆ ◆ ◆

When he pulls up outside the flat, Matthew is surprised. So, life has gone very wrong for Melody Sage. He gets the familiar mixed emotions that sink estates always stir. He feels sorry for the people stuck here and yet? Years on the beat showed him the darker side, the consequence of the anger these places fuel. You can almost smell the rage in the air. He doesn't know this area but he certainly knows the drill. Watch your car. Watch yourself. Keep your hand on your phone in your pocket.

Three teenagers stand in a huddle on a corner ahead of him, one leaning back against a red-brick wall. They're whispering, then lean in, heads almost touching and clearly exchanging something. One glances towards his car and Matthew pretends to search for something in the glove compartment. The trio walk away.

Matthew waits until they're out of sight before approaching the maisonette block. The small front garden is littered with junk – an old sink, two mattresses and various plastic boxes and crates, all filthy. Amid all this is the paradox of a motorcycle covered with a deep green protective cover. It's clean and the wheels peeping beneath the cover look polished. So someone here cares for something after all.

Melody's address is listed as 1a – the left hand of the ground floor flats or maisonettes. Matthew tries the bell. No sound. He uses the door knocker, quietly at first but then more loudly as he catches sight of a silhouette against the closed curtains.

He lifts the flap to the letterbox and calls through. 'Police inquiry. You need to answer right now.' A white lie but he knows it will work. Sure enough, a woman of about the right age opens the door, scowling. Her pupils are enlarged and there are dark circles under her eyes. Her hair is unwashed, dragged into a tight and unflattering ponytail, and she's the unhealthy end of skinny.

'Melody Sage?'

'Who wants to know?'

'I'm a private investigator looking into some harassment concerning the Colman convent school closure.'

She moves to close the door but Matthew puts his foot in the way.

'You said you were police.'

'No, I didn't. I said I was here about a police inquiry. And trust me, there *will* be a police inquiry into the drugs in this flat unless you let me in right this minute.'

She pauses, staring at him, before finally backing away indoors. Matthew follows her into the sitting room, taking in the familiar chaos of an addict's landscape. Piles of dirty plates and cups and bowls litter the surfaces. Melody glances to a corner table and Matthew follows her gaze to a biscuit tin alongside a metal ashtray, a spoon and lighter. So that's where she keeps it. Heroin, he suspects.

'I hear you were expelled from the school a long time ago and I wondered how you feel about that? Feel about this big party coming up? Seeing as life's not going so great for you personally. Upset you, has it?'

'I have no idea what you're talking about. Why the hell are you even here?'

'Like I say, there's been some unpleasantness. Some harassment over this final party coming up.'

She scratches her skull and shrugs. Matthew thinks of Sally and Beth and looks again around the room and at the contrast of this mess of a life. Sad.

'OK, so I know you know about the party because I saw your post on Facebook saying – what was it? – *about time they knocked that place down*. So I'm here to tell you that if there are any more nasty posts or phone calls linked to any single one of the people going to that party, I'll be straight back here with the drug squad. Do we understand each other?'

She says nothing but continues to scowl and gives him the finger, tilting her head defiantly to the side.

'Good. Excellent. We understand each other.'

Matthew then turns and leaves, wondering as he fires the key to unlock his car when exactly Melody took the wrong turn in life that led her here.

CHAPTER 23

BETH - NOW

And so now I learn that greyness can creep up on you. *One o'clock. Three o'clock. Dinner time, Mr Wolf.*

I have always hated the colour grey, ever since those stupid blankets in school. But I've never thought of myself as anyone who would get depressed. Not truly medically depressed. And so I don't at first see this for what it is.

I just see this grey fog around me and assume it will pass.

Day after day I look around at all the familiar things: the boys' school, the corner shop, our house and the lamp at the end of the street. It's like viewing everything through a new app that has taken away the colour and the contrast – my whole surroundings suddenly switched to black and white. And *grey.*

I'm wondering just how much Sally has really told Matthew. Why has she even confided in him about Melody and Jacqueline? We've argued about that and I hate that all this is coming between us.

I can't seem to sleep properly at night or concentrate properly during the day. One morning I even find myself packing teabags into the boys' lunchboxes. And the whole family keeps asking me if I'm all right.

In the past I would have confided in Sally about this strange phase – all this peculiar *greyness* – but she's now so wrapped up in Matthew, I hardly see her. She's cancelled some of our regular girls' nights, which has never happened before.

Carol's number is unsurprisingly unobtainable. I tried phoning Deborah again but she was just evasive. *Best leave it, Beth. Leave it up to her. Please.*

I find myself wondering if Deborah really could be behind the messages after all? And then I think of the bluebell picture on Facebook. No. She couldn't know about the bluebells. *Could she?*

◆ ◆ ◆

Things are still strained between me and Adam. I feel guilty for not telling him the full story about how we met Matthew but I can't talk to him properly without giving myself away and so I keep it all bottled up inside.

I can tell that he's worried too. He keeps whispering with the boys and checking up on what I've eaten. And then he suddenly announces that he's invited Sally and Matthew round.

What the hell?

'We should make an effort to get to know Sal's new fella better, Beth. For her sake, don't you think? And it'll do you good to see Sal, seeing as she's been so busy lately? *Yes?*'

I look at Adam's face through the grey fog, trying to appreciate his effort. He's organised a barbecue and puts on his Homer Simpson plastic apron. It normally amuses me – my lovely Adam who, alongside a barbecue, thinks that a cartoon apron and long-handled utensils will magic him into a master cook. But I can't find my smile today, can't remember where I put it.

I check my watch. Just half an hour before Sal and Matthew arrive and still the charcoal is red.

'I think I'll just pop the chicken in the oven to give it a bit of a start.' I try to sound relaxed. Do not want any kind of argument.

'What's the point of a barbecue if you cook everything in the kitchen, Beth?'

'I'm not going to cook everything, just give it a start. You can still blacken it on the grill.'

'I do not blacken food.'

He's blowing on the coals now, sending smoke billowing back into his face, which prompts a coughing fit. I remind myself that he's trying to make an effort for me and so say nothing more.

Sam stands alongside his father, unimpressed. 'You haven't used that stinky marmalade, have you, Mum?'

'It's *marinade* and yes, I have.'

Both sons grimace as their father winks. I force a smile – painfully aware of the muscles. Out of practice.

Adam continues the infuriating habit of asking me constantly if I'm OK and spotting the smile now obliges on cue, 'You OK?'

I nod before wandering into the downstairs cloakroom and stand on tiptoes to check myself in the mirror. Strange to feel nervous over seeing Sally. I've changed twice already – trying shorts at first, which seemed to make my legs look stumpy, even though Adam insists they're still my best asset. I am now in three-quarter-length trousers with a short-sleeved linen shirt. Adam keeps asking – why make such a fuss? *It's only Sally.* He's in his oldest, most faded shorts and a white tee shirt with a hole under the arm and I envy how shabby and relaxed he looks.

The point being that it *isn't* only Sally. It's Sally and Matthew. The new Sally-in-a-couple Sally. The Sally who wants to close the door on the whole Carol saga and who has not even noticed what is happening here. And I know they'll turn up – Matthew rabbiting on about all the work he's doing on Sal's cottages and she'll be relaxed and glowing as if I'm the only one with a madness in my head, and I will feel like I always do these days.

Grey.

I move back outside with a glass of wine to calm myself and stand next to Adam, touching the back of his neck which makes him stretch, imagining a fly.

'So what do you think of Matthew really?' I lower my voice as the boys disappear to the lawn for goal practice, biting my lip as Sam sticks out his foot in a bid to trip his brother en route. I have had to tell Adam how Sally really met Matthew, though I've been light on the details. Dodging any tricky questions.

'What's there to think? I've only met him once. Seems a nice enough guy, though why the hell you ever needed a private investigator to find Carol, I still don't understand.'

'Oh, I don't know. He just doesn't seem the family type to me.'

'Excuse me? Family type? What do you mean *family type?*' He's pulling his warning face. 'I hope you haven't been saying the wrong thing to Sally. Meddling. Is that why you two have fallen out? Is that what's upsetting you, Beth?'

'We haven't fallen out.'

Sam has gone too far now. Out of the corner of my eye, I see Harry nursing his ankle and I shout for them to *get along or go inside.*

'Look, Matthew just seems a bit odd about kids. Doesn't seem to like them much from what I can see.'

Adam, meanwhile, pulls another face. 'Well, he hasn't got any, has he? Kids, I mean.' He's blowing again on the coals. 'Anyway, other people's kids are always a complete nightmare.'

'Sam, this is your last warning!' I turn back to Adam. 'No, I think it might be more than that. He always seems . . . Oh, I don't know – whenever I've talked about the boys, he's always seemed really awkward.'

'Oh, for goodness' sake, give the poor man a break. Single guy syndrome. I knew nothing about kids until it was too late.' He winks and I try once more to find a smile as he puts the grill in place over the red coals. Then his expression changes and he turns to me with a warning in his eyes. 'Now you won't go saying anything about Matthew to upset Sally today, will you?'

I return to the kitchen and discreetly put the chicken in the oven.

◆ ◆ ◆

In the end, Sally and Matthew arrive almost an hour late, by which time the meat is a healthy colour, under caveman supervision, the boys have served two punishments indoors and are now back on the patio, moaning about how hungry they are, and I'm feeling a little light-headed from too much wine on an empty stomach. Just as I fear, the golden couple are radiant. I swear that Sal has lost half a stone in the past couple of weeks and Matthew looks as if he's stepped off a yacht: cream shorts, worn deck shoes and a white tee shirt.

Adam is charm personified and the boys cheer up to pester and amuse while I potter in the kitchen. For a reason I can't explain, I now feel *out of it* once more. A spectator, disconnected. In our pre-Matthew life Sally would have joined me inside and my irritation grows as I watch her through the window, laughing and gently touching Matthew's neck (who does not mistake this for an insect) as Adam pours them more wine.

They keep catching each other's eye and smiling and I'm thinking – *oh right, so you're properly together now*. It annoys me that Sally hasn't told me this, has stopped confiding in me.

After dressing the salad and slicing the French bread, I find I can't help myself; I call out to Sally to ask for a hand. I must have got the tone wrong for there's wariness on her face as she joins me and helps put the bread into a basket.

'Sorry I couldn't make Julio's on Thursday.'

I say nothing to help her.

'Matthew got these tickets for a jazz concert. They were quite expensive so I didn't like to say no. We'll do next Thursday. Definitely.'

I smile, not believing her. 'So it's still going well with him?'

She blushes and I raise my eyebrows.

'He's amazing with the cottages, Beth. Got loads of contacts in the trade. His dad was a builder so he worked with him years back, before the police. I've landed right on my feet.'

I spread butter on a piece of bread, offering Sal a slice too.

'I'm surprised he finds the time.'

'Oh, he picks and chooses what he takes on at the agency. It's still quite new and there's not always the right kind of work about.'

'Oh.' I let the word hang in the air and we join the others to serve lunch, which goes quite well until the boys ask Matthew if he likes football. At first he just shrugs until Sal intervenes.

'Spends half the weekend glued to it.'

'Will you go in goal for us?' Sam throws Matthew the ball and normally I'd chastise him for being so pushy but for once I'm grateful for his intervention and watch Matthew carefully.

It's just as I expect. He looks ill at ease and won't look my son in the eye. 'Maybe later. When my lunch has gone down.' Still he does not look at Sam.

'Oh, leave the poor man alone.' Adam steps in to take the ball and heads to the lawn himself.

'Bit of a pain, kids?' I can't help myself.

Matthew does not reply. Sally glares at me.

'Best thing we did though – having the boys.'

Sally and Matthew just sip their drinks. Only later in the kitchen as Sally helps me load the dishwasher does she tackle me. 'Why did you do that?'

'What?'

'Embarrass Matthew like that. Always going on about him not being the *family type*?'

'I don't.'

'You do. Every time I talk to you about him. Ever since that stupid trip to Kent. It's not a sin, you know, not to be into kids.'

'So I'm right then. He doesn't like children?'

Sally looks distressed and I realise too late that I've gone too far. Too much wine. She slams the dishwasher door closed.

'Look, Beth. I really don't know what's got into you lately but I'm tired of it all. If you ask me, you're just bloody jealous. For once, just *once*, I've got something going for me that doesn't involve you and you can't bear it, can you? You just can't be *pleased* for me.'

She's really flushed now and I'm shocked. 'Sal, I'm sorry. I'm just concerned . . .'

'Oh, don't patronise me. You're not concerned. You're just angry at the whole bloody world because of Carol and what . . . we . . . did.' She has lowered her voice to a harsh, spitting whisper and stares right at me. 'You just can't see it, can you, Beth. You've made it worse. You should have left it alone. We can *never . . . fix . . . it*. We did something bad. No. Worse than bad – unforgivable. And you just can't accept that, can you?' She heads off into the garden to find Matthew. 'Come on, Matt. We're leaving.'

'What now? Already?'

'Guys, guys, what is this?' Adam is at a complete loss.

It is all at once terrible and humiliating. Sam and Harry stare wide-eyed as Sally grabs her things and marches to the car – Matthew clearly embarrassed, shrugging his apologies.

As they pull away, Adam, still clutching the boys' football, turns to ask me *what the hell is going on, Beth?* and I just run upstairs so that no one will see me cry.

CHAPTER 24

CAROL - NOW

Saturday

I took Emily to the market today and made her do all the ordering and bartering – for the sake of her French (which is quite good, actually) – and bought her a little bracelet from Madame Bresain's stall. Cheap but pretty.

And then she said something very strange. Quite hurtful, although I know she didn't intend it to be. She asked me why the phone never rings at my house – neither a landline nor mobile. And didn't I mind? Told me that the phone rings all day at her mum's – friends, relatives, hairdressers, caterers. She couldn't understand the quiet at mine. Why no one even popped by.

It was like a slap to the cheek – coming from such a little kid, with such a crap life herself. So I lied to her. I told her that all my friends and relatives are still in England and I see them heaps when I'm over there. Heaps.

She said, 'Oh, I see . . .' in a tone that said she saw rather too well.

So last night I went up into the attic and went right through the box, which I haven't done in years. Like Dorian Gray. I've hidden it so well, under so many piles of curtains, the dust nearly choked me. But it's all there. Safe.

The Whistler postcard. Even that picture from Paris, the sketch I meant to get copied and post on but never did. It shocked me how young we all looked in it – Sal and Beth and me. How young and innocent and normal we all looked.

Monday

Today Emily was rooting around the house and found my watercolours. It didn't occur to me to hide them away. I was embarrassed at first but she was really fired up about them. Paints herself, apparently, although she prefers pen and ink drawings she says. Black and white more her style.

I'd forgotten there were so many in the case, some from years back when I was still struggling with the washes, and then she made me get my kit – the easel, the paints, the lot. And before I know it we're in the garden, painting the view from the shade by the vine and she's keen as mustard. Really patient. Really paying attention.

Then it all went horribly wrong.

She found two pictures I'd started years back. One trying to copy the Whistler with washes of grey and pink with pencil over the top of the three figures and the tree. And a second of a single bluebell in a vase.

'What are these? They're lovely.'

'Nothing. Nothing. Give it back. It's nothing.'

And my knees almost went from under me for I honestly have not thought of it all so much, not since she's been here.

I found myself panicking, lying to her. This horrible pounding in my chest. Boom. Boom. Boom.

I've said that she can't come over in the morning because I have something on.

Thursday

Emily is going home tomorrow and I'm telling myself that it's probably for the best. We're both pretending to be fine about it and she has set a challenge: I have to finish three lengths of butterfly before she will leave.

It's nigh on killing me and I joke that she'll just have to stay, only I'm not sure I am really joking. I'm so worried about her. The divorce. And yes – I'm sorry that I got upset with her over the pictures. I'll miss her.

Ella came over briefly with flowers to thank me for being so brilliant about the pool and to say that the repair man reckons the part should be here soon and it should be fine before the changeover day with the next set of guests.

Emily was different while she was around, which pleased me. I had rather hoped that she's not the same with others as she is with me.

Friday

It's an evening flight so Emily came over very briefly this morning to say goodbye and we both tried very hard to be cool. I did my three lengths of butterfly. She said the style was utter crap but not bad for someone of my age.

And then she gave me something that almost made me lose it – a little pebble that she'd painted really beautifully as a thank you gift. A background of pale blue with dolphins leaping through waves. She wasn't grown-up at all when she handed it to me. Just a little girl. And I was thinking – is that how we were when we met? Me and Sal and Beth? That young?

I couldn't speak.

She's asked if she could write – or ring? Maybe even visit again some day?

And only then did it hit me – that I'm afraid that if she gets to know me too well, there will be more moments like over the paintings; that she will see the truth deep inside me. The darkness and the blackness. I can't risk it.

I just can't.

CHAPTER 25

MATTHEW - NOW

Last night it was amazing. This morning? Matthew has his arm around Sally's shoulders, glancing around her bedroom.

She put on a wrap first thing when she made them coffee and is still wearing it. He's sad about that but won't say so. She's all of a sudden awkward as if pulling away and a worry burns inside him that she's having second thoughts.

It's the third time he's stayed over and her Plymouth waterfront home is still a puzzle – like something from a lifestyle magazine. Impressive and yet almost too perfect with it. Like a hotel. Marble bathroom with huge power shower, a kitchen in white gloss with no door handles.

How do you open anything in this place?

Press, Matthew. You just press the door. Like a tumble dryer . . .

The bedroom has fitted sliding wardrobes along a whole wall so there's no clutter. Nothing out of place anywhere. Matthew continues to look around the room and understands why Beth teases her so much. Ah yes – *Beth*.

'Look, I don't want to pry, Sally, but this bust-up with Beth – is it my fault? Because I know how much it's upsetting you and if I'm to blame for that . . .'

She pulls away to place her coffee cup back on the bedside table and Matthew has to remove his arm from her shoulders, pretending that he's fine with this when he really wants it to be last night again. Close. Fine. Dark. Just them. No Beth. No Carol. None of this awkwardness . . .

'It's not your fault.' She opens her mouth as if to continue but then changes her mind and finishes her drink. 'Shall I fetch us more coffee?'

Matthew waits and then puts the back of his hand very gently against her cheek. For just a moment she leans into his hand and he feels this very strange but all-pervading sense of sadness; he would like to tell her about this. He wants to tell her that they must not let this slip away from them – how they were together last night – but he's a man who's learned to be afraid of honesty. Ironic, he thinks, that he pursues truth for a living. 'Yeah, sure. More coffee would be lovely.'

When she returns with their fresh drinks, he tells her more about Melody Sage. How sad it is to think of them all together as young girls and now leading such different lives. He repeats that he considers it unlikely that Melody sent the Facebook message or made the call to Beth's boys' school but he's glad to have put out a gentle warning all the same.

'It's good that things have gone quiet,' he says finally, and she forces a small smile before immediately changing the subject.

They talk instead about the work at the cottages. Matthew, whose father was a general builder, has been helping out one day a week and Sally worries that she's taking advantage. The truth is, Matthew loves to be there, sharing a flask of coffee and sandwiches with Sally as she marches about, all fired up and drawing up plans and lists. She has a builder commissioned to do all the major work – damp-proofing, plumbing and the major electrics – but Matthew is keen to help where he can. Any excuse to be near her.

'Look, you mustn't feel you have to help so much. I wouldn't want you to be missing cases . . .'

'Oh, please. Like I told you, I'm only getting about three days per week of decent commissions. I'd much rather help with your cottages than work with mad people.' He's told her about Mr Ellis and *the little people* and expands again now to try to make her laugh, rabbiting on about the many strange cases he's offered, when suddenly Sally interrupts him.

'Can I ask you something, Matthew? About a case, about the law?' Her tone has changed.

'Of course. Anything. Ask away.'

There's a long pause, Sally smoothing the fabric of the duvet.

'The age of criminal responsibility is ten – right?'

Sally is now pointedly looking at her coffee cup, not at him, and Matthew stares, a chill suddenly in the air as he worries again that he may have seriously underestimated this whole thing with Carol. He originally suspected drugs maybe. Self-harm? Some kind of mental health issue? Now he finds himself both willing her to continue and yet concerned at exactly what she might be about to say.

'And children are treated differently by courts?'

'Yes, that's right.' Matthew speaks deliberately slowly, the little ball of dread growing in his stomach. He realises only in this moment that he'd not imagined a crime. At least not a serious crime.

'But what if something from childhood doesn't come to light until the person is an adult? What then? Is there leniency? *Are allowances made?*'

Matthew pauses. He wants Sally to look at him so he can try to read her expression. 'Do you want to give me an example, Sally? The details? Hypothetically, I mean?'

Matthew fancies that he sees tears forming in Sally's eyes, just as they did at that first picnic. Her hand is actually trembling. He badly wants to know exactly what they're really dealing with but doesn't want to get it wrong again. Finally she turns towards him and shakes her head. 'I can't, Matthew. I'm sorry. I just need to know what would happen. Hypothetically, I mean – in terms of the law.'

CHAPTER 26

BETH - NOW

Precisely how long after the barbecue I stop washing is hard to remember. Two, maybe three days.

It's such a horrid thing to admit to – so unlike me. At school I was almost OCD over cleanliness – the one bribing girls to give me their turn on the shower rota.

'Beth's just been in then,' they'd all laugh in the communal bathroom as bare feet trekked through my patch of talcum powder like footsteps through snow.

But now? In these long, empty days after being dismissed on the phone by Carol, the strange threatening messages and the row with Sal? Washing suddenly seems like too much effort. Sometimes I step into the shower room, towel at the ready, and then I just can't summon the energy to take the final step up into the shower basin. I can't see the point.

I manage everything else – just about, although the boys tell me one day that I've packed teabags in their lunchboxes again. I cover just enough research to keep Cruella off my case but cry off filming with the excuse of a virulent stomach bug.

I suppose it only hits me just how serious this has become when Adam suggests a visit to the doctor with him. He hates doctors.

Next I notice him changing the bed and I know that things must be very bad. We believe in equality but have somehow, since the boys, shared out the tasks to gender stereotypes. Adam never normally changes the bed. He chops the logs and empties the bins. I do the cooking. I change the beds.

And before I know it, when the boys are at a friend's house one evening he leads me into the bathroom and he's set candles all around. There's a strong scent of vanilla coming either from the candles or from the bath, which is foaming almost to the top.

'A bath will do you good, Beth. Make you feel better.'

He helps me undress like a child and I say nothing, too tired to resist. Then I'm sitting in the bath and Adam has found a sponge and is using it to wash my back – at first just warm, delicious water which he allows to cascade down my back like a waterfall, then creamy soap which he swirls in large overlapping circles.

I close my eyes and try to feel my gratitude, to shape it like a sculpture – give it some form that I might be able to show to Adam. But I cannot.

'Do you remember you always used to talk about visiting China, Beth?'

I frown. 'Yes.' It's true, although I'm puzzled, have not thought of it in years. At school I became obsessed with mountains. Longed more than anything in the world to one day visit Guilin with its magical peaks.

'Wasn't there some book you always wanted? By a photographer? Maybe we could try to get a copy. Start saving. Plan a special trip for your fortieth?'

I look towards him. Ah. So he thinks all of this – this odd and alarming phase – is because I'm worried about getting older. I feel guilty again, cannot tell him *That's not it, Adam. I'm not who you think I am. The wife you think I am. The mother you think I am . . .*

'What was the place you wanted to see?'

I stare down at the bubbles and turn the word over in my mind. 'Guilin.'

'That's it.'

I close my eyes to feel the water down my back. It was in the school library – the book – by a photographer called Hiroji Kubota. Sister Veronica had directed me towards the photographic section when I'd exhausted the stock in the geography aisle.

The cover photograph was just extraordinary. Half a dozen men on little raft-like boats in the darkness with lanterns to guide them. I always presumed they were setting out on a fishing expedition, but whether it was a lake, a river or an estuary I couldn't tell. Their lights reflected on the water and beyond them in the distance they were watched by a range of mountains I positively ached to touch. They rose up like giants, silently guarding the fishermen in the darkness, arching their huge backs as if smiling down on them.

'I could never pronounce the names.'

'Sorry, darling?'

'The places in the book. I'd love to see them but I could never pronounce the names.'

'So we should start saving.'

'Maybe.'

There's a long pause.

'We must visit your mum, Beth.' He has rinsed the sponge now and the waterfall is back – first down my left shoulder and then my right.

Good idea, Adam. Good idea.

'What do you think, darling? Next weekend?'

I try to find my voice but it is lost somewhere, deep in the water, drifting to China and back, and so I just nod my head and he smiles encouragement.

I sink deeper into the water and he warns me not to let myself get cold, to enjoy my soak but – *don't get cold, Beth*. He points to a white towel, laid ready on the toilet seat.

Poor Adam. He doesn't know that I'm already cold. *You'll catch your death.* It's my mother's voice and I turn, confused, to the doorway where Adam stands – smiling with his mouth and worrying with his eyes.

◆ ◆ ◆

Four days later we're at my mother's and there's no messing about. She doesn't panic but announces to Adam that she'll be coming to stay with us for a bit and she'll *have a lift straight back with us, if that's all right*.

At the doctor's with me, she is blunt. 'My daughter's depressed. It's been going on for a while, apparently. Never happened to her before. She's normally such a sunny girl. But there's no stigma, is there? Tell her, doctor. This can happen to anyone.'

The doctor confirms that, yes, a period of depression can happen to anyone and asks then to speak to me alone. At first my mother is reluctant to leave the room but I manage a smile, which I hope she'll read as relief, and when I judge that she's a safe distance away – back in the waiting room – I'm suddenly crying. No – worse than that. I am sobbing as if a lifetime of shame and guilt is pouring out of me. Normally I'd find this humiliating but on this occasion I don't especially care what the doctor thinks. It doesn't seem to matter.

I cry for quite a long time, accepting tissues that the doctor hands to me, one at a time, and then when I have finally regained control we talk. There is a series of questions and I find even I am alarmed at my answers.

He's asking if there has been any unexpected stress lately. *A trigger?* I lie. I know perfectly well what has caused this but I tell him I have no idea.

He recommends urgent talking therapy but I don't want that and so eventually he decides reluctantly on a prescription and spends some time explaining the medication, which he assures me is mild and not addictive. A temporary crutch. He wants to see me again soon.

Back at home, my mother takes over my kitchen as if it's her own and I sit with a cup of tea at the table, watching her busy herself just as I did as a child.

It hits me only now that whenever I think of my mother, I always picture her standing up. Standing at the cooker. Standing at the spin dryer. Standing at the table, waiting for plates to clear and cups to be drained. Even when she used to phone for our weekly call when I was at boarding school, I knew she would be standing at the extension in the kitchen, not sitting in the lounge as my father would.

She's from a generation of mothers who seem incapable of sitting down for too long. As if it may somehow devalue them.

'Where's your colander, love? I thought I'd do us a fish pie. I've found some cod in the freezer.'

I stare at her back as she searches my cupboards and feel such overwhelming love for her that it frightens me – today the love of a small and helpless child, reaching out to her with sticky fingers.

She feels my stare on her back and turns, her eyes wide with concern. 'It will be all right, Beth. It will pass, love.'

My mother sits opposite me then and holds my hands across the table as I stare down at the pattern of ring marks on the scrubbed pine.

'When I turned forty, I left your father.'

This statement – as shocking as it's unexpected – pulls me suddenly back to the present. 'You *left* Dad? What do you mean, you left Dad – when?'

My mother fidgets, adjusting an apron she's found in the utility – an apron I'd forgotten I even owned: thick cotton with a motif of large strawberries in a pale blue bowl. 'When you and Michael were both at university, I turned forty and suddenly thought what's the bloody point of it all.'

I'm still staring at the strawberries, desperately searching through the back files in my brain, trying to place this story in the correct drawer. I wonder if she's making this up to try to make me feel better – to empathise with the midlife crisis she and Adam mistakenly think I'm having. 'I don't understand. What are you talking about, Mum?'

'We had our kids so much younger, my generation. And things were so different. None of this juggling or whatever you call it now. Career women and all that. We had our babies, you kept us busy and that was that. And then—' She pauses and looks away. '—and then the babies grew up.'

Her gaze is through my kitchen window to the line outside, where washing she's been supervising since her arrival is flapping in the wind. It's an unfamiliar sight and sound in our house – the tumble dryer normally used for everything.

I picture her suddenly with her twin tub and her hands, red with hot water, and yes, I remember it. A very different kind of motherhood.

'When you both left home, it was even worse than when you were at boarding school. I started sleeping in your beds. And then I went a bit manic about the house. Cleaning all the time. Place stank of bleach but nothing seemed to be clean enough. And your dad went on and on at me to pull myself together.'

I could hear his voice. *Sit down, love. Why don't you just sit down . . .*

'And so I left him again. I went to stay with your Auntie Eve and I had no intention of coming back.'

'But why didn't you tell me, Mum? Christ. I had no idea. I'd have come home from uni.'

'Precisely why I didn't tell you; I didn't want that. So. Anyway. I stayed with Eve for quite a few weeks and then she took me to the doctor. Valium they used to prescribe in those days. Fortunately it made me vomit so I gave it up. Just as well as a lot of women got hooked, you know. Anyway, after a few weeks, I just seemed to feel better.'

'And what about Dad? What on earth did Dad do?'

'Oh, he managed. Lived off fish and chips. Missed me. Did us both good in the end, I reckon.'

Something then echoes in my head.

'You said – you left him *again*. So it happened before?'

I pause then to once more watch the towels flapping in the wind. Dear Dad. He must have been so lost without her. How I miss him. His cheap aftershave. *Wanna mint, Beth?* I can see the pack of Polo mints tucked into his shirt pocket – the foil and paper shaped by him into a perfect coil, like his trick with an apple, peeling the skin so it wouldn't break.

'There was a bit of silliness when you children were little.'

'Silliness?'

'Your father got his head turned. Young girl at work.'

'You're kidding me?' I'm truly shocked now. I had never, ever imagined my father to be the unfaithful type . . .

'We had a month apart back then too. It blew over. He saw sense.' She pauses as I try to take in the shock of this. My parents apart. *Twice.* I'd had no idea.

'Marriage can be difficult, Beth. Not all a bed of roses.'

And now I see. She thinks there's something up between me and Adam. 'This isn't like that, Mum. There's nothing wrong between me and Adam. And I don't mind being forty. Really I don't.' I can't tell her what's really wrong – that I'm not the daughter she thinks I am. Not the person that anyone thinks I am.

'Maybe not, dear.' She smooths my hair. 'I'm just saying that I'm here now and it's going to be all right, love.'

I reach out for her hand again now and squeeze my thank you. I don't know what shocks me more – that my smiley, optimistic mother, the champion of the silver lining, could ever have felt the way she describes or the fact that she's waited twenty years to tell me.

CHAPTER 27

CAROL - NOW

Monday

Things go from bad to worse. Not only am I missing Emily more than is rational but the crows are back and although he will not accept it, our neighbour Jonathan is entirely to blame. He has sown some new crop in the largest of his fields as an experiment but can't be persuaded to take any precautions against the birds.

I have tried reasoning with him. Explaining how filthy and utterly disgusting they are, how much damage they can do, but he won't take me seriously. His farming, he argues, is for fun not profit. An experiment. So where's the harm in a few crows around?

Harm? Is he serious?

Yesterday I came home to find one sitting on the top of the telephone pole, ripping some poor little bird to shreds. The prey was still alive, struggling as the crow tore at its flesh. I threw a stone but the crow was too high. Just stared at me with that superior look I so hate.

I had to go into the downstairs toilet to throw up.

When Ned gets back from Spain, I must persuade him to talk to Jonathan.

There are all sorts of contraptions these days – electronic devices with timers to set off tiny explosions to scare them away. Not expensive – I've checked.

Meanwhile I have made two scarecrows for our own land. Basic – just old clothes stuffed and attached to broomsticks. I've put one by the vine and the second at the end of the drive. The postman gave me the most peculiar look when I was setting it up. I tried to make a joke, of course, but for me, it's more serious than any of them can know.

I couldn't bear it if they bring back the dreams. Not now. Please not now. Bad enough that it's so quiet with Emily gone. But the crows.

If the crows stay, I don't know what I shall do.

CHAPTER 28

BETH - NOW

It surprises the whole family how easily my mother fits into our lives. Adam certainly seems relieved to share the burden and worry of my depression with someone else.

As for the boys? Sam grumbles at first about having to share his room with Harry but my mother's cooking soon wins them over. Within no time at all the house smells of my childhood – bread-and-butter pudding, Lancashire hotpot. Suddenly the boys say stew is not so bad after all.

In the evenings the TV is turned off as my mother plays Scrabble, Cluedo and Monopoly with the boys, asking after their day in a tone that brings the miracle of conversation.

All this I watch from the sidelines. I watch Adam shower, dress and kiss me goodbye every morning, wishing I could step across the void between us.

But mostly I watch my mother. I watch her shop and bake – rolling pastry on my large kitchen table with clouds of flour hanging in the air – seeing my whole life this way just now. Hazy. Yes, as though through a fine cloud of flour.

At first, while the boys are in school, I pretend to keep up my routine of work, trying to research the latest list of programme ideas from Stella. But it's futile. I can't concentrate and wander instead through cyberspace, searching out recipes for bread-and-butter pudding and Lancashire hotpot.

In the end, when the emails and messages from Stella move through sarcasm to anger and finally hysteria, I reluctantly follow my mother's advice to allow the doctor to *sign me off*. Even in my detached state, I guess (correctly) that this will be professional suicide. I'm already the subject of gossip after fleeing the set during the 'Friends and Reunions' recording.

'How awful for you.' Stella's tone on the phone is unconvincing. A beautiful irony that our programme supposedly examines people's personal traumas when the producer cares not a jot for mine. At least they pay me. *A maximum of three months on full pay, thereafter subject to freelance contract.*

'Never mind about all that, dear. We just need to get you well,' my mother says. And so, like a child, I let her shape my day. She reminds me when to eat, when to wash and we share the household chores, listening to plays on the radio. In the kitchen, I let her teach me the things I so resisted as a sulky teenager, finally mastering the mystery of suet.

The boys cross their eyes in alarm. *Dumplings?*

'If the wind changes, they'll stay like that.' My mother and I speak over each other and she catches my eye, smiling encouragement.

'At least *try* them.' I pout to make Sam laugh and he pushes the dumpling around his plate and holds his nose to sample a morsel. Silence. Which means he likes it, although it'll be a while before he will say. I remember how he would do this as a toddler, stealing food from other people's plates behind my back rather than admitting he liked something new that I'd asked him to try. Pride. Mischief. My little Sam. I say nothing but smile back at my mother, enjoying the memory in my heart and the feeling on my face.

And so we fall into a glorious old-fashioned routine. Home-made apple pie on a Wednesday night. Stew (back in favour thanks to dumplings) on Thursday. Fish on Fridays. Yes. The homely smells of my past.

My mother, meanwhile, asks nothing of me. No questions. No pressure. And not until the third week of her stay, when I begin to style my hair and use a little make-up again, does she even test the water.

'I'm surprised you haven't heard much from Sally?' She's pouring me tea from a large blue-and-white teapot recovered from the back of one of my cupboards, disapproving of my habit of putting teabags straight into the mugs. I let the question hang in the air for a moment then sit down opposite her.

'I've upset her, Mum. Badly, I think.'

'Oh, I see.' She pushes my cup towards me and waits. It was just the same when I was a child. She would wait like this, when I came home from primary school sour or grumpy. She would not push or prod or force the issue. She would just make tea, open the biscuit tin and wait.

I sip my tea now, remembering the flowers I sent Sally by way of an apology after the barbecue – remembering the strained telephone call when she'd assured me everything was all right between us, when it so clearly is not.

I remember too the day I drove secretly to Sally's cottages to check on their progress, half hoping, half dreading bumping into her and Matthew. It astonishes me how quickly they're being transformed. The new thatch is in place now with a signature creature for each cottage – a pheasant above one, a squirrel on the second, an owl watching over the third and the beginnings of a rabbit on the fourth.

'We got it into our heads to try to find Carol. Over this school closure. I got a bit obsessed.'

My mother sips her tea while I weigh up how much I dare share.

'We hired a private detective.'

'Good Lord. Why ever would you do a thing like that?' Her reaction is the same as Adam's. Of course I can't tell them why . . .

'I do know it sounds drastic. But I promise you I meant well, Mum. And we found Deborah. You remember Deborah? Carol's mum.'

I tell her only the part of the story that is safe. The trip to the bingo hall. Deborah's rift with Carol, her drinking and loneliness. My childish jealousy of Sally and Matthew. The row at the barbecue.

For a long time my mother says nothing. Then she pours more tea and takes in a long breath as if something has been decided. 'When you were a little girl you set up a doll's hospital, do you remember?'

I frown, no idea what she's talking about.

'You took in everyone's toys and mended them.' My mother stirs sugar into her tea. 'We'll invite Deborah to stay,' she says. 'I always liked Deborah.'

'Oh no, no, no, Mum. There's no *way* she'd come. I've upset her – done quite enough damage.'

But my mother's expression is fixed. Her mind made up. 'She's lonely you say? Some rift with Carol. Well, she can only say no, can't she? And I know you. You're not going to solve this guilt trip or whatever it is at the root of what's bothering you unless we *do* something.'

I can feel my lip quivering and my heartbeat increasing. I'm fighting not to let my mind go back there, to that day long, long ago when I almost telephoned her. My lovely mother.

What I wish instead is for a time machine, not to remember what truly happened but to go back and actually change it all. Undo the bad thing and do the right thing instead. Make the phone call. *I need you, Mum. You need to come home . . .*

It's not my mother's fault that she underestimates this.

'No, Mum. Believe me, it's too late. It's all best left alone now. Honestly.'

CHAPTER 29
CAROL - NOW

Wednesday

Ned is back in Spain at the moment. We had a terrible row about my eating and he wanted me to go with him. I never mean to be this difficult but I can't help myself . . .

His new venture is a development of a dozen luxury properties, all with sea views. He seems to think that we should earmark one for ourselves as a treat and he wanted me to go to help pick which one. But I couldn't face it. I've told him over and over there's no way we need another place to be worrying about and I fear I'd hate Spain (even hotter than here) but I bet he keeps one of them as a 'surprise'.

So this time he's left Pierre to keep an eye on me. He says it's to make sure that I look after myself. He means — eat.

How many times do I need to tell people that I eat plenty. Loads.

Also Ned is trying to persuade me to book a trip to visit my mother. It's almost as if he knows we've been in touch. He keeps saying that it would do me good — to return to England and touch base with my mum. How can I tell him it's the last thing in the world that I want?

Just as I'm trying so very hard to put the whole nightmare that was school and Beth and Sally entirely out of my mind, there was a card today from Emily, which did not help.

Her parents' divorce is going to be as ugly as she feared, poor thing, and her mother is suggesting boarding school. And she wants to know what I think.

'Were you happy at school? Do you think it's a good idea?'

I have started my reply over and over but can't find the right words to counsel her. How to explain what school was to me. The best. The worst. The best. The very, very worst.

It's all so impossible again. Like this pounding, pounding in my head.

For now, to try to distract myself, I continue to do battle with the crows. At least Pierre is on side. Ned has him working full-time for us now. Odd jobs as well as the cooking – mostly to keep closer tabs on me, I suspect. Pierre lives not far from us and the crows are stealing the vegetables from his own garden at home so he has offered in all seriousness to bring a gun and shoot them for me. I am all for the plan but am worried by his enthusiasm. Also Ella would probably call the police.

Until Ned speaks to Jonathan again, I am making do by changing the hats on the scarecrows every few days. It seems for now to be tricking them.

CHAPTER 30

BETH - NOW

A week later both my sons are at the sitting room window as Deborah's taxi pulls in.

'Don't stare, boys. It's rude.'

'She's got very weird eyebrows.' Sam is stretching his own eyebrows into a high arch.

'Come away, both of you. You'll make her feel uncomfortable.'

'I don't get where she's going to sleep, Mum? We don't have enough bedrooms.'

'Shh, boys! She's coming up the path.' I clear my throat and smooth my skirt, the muscles in my stomach in some kind of spasm. I can't believe my mother has persuaded Deborah to visit. All she will say is that *honesty is always the best policy*, which terrifies me. How much has she shared with Deborah? Hiring Matthew? My falling-out with Sally? My depression? *Jeez.*

The doorbell sounds but no one moves. It rings again until my mother appears from the kitchen, beaming and drying her hands on the strawberry motif apron. 'I'll get it.'

I signal to Sam to put his feet down and follow my mother into the hallway. Adam appears for a quick hello, offering to take Deborah's suitcase upstairs – an excuse to retreat, I suspect – while my mother leads Deborah into the sitting room to introduce the boys. They manage only nods.

In the kitchen my mother sets out the mugs and plates as if it were her own home, which indeed is how it has come to feel in recent weeks. 'So how was the journey?'

I notice Deborah looking curiously at me over the apparent role swap but the moment passes as the two women are soon in animated discussion about trains and taxis, the awkwardness of tipping and how much easier and more efficient travel was when there was just one rail company and real people on the telephone. I sit at the kitchen table, fidgeting until my mother leaves to take a plate of biscuits through to the boys.

'It was very good of you to come, Deborah. The thing is, I felt so very bad – upsetting you. Over Carol.' I watch her expression closely but there's nothing to suggest she's cross with me, angry enough to have hit back. No, I still don't think she posted the Facebook message.

Deborah leans forward then and puts her hand on mine. 'I'm not going to lie,' she says. 'I was very surprised when your mother rang with this invitation. I said no at first but the truth is—' She pauses, smiling. '—well, I always liked your mother and she doesn't seem to understand the word *no*, does she?'

'So you're not still angry with us? Me and Sally?'

She tilts her head. 'Look, it was a big shock to see you and Sally. I embarrassed myself. I was upset, I admit it. But no, I see now it's not your fault how bad things are between me and Carol.'

'And you've not heard from Carol since?'

'No. Ned called me out of the blue – said he's worried about her. That she's not eating properly. He's trying to persuade her to come over but she's not interested. He's asked me to write to her but I don't much see the point. I know she won't reply.'

Deborah sips from her mug, tapping her nails on the side. 'Your mum tells me you've been unwell?'

So that's why she agreed to come. I feel my face flush. 'It's getting a bit better, Deborah. Thank you.'

'Well, that's very good to hear. I'm glad.'

My mother is soon back in the room, shouting through to the boys to *watch the crumbs on the carpet* and suggests that Deborah might like to freshen up.

'I'll show you where you're sleeping and we can plan the weekend.'

I watch the two mothers disappear up the stairs, noticing how their frames match almost precisely. The flat bottoms and stretched waists. It feels so very weird, this. They met only rarely at St Colman's – concerts, fund-raisers and other events for parents – but I am remembering only now that my mother and Deborah had clicked rather well back then. I presumed in the self-centred space that is adolescence that it was the common issue of our friendship – mine and Carol's. But perhaps it was not about us at all.

The two women are in animated and easy conversation as they reach the top of the stairs and I wonder if perhaps my mother needs this visit too? More lonely and bored than I have noticed. I remember the story of her leaving Dad, of his 'silliness' in the marriage, and wonder how much more about my mother I have missed.

I pour myself more tea and wander into the study to offer Adam a cup. Sunlight is streaming in from the window, highlighting dust particles in the air. Adam is at the computer and removes his glasses to look at me.

'You look better, Beth. Really. It's good to see you looking a little better.'

'You don't mind about Deborah, do you? I mean, I know it's a big ask with my mother here as well.'

'Of course not. I'll be sociable – introduce myself properly later.'

I check his eyes – still worry in them – and watch the dust circling in the current of air. There's a strand of hair falling on to his forehead and I move forward to brush it away and kiss the top of his head. He's surprised and reaches up to take my hand, kissing the back of it, which inexplicably makes me want to cry. I am not a crier by nature – truly hate the memory of breaking down at the doctor's – but I feel so guilty that I've not been honest with Adam. I straighten the papers on his desk, fighting the moment, as I do later when he catches my eye across the kitchen table to smile really intimately as we feast on my mother's home-made lasagne and I confess to Deborah that I'm luxuriating in my laziness, allowing my mother to take over my house and do all my work. 'I should be ashamed, I know,' I say, 'but she's marvellous. The boys have never eaten so well.'

With the meal we share a bottle of wine and when it's finished I make a little face at Adam to discourage him from opening a second bottle – hoping I'm mistaken about Deborah's drinking. Maybe the image of her swigging from her secret bottle has become exaggerated in my dreams, fuelled by the paranoia that began in the days when Sally drank so heavily after losing her baby. Maybe Deborah doesn't have a drink problem at all but I'm nervous. What if she becomes truly drunk while she's staying with us? How will I explain it to the boys?

In the event, I am right to be concerned; there's embarrassment to come, but not from the source I imagine.

We stay up late that first night – Deborah stunning the boys by proving a highly competent and competitive Cluedo player – and it's gone 9 a.m. the next morning before Adam and I wake. I regret not having any time alone with Deborah to talk more about Carol but am pleased that she feels relaxed in our home and is enjoying herself. It's going much better than I'd expected.

The boys have already been picked up by the school minibus for their special Saturday football club. It costs quite a lot but they love it and with the full school supervision I feel that they're safe there. The collection and drop off option is a bonus when we're busy. All is calm by the time I venture into the kitchen to find my mother and Deborah clearing up the remains of a full fry-up.

'You gave the boys a cooked breakfast?'

'You can't expect them to play football on cereal.' My mother pours me a coffee. 'My daughter is the food police, Deborah. You enjoy your bacon roll and ignore her.'

I blush as the two women put sauce in their snack while I pop wholemeal bread into the toaster.

I rummage in a drawer for my National Trust card and there's genuine enthusiasm when I suggest a visit to Buckland Abbey where Sir Francis Drake once lived, but an uneasy silence when I suggest a meal out this evening.

'Oh, you don't want to go to all that expense.' My mother is giving Deborah a knowing look.

'Well, we could eat in and pop out for a drink maybe? Or a film?'

Again they're silent until finally my mother passes the toast. 'The thing is, Beth, Deborah and I – well, we quite fancied a night out together. Just the two of us.'

'Oh, I see.' I turn my back as I butter the toast to conceal my surprise. 'So what did you have in mind?'

'Deborah's offered to take me to the bingo. The thing is, I've never really tried it. I know it's all online these days but we don't like to trust our credit cards on the internet. And apparently the club she belongs to has a branch in town.'

'*Bingo?*' My tone comes out all wrong and I try immediately to backtrack, to spare offending Deborah. 'Great idea. Why not? I'm sure you'll love it, Mum. We'll give you a lift.'

'Lovely, dear.' My mother looks really pleased then and pushes the jar of jam towards me like the winning move in a game of chess.

And so after an outing complete with cream tea, they go to the bingo, which Adam thinks is all perfectly hilarious until it's 11.45 p.m. and I'm pacing the sitting room like an anxious parent waiting for a teenager.

'They could have had an accident?'

'Oh, for goodness' sake, Beth – they're grown-ups. Fit and healthy. Probably having a drink.'

'My mother doesn't drink and they don't have phones – something could have happened.'

Somehow Adam manages to distract me with a late film but once midnight has long since passed, I catch him peeking through the curtains himself as I bring coffee in from the kitchen.

'You think we should phone the bingo hall?' I say. 'They must have shut hours ago. We should never have agreed to let them get a taxi home.'

Adam does not immediately answer until there's the chugging of a diesel engine outside and we both peer through the window to see a large black cab pulling up.

'See?' Adam fails to conceal the relief in his voice. He picks up a paper, pretending to read. I've given my mother a key to save disturbing the boys with the doorbell. But oddly nothing happens. After several minutes, there's finally a soft tap at the door and I rush to find Deborah on the doorstep, her face flushed with alarm.

'I think we'll need a hand.' She looks straight past me, widening her eyes as a signal to Adam as he appears behind me.

'What's the matter? Is Mum all right? Has she hurt herself?'

'Not exactly . . .'

And then we see the taxi driver, who is struggling to assist my mother from the car as the appalling truth hits home. My mother is drunk. Not just tipsy but so obviously, blindingly drunk she can barely stand up.

'Hellooooo, Beth, my *darling* girl!' She swings her handbag with such force that it completes a full 180 degrees before falling straight back down to hit her on the head. She looks up at the night sky then, puzzled. 'Was that a bird? Beth. I think a bird is trying to attack me . . .'

Adam rushes forward, thanking the taxi driver, who is still straining to support my mother's weight. Between us we then somehow manage to walk her to the house, urging her to no avail to keep her voice down. By the time we reach the doorstep, both boys are gawping through the upstairs curtains. As we manoeuvre my mother into the hall, they're at the top of the stairs.

'Is Granny *drunk*?' Sam's tone is one of admiration.

'Back to bed, both of you. She's just a bit unwell.'

'She's not – she's drunk. Harry! Come here, Harry. Granny's drunk! We need to put this on Facebook.'

'Facebook?' I say. 'You're not on Facebook. You're too young.'

'Oops.' Sam pulls a face.

'Seriously? Adam, did you hear that?' I turn to my husband, appalled. 'I thought you had to be thirteen for Facebook? Right,' I say, 'you're busted, Sam. Phone is confiscated – you put it straight in my room. And I shall be speaking to you about this in the morning.'

Putting my drunken mother to bed is tricky. I can't manage to undress her without Adam's help but know she'll be mortified to imagine him even glimpsing her Marks & Spencer slip. In the end I just loosen her skirt and untuck her shirt. She sings 'Green, Green Grass of Home' through most of this while I leave a plastic bowl on the floor (just in case) and a glass plus large jug of water beside her bed with a box of aspirins. Finally I retreat, wincing at the hangover that awaits her.

Adam tactfully goes straight to bed then, ushering the boys on the way, leaving me to deal with Deborah.

'Beth, I am so sorry. What must you think of me? Letting this happen.'

'It's OK, Deborah. She's asleep now. It was just a bit of a shock. I've never seen her drunk.'

'I honestly didn't realise we had had very much. She seemed absolutely fine. Truly, Beth. We found this really nice little bar after the bingo. And then with the fresh air, she just sort of *went*.'

Deborah still looks mortified but I rerun the picture of my mother beside the taxi, hitting herself on the head with her handbag, and smile.

'It's all right,' I say. 'She's safe. I rather think she'll dine out on it once the hangover's gone. I don't think she's used to alcohol.'

Deborah pulls a small folding mirror from her bag to finish repairing her face. I can hear the kettle boil and she nods gratefully at the offer of coffee, snapping the mirror shut and zipping it neatly away again, raising her voice as I walk through to the kitchen. 'So is this where we talk properly? Yes?'

'I'm sorry?'

'About Carol, Beth. I take it you want to talk about her. Properly, I mean. That's why I'm really here?'

I busy myself with the cups and spoons, opening and shutting cupboards, not quite sure suddenly what I'm looking for.

'Of course,' she says, 'I try not to let on to Carol how very worried I am. But I've been seriously worried for years. She doesn't eat properly, you know. Ned's right to be concerned. She's lucky he's so patient.' Very soon she's putting extra sugar in the drink I hand her: two heaped teaspoons. 'I sometimes think it started with that stupid Ouija board nonsense at school. Do you remember? When you all nearly got yourselves expelled?'

'Sorry?'

'You know that she never let it go, Beth. That it was just the start of it all. The whole spiritualist and ghosts thing. She got it into her crazy head that it was her father trying to contact her.'

I stop blowing on my own drink. 'Her *father*? But why on earth would she think that? The Ouija board stunt was just a stupid prank, Deborah. And she never said anything to us . . .'

'His nickname for her was "Princess". His little Princess. I take it she didn't tell you that either then? She told me the board spelled it out. Stuff and nonsense, I said . . .'

'Oh, heavens. No, she didn't say anything to us about that. She wouldn't talk about it.'

I remember now Carol's face as Melody was spelling out the letters – P-R-I-N-C-E-S-S. But it was just a black joke, a stupid coincidence. Melody had this fixation with Princess Grace.

'I swear we didn't know about the pet name, Deborah. That was the other girl, Melody, mucking about. The one who got expelled. We tried to tell Carol at the time that it was a joke. We had no idea . . .'

'Yes – well, she took it very badly of course when her father died. Completely broke her heart – the accident. Such an awful time. She was only six. She used to lay a place for him at the table, you know. For months.'

'Really?'

'Yes – not just forgetting. On purpose. As if he was coming back. She saw some rubbish on the telly and started talking about mediums, even back then. I handled it all wrong. Told her that it was all nonsense. Just couldn't bear it. One day I grabbed the table mat and the cutlery from her. Just couldn't bear to see her like that. I thought it was time for her to try and accept it.' Deborah is staring at the floor now. 'She became completely hysterical, Beth. Shouting at me that it was *for her daddy. A place for her daddy.* And she clung on to the table mat and the cutlery until the knife cut deep into her hand. Three stitches it needed.'

I've closed my eyes.

'Of course there are counsellors these days. More help. Back then we just made it up as we went along. I'm sure I did way more harm than good. But when we came into that little bit of money, I really hoped boarding school would help her. More company of her own age. Friends. That she wouldn't feel his absence in the same way she did at home. And then after that Ouija board nonsense, she was – *well*. First – this obsession with spiritualism. Weird churches. Mediums and all that nonsense. I thought it would pass. But later it was as if there was something else . . .' And now Deborah looks very directly at me as I open my eyes again. 'And that's really why I came, Beth. I've been thinking about this a lot and I'm hoping that you might be able to help me? Throw some more light?'

She waits for a while and when I don't answer begins picking at some imagined piece of fluff on her skirt as I watch her hand, mesmerised. There's nothing there – on the skirt. No fluff or stray hairs. But still she pick, picks at the fabric so that I again have this overwhelming urge to reach forward to still her hand. Staring at it, I can't quite believe how familiar her hand looks. Genes, I suppose. Carol's hand was identical. Long, slender fingers with very oval nails. I remember her pick, picking at the grass that awful day she *told* us. Still in the fourth form.

◆ ◆ ◆

We were all lying on the grass together in the grounds of the convent. Me and Sally and Carol. In the distance, one of the nuns was on the ride-on lawnmower. I remember how the back wheel lifted slightly for a second and I waited for it to right itself as the machine turned and I tried to take in what Carol was saying. All the while her hand pick, picking at blades of grass.

'But you *can't* be pregnant, Carol. Don't be silly! You don't even have a proper boyfriend. How can you possibly be pregnant?'

I watched Sally's mouth shape the words, unable to find any of my own. A kind of multilayer shock – surprise not just at what Carol was telling us but at the sense of betrayal. She'd been so upset since the Ouija board debacle – withdrawn and not herself. But to keep something like this from us – some boyfriend so serious that *this* could happen. Until that moment I honestly believed the three of us shared everything – knew anything of any importance about each other. And here suddenly was a Carol we did not know at all.

We were fourteen. Still children ourselves. How the bloody hell could she be pregnant?

'But who, Carol? *Who?* And why didn't you tell us? I just don't understand?' Sal's face was now completely white, her voice rising over the pitch of the diesel motor, which spluttered as it was manoeuvred precariously in the distance, weaving from right to left now across the hockey pitch.

Carol was still picking at strands of grass, her voice in contrast steady and cold. No tears. No emotion even. I reached out my hand to hold hers. Make her stop. To still her. Make her look at me.

'It doesn't matter,' she said. 'Just a boy – a neighbour. In the holidays. An experiment. A mistake. We got carried away . . . I didn't *mean to*. The thing is – I don't like to ask but I need you to help me.' And only then did she look up – not at Sal who was doing all the talking but at me.

'It'll be a mistake, a false alarm. Maybe your period's just late.' Sally's words were coming faster and faster as Carol pulled her hands from mine, rubbing the palms together to free them of the strands of damp grass that clung to her fingertips.

'I've done a test,' Carol said. 'Three, actually. It's not a mistake. I need to get rid of it before it's too late, don't you think? Will I be allowed to do that without anyone telling my mum?'

It was the steadiness of her voice that chilled me the most.

'Get rid of it? Oh, good grief.' Sally's Catholic shock was now in full gear. Also fear. 'But you *can't*, Carol. Surely you don't mean . . . You can't possibly mean . . .'

For just a second Carol seemed to have to steel herself – biting her lip to steady it – but the moment passed very quickly and then she was staring directly at me again.

'But your mum won't let you, Carol,' Sally said. 'I mean, it's a sin, isn't it? A *mortal* sin. And even if we all went to confession – I mean, we can't.'

'Don't be mad,' Carol said. 'I can't tell my mum. Nobody's going to bloody confession. Nobody's to tell *anyone*. And it's not a sin.'

And now the air felt really cold and the enormity of what was happening began to register, for I realised what Carol was really asking of us.

'So is there anything you can think of, Beth? Anything you can tell me? I've wondered whether it was drugs that changed Carol.' Deborah clears her throat. 'I mean – you read so much about drugs. I don't mean now. Ned would tell me if there was anything going on now, I'm sure. But I don't want you to think I'd be terribly shocked if you experimented when you were younger? With drugs? Was that what upset her, changed her – back in school, I mean? Is that why she suddenly left? Stopped eating properly?'

I feel the coffee drip on to my trousers and quickly right the mug and stand up. Deborah smooths the fabric of her skirt one last time, stretching it over her knees as I blot my trousers with a tissue.

'No, I'm sorry, Deborah. Actually, it's getting very late. Sorry – stupid of me with the coffee. Look, I can promise you there were no drugs in school. At least not around us.'

'Good. That's good then.' She stands suddenly, her shadow stretching long and lean – slimmed by the lamp behind her. There's this strange contradiction: her face in this cruel light looks old, her shadow young. There's this hollow ache deep inside as I realise how very much I like her.

And that I hate myself more than ever for all these years of lying to her.

CHAPTER 31

CAROL - NOW

Wednesday

At last the temperature falls a little and I feel I'm turning a corner. Quite by chance I've come across the most extraordinary book on tarot. I really think this could be it. Don't know why I didn't think of it before – no more cheats and charlatans. No more money-grabbing mediums who could no more read the paper than the future . . .

I don't know why I was so against it in the past. Tarot. There's a great deal more to it than I realised. Not random. Not some trick, which is what I imagined, but an ancient art that I can learn myself. What I realise now is that I need to stop focusing on looking back and look forward instead: for me, for Emily, for everyone.

This could really help me; I feel it. A clue to what truly lies ahead if I can just make all the nonsense with Beth and Sally STOP.

I've sent off for a proper pack of cards through a website plus another book written by the most amazing woman. There are seventy-eight cards which form an 'arcana' – a symbolic representation of ancient wisdoms. Fascinating.

There's the major arcana and the minor arcana (haven't quite figured it all out yet but I'm researching online until the book arrives) and the rest of the cards are divided into suits of earth, water, fire and air.

It's pretty complicated, of course, and I'll have to work hard. Study. But the beauty of this is it's at my own fingertips. I really wonder that I've not thought of this before.

The website says the woman will also do readings by email but I'm not sure if that's such a good idea; passing on my real details, I mean. We'll see.

I honestly feel so much more hopeful today.

Oh – and the news on the crows is good too. Ella (probably feeling guilty after all I did to help over the pool) has promised to have a word with Jonathan for me. I think she's secretly worried that Pierre is serious about shooting them so she's happy to talk about more scarecrows or maybe even a mechanical device.

I've been reading up on them too. They're carrion crows, just as I feared – some war just now, it seems, between the carrions and the hooded crow. Territorial battle lines across Europe. Well, here's hoping they fight it out among themselves. Wipe out the whole wretched species.

CHAPTER 32

MATTHEW - NOW

'No way, Matthew.'

He watches Sally wincing as she pulls the supportive stretch bandage up over her sore ankle. Matthew is surprised by her reaction. She was supposed to be visiting her mother today but a slip on the wet floor in the bathroom has put a spanner in the works. It's a sprain and she clearly can't drive. He's offered to chauffeur and thought she would be pleased.

'But you said she'd be really upset if you cancel.' Matthew widens his eyes, willing her to look at him properly. 'I don't mind, honestly. I'm free today and it's only a couple of hours.'

She pauses and lets out a little huff of air. They're both sitting on the end of her bed. It was another really good evening together. No. Better than good . . .

'It's not that I don't want you to meet her, Matthew.'

'It's just that you don't want me to meet her.'

At last she laughs.

'Look, I get it's a bit early to *meet the parent*. I'll drop you off and make myself scarce, if you prefer. Call back later.'

'Don't be silly. You're not a taxi driver. I can't ask you to just drive all that way and not even come in for coffee.' She looks at the floor, pauses, then back up at Matthew.

A text buzzes into her phone suddenly. She opens it, her face darkening. 'It's from *Beth*.'

Matthew watches her closely. He knows that Beth sent flowers to apologise for the row at the barbecue, but he also knows that they haven't spoken since. Sally scrolls back as if rereading and then bites into her bottom lip.

'It's not good, Matthew. She's had some kind of big row with Sam this morning – her elder boy. He's been on Facebook secretly. Lied about his age. She's been through his profile and found he's been posting pictures and stuff about his school and the family.'

'Oh dear. Not good, but I'm afraid it's not uncommon. Kids setting up accounts . . .'

'No, no. It's worse than that. He's had a message. Look, Matthew . . .'

Sally holds out the phone to share a screenshot sent by Beth. It's another message from the fake Facebook account, the one with the bluebell as a profile pic:

Tell your mum to LEAVE IT ALONE . . .

'It was sent a while back. Sam didn't tell her because he didn't want her to know about his account. He thought it was just some random nutter or one of his mates fooling around. Beth's really worried. She's asking if we can meet up to discuss it.'

'Of course. I'm happy to. We can go right now if you like?'

'OK, good. But not right away. First we need to deal with my mother. I'll message Beth to say I'll ring her straight after we've been to Mum's.'

'So you've changed your mind? About me meeting her?' Matthew tries not to let it show on his face just how happy he is.

'Apparently.'

◆ ◆ ◆

On the drive Matthew tells Sally more about his visit to Melody Sage. He's used a mate in the force to check out her boyfriend via the motorcycle licence plate. A bad choice of partner. A conviction for actual bodily harm and two counts of possessing Class A drugs. But Matthew doubts the couple have any involvement with the messages to Beth – or the one to Sam's profile.

'She knows about the school closure, this Melody,' he says. 'But I can't see the motive – why she'd be bothered about you all after all these years. Doesn't fit.'

'Jealousy?'

'Maybe. But I honestly feel it's unlikely.'

'So do you think we should be worried? Two Facebook messages now and the phone call to the school.' Sally's voice is strained.

'I honestly don't know how to answer that. Not least because I don't have all the facts about what really went on between you all.' Matthew has lowered his voice. He knows there's no point in pressing her but is getting more concerned and frustrated and so lets the comment hang in the air. 'It could still just be a troll. Nasty . . . but harmless. I want to dig some more.' He's looking right into her face as he speaks.

'So, my mother.' Sally tilts her chin. 'I told you she had some issues, so best you know the score.'

Matthew lets out a long sigh. He opens his mouth to change the subject back again to Beth and the messages but thinks better of it. It's an unsettling turn of events that someone has contacted Sam – an innocent child – but he'll look into it quietly and try not to alarm Sally more than he has to. She will just have to tell him the truth about Carol in her own time. Or he'll find it out for himself. 'OK, fire away. So, your mother?'

'. . . has had a bit of a problem for years.' Sally still has her head tilted up at a strange angle. 'Hoarding.'

'What – you mean like collecting?' Matthew's own mother is obsessed with small china jugs. Has scores of the things. He's just about to share this to make Sally feel better.

'No, not collecting – proper hoarding. Rooms full of old newspapers and catalogues and magazines. *Bonkers* hoarding.'

Matthew is taken aback, has no idea what to say.

'The truth is, I should visit her more often. I stay away to avoid a row. For years we've been at loggerheads because she wouldn't get help. Was in denial.'

'Oh, goodness. I'm sorry, Sally. I didn't mean to intrude when I offered to drive you.'

'No, it's OK. Really – it's best you know. Anyway, the point is she's in counselling at last. That's why she wrote to me, asking me to visit. She reckons she's doing better. Wants to show me and to apologise for being so stubborn. But I'm just telling you in case it's a load of baloney and it's still wall-to-wall newspapers.'

Matthew bites again into his bottom lip and runs his hand through his hair. Crikey. *Hoarding?*

'Look, you don't have to come in, Matthew. It's all a bit full-on, isn't it?'

'It's OK, honestly. I can handle it. I was in the police, remember. I've seen everything.'

'I didn't say she was a *criminal*, Matthew – just a bit troubled.'

'Sorry, sorry. I didn't mean it to come out like that. I just meant that there aren't many things that can surprise me.'

They drive for a further five minutes in silence until Matthew builds up the courage to ask if there was a trigger for her mother's behaviour.

'Oh yes. My father.'

Dear Lord. Matthew wonders what the hell is coming next. Suddenly he realises how lucky he was with his own parents. Nice, steady and boring suburbia.

'Dad was a drinker. No. That's an understatement. He was an alcoholic, Matthew. I was terribly ashamed about it all when I was younger. I had the girls to stay a couple of times when we were in school – Beth and Carol – and he would sit up drinking whisky and get completely blotto. Humiliating. Awful. Anyway, he eventually left my mother for another woman. Managed to kill himself, drinking and driving . . .'

'Dear Lord. Sally. I am so, so sorry . . .' Matthew reaches out with his left hand to squeeze her arm. 'Crikey. Have I put my foot in it, pushing you to let me come today? Making you feel you have to tell me all this?'

'No. The truth is, she would have hated it if I'd cancelled. I'm grateful. I've been trying so hard for her to face this and get proper help. I just hope all this baggage doesn't put you off me.'

'Well, actually, it has, completely.'

She flicks her head to check his expression. Matthew winks and blows her a kiss before reaching across again to hold her hand.

For the final half-hour of the drive, Matthew plays the radio and finds himself thinking back over their dates. He recalls how careful Sally always is with her own drinking. Two small glasses of wine her maximum before switching to fizzy water. He feels a little punch inside, imagining her shame when she was a teenager. Beth and Carol seeing her father overdoing it. He changes gear but then reaches back to clasp her hand again and is pleased when she squeezes it in return.

◆　◆　◆

Sally's mother's house looks fine from the outside. Neat borders in the front garden. Mown lawn. Sally says a neighbour helps with the garden. She rings the doorbell and is clearly nervous when her mother answers

179

the door. Mrs Preston is much taller than Matthew expects. Slim and smart with her hair up in a chignon and carefully applied make-up.

'I've brought a friend. Matthew, this is—'

'—Wendy.' Sally's mother's handshake is firm and warm and her eyes widen. 'Come in, come in. I've made a cake!'

The hall is free from clutter as far as Matthew can make out and in the kitchen, Sally is glancing around in obvious amazement.

'So you didn't believe me?' Wendy is beaming at her daughter and then at Matthew. 'Has she told you?'

Matthew is too embarrassed to answer but Wendy steps back, sweeping her arms to show off the tidy space.

'All in the past now. Ten years of newspapers – gone. All the shopping catalogues and the magazines too. My counsellor is delighted with me.'

'I don't know what to say. It's fabulous, Mum – really fabulous.' Sally steps forward to hug her mother again.

'Upstairs is still a pickle, I'm afraid. Baby steps. Can't do it all at once. But it's a start, no?'

'Better than that – it's brilliant, Mum. I'm really proud of you.'

'Good. It's been tough but I'm getting there. So let me put the kettle on, then you can explain the limp. And why when I telephoned your office, they seemed to think you don't work there any more.'

CHAPTER 33

BETH - NOW

And then comes the explosion in my life.

The day starts like any other. A trick to make me think this is a normal day. Adam makes us tea, which we drink in bed. I take in his profile. That little mole on his left cheek. I think quietly that he's still a very handsome man but, to my eternal regret, I do not say this to him. I do not say anything much to this man who I love and yet lie to – this man who is the best thing to have happened in my life.

Instead I hurry down to make toast and I get distracted, nagging the boys to get ready for the school run. Adam has a dental appointment this afternoon and mumbles something about leaving school early. He has a free period last thing, says his head of year doesn't mind. I think he says he'll walk to the dentist, leave the car at school. But I'm not really listening properly. Paying attention – paying *him* proper attention. One of the boys can't find his PE kit.

And now six hours later, I'm in a taxi in shock, realising only now that I did not even ask the policeman on the phone how badly hurt Adam is. I'm numb, listening in a daze to the high, shrill voice of this crazy woman, gabbling at the driver. Repeating herself over and over . . .

'I don't even know how badly hurt he is. I didn't ask. I should have asked, shouldn't I? Why didn't I think to *ask*?'

I'm hardly able to compute that this is *my* voice. It's as if there are two of me in the taxi. One watching in silence. One talking too much. Babbling Beth – ridiculous and hysterical, with a parallel version of myself sitting alongside, entirely outside my own body – while in the rear-view mirror, the taxi driver keeps checking my face.

Both our faces?

'The thing is, they probably aren't allowed to say too much anyway. On the phone, I mean. About how he is. There's probably some rule about that. So even if I had asked, they probably wouldn't have told me. My mum just saw your taxi pull in across the road and said – go. Grab that taxi. Get to the hospital, Beth.'

And now the driver's expression changes and he puts his foot down. 'Not far now, love,' he says. 'Try not to upset yourself.'

◆ ◆ ◆

I do not deserve him, Adam. That is the truth of it and that is what I am thinking . . . too late. So self-obsessed, so wrapped up in the bloody past and all my black and stupid mistakes that I've not thought of him and all of these pictures often enough, the images flashing in front me right now. In this cab.

This first picture of us together – me just nineteen years old the night I met Adam. My beautiful man. Look: him so young. The same little mole on his left cheek. Hopeful and lovely . . . That clear autumn evening back in university. Cool and gorgeous outside with all the stars shining, while inside a mediocre band is much too loud and I'm feeling stifled. Unable to breathe.

It was back in the days when people still smoked too much and there was this heavy fug in the air. The sound system was terrible and

I felt uncomfortable. Head pounding. Sort of hemmed in. So while my friends queued for more drinks, I said I was bailing and struggled through the crowd towards the door, eager for some fresh air.

And that's when I met him. My Adam.

He was in the small reception hall, crushed close to a door which I remember was painted the most disgusting shade of green. Phlegm colour. It turned my stomach and I needed Adam to move to let me pass through to the cool outside.

'*Sorry.*' He hadn't heard me, engrossed in loud conversation with a tall thin student with thick black glasses. I pinched his arm slightly to attract his attention.

'Sorry. *Can I come past?*'

And then he turned, at first frowning and irritated but then his expression changing. For a few seconds he did nothing at all but then helped me jostle through the bodies to the doorway.

The relief of the cool air and that clear sky was at first so welcome that I didn't notice he'd followed so that when he stepped in front of me, holding out his hand, I was startled.

'Adam,' he said. 'Hello. Sorry – didn't mean to make you jump. It's just you looked a bit pale in there. Are you sure you're OK? I've seen you around campus a few times. Meant to introduce myself before.'

I was confused. The handshake was bizarrely formal. And what was he saying here? That he'd been watching me? *Fancied me?* What? I found myself appraising him with greater interest. Without the phlegm-coloured background, he wasn't bad – tall with very dark, very curly hair cut short. Most people would not describe him as classically handsome but he had an open, warm face and very direct brown eyes. Then he smiled and I swear I've never seen such perfect teeth. Could not help myself and stared for quite some time directly into his mouth. Only when he shut it suddenly did I realise I'd been staring long enough to make him self-conscious.

'I'm so sorry. It's just you have very nice teeth.'

Next he was laughing and I made things much worse by babbling on about how I had rather overcrowded lower teeth ('See?' – I showed him) and always wished I'd been made to wear braces, and that's why I tended to notice other people's teeth before anything else. An obsession.

'Shall we walk?' he said.

'Sorry?'

'You look as if you need the air. And it's such a clear night. Please.'

I remember thinking what a nice voice he had, compared to my gabbling. Rich and deep. Steady and safe.

So we walked and we talked. We sat on a bench and watched the stars and Adam confessed he'd seen me several times at functions and had wanted to introduce himself, but I always seemed to be surrounded by so many people and he'd never found the courage.

He told me, without the slightest embarrassment, that he liked to watch me from a distance because I always looked so happy and animated in conversation that my face actually glowed. 'No, really. Your skin glows, Beth. I'm not kidding . . .'

◆ ◆ ◆

'Nearly there now, love.' The taxi driver is still watching me through the mirror.

'I thought driving myself would be quicker,' I say, 'but my mum said that was a bad idea. She was the one who spotted your cab. Sorry, did I say that already? She's with my children. We haven't told them yet. I don't know what to tell them. I've left a message for Sally though. We had a bit of a row so I don't know if she'll answer. Stupid how these things happen, isn't it, even with really good friends? And then, just when you kid yourself that everything is going to be fine . . .'

'Like I say, not far now. Just round this corner.'

'You always think this sort of thing happens to someone else, don't you? A call from the police and the hospital like that. The shock of it.'

'Right. Which entrance do you want?'

'I don't know. I really have no idea.' The voice is cracking now. 'They didn't say. It was an ambulance that brought him in. What do you think?'

◆ ◆ ◆

Adam wanted our first date to be away from the campus so we drove in his grey Mini Cooper to a pub about five miles from the university. It was raining and only one of his windscreen wipers worked.

The pub faced a small neat village green and inside there was a huge black dog sprawled by an open fire. Instinctively I moved towards the warmth but Adam gently steered my arm.

'The dog farts,' he was whispering, guiding me to the other end of the bar to a small circular table in a little alcove which had old farm implements hung all around the wall on large black hooks. Then he sat down opposite me.

'At last I have you all to myself.' And he said it not as some cheesy chat-up line, which it sounds as I tell you this now, but with the triumph of someone who had been *waiting*.

And that's precisely how it felt when I fell in love with Adam. As if he'd been *waiting* for me.

We moved in together just three weeks later. I was no virgin but went to Adam's bed with the low expectations of a girl whose only experience of sex was rather swift and unsatisfactory fumblings with a student doctor who'd waited tables with me during a summer holiday job in the lower sixth. He had the most beautiful jawline and mistaking lust for love, I lost my virginity in his car on a wet summer's night by a lake. His windscreen wipers worked perfectly but his lovemaking did not. I will never forget my aching disappointment and although we visited the lake often that summer, I never understood all the fuss.

Until Adam.

Night after night he would sneak through a window into my block and so utterly shocked was I by this very different experience that I would sometimes cry with the relief. The contrast was so extreme that I felt as much despair for the unknowing as relief for myself. *What if I had not found this . . .* And he would kiss my eyelids then smile at me with his perfect teeth and we would fall asleep at night – lips still touching so we could feel each other's breath.

When I told Sal on the phone that he was definitely *the one*, she laughed – dismissing it as the afterglow of my first decent sex. But when she came to visit and saw us together, she took me aside and looked at me so seriously it unnerved me. 'Listen to me, Beth. You hang on to this one. You hear me? I'm not mucking about. Are you listening?' She had both her hands cupped around my face. 'I've watched the way he looks at you.' She hugged me really close then. Bear tight. 'I'm the only one who looks at you like that. You hang on to him. *Yes?*'

So after college, we set up home in Essex where Adam found his first teaching post. History was both his subject and his great passion and at first in the holidays we took research trips: Rome, Greece, Vietnam, Cuba. I thought that with him I would one day get to my precious mountains, to China. But as time went on Adam began suddenly to worry about money. It was the only thing we argued about.

He was the only child of a warehouseman and a cleaner and money had always been a struggle. They lived in an immaculate council flat on a rather undesirable estate and as we watched his father each year preparing the most beautiful hanging baskets, all of us knowing full well they would be destroyed by vandals, I grew to understand why Adam wanted a different life for his own family.

Although he loved teaching, he complained about the pay and the prospects and once we started to talk about our future and the possibility of a family, he started to fret. Instead of travelling in the holidays, he began saving. Suddenly it was all about mortgages and catchment areas. He started to take private pupils at weekends, even 11-plus tuition of which he quietly disapproved.

'I'm fed up with being broke,' he would say, as if it were his fault.

Meantime I took a series of dead-end jobs – in a museum, a travel agent's and finally a bank. They were all dull but with Adam I did not care. We had our little home and our dream. Our future.

But Adam seemed to feel that he was letting me down. He told me once that he did not deserve me but the words so chilled me that I made him swear he would never repeat them, made him promise too that he would never leave me. So we married.

We had our beautiful babies. And Adam at night would rock them in his arms and smile his big smile at them and for a long time I forgot my mountains. My dream of visiting China.

He taught me so much – to feel beautiful, despite the teeth, and to play cricket, the latter lesson approached with all the seriousness of a born teacher. At school I'd been a rounders disaster and on the beach always hopeless at cricket. Never able to hit the ball. It was a complete mystery to me how a bat so thin could hit a ball so small.

But Adam was patient. 'Relax. Stop worrying. And just *keep your eye on the ball.*'

I remember the day it first worked – the delicious sound as the bat engaged and I hit that ball right across the beach.

I remember the exhilaration and the sense of complete happiness. As I smiled my crooked smile, Adam smiled his perfect smile, and the baby in the rucksack on his back smiled a gummy, toothless smile.

Now at last we arrive at Durndale Hospital and I'm so flustered suddenly that I jump out of the taxi and run up the steps to the main entrance, without even paying the poor man. I trip about halfway up the flight of steps, grazing my knee. It's the taxi driver who helps me to my feet. Only then does it hit me that I have only ten pounds in my purse.

'I'm sorry. It's not enough, is it? For the fare.'

And he looks right into my eyes then as they fill with tears and shakes his head. 'It's fine. A tenner is fine. You go on inside. Hurry now. And good luck.'

Next there's the sound of a siren from an ambulance outside. And all the voices pulling away – far, far away. And me standing at the reception desk. Giddy. Surrounded by people – pushing, hurrying. Frantic.

I close my eyes and there's another memory. The very worst this time. I'm back in that room with Sally and Carol. Fourteen years old. I'm thinking of the word 'ambulance' here too, in this terrible room. With the smell of blood. And the smell of panic . . .

'That's it. I'm calling an ambulance, Carol.'

I try to pull away from the bed but Carol is clutching my pyjama top with one hand – her other clasping her stomach, still doubled up with the pain.

'No, please no, Beth. I'll be all right.'

'All right? *All right?* Just look at you, Carol. You could be dying for all we know.'

'Oh Lord, is she dying, Beth? Do you really think she's *dying?*' Sally's holding the cotton flannel we've been using to try to cool Carol's forehead, her face ashen with terror.

'*Nobody* is dying.' Carol's face twists with a new wave of pain. 'I'm having the baby. Or losing the baby. I don't know which.'

Sally begins both to sob and to retch, her shoulders heaving over and over so that I fear she's going either to faint or be sick or both. It's too much for me, my legs buckling so that I have to sit alongside Carol. We have stripped the stained bedding but the sanitary towels I've found are clearly inadequate. There's more blood suddenly. A lot of blood . . .

'I think we'd better all move to the bathroom,' Carol says.

'No, Carol. We can't do this on our own,' I say. 'Not here. Not without help. We've *got* to get some proper help for you. Get you to a hospital. I'll ring my mum.'

'No, Beth. I'm begging you. Please, Beth. I'll be expelled. I'll never see you again. And my mum – it will kill her. *Please.*'

Carol has been bleeding on and off for two hours. It's the end of the Easter break and we're all staying at my home – the original idea was to get some space together, away from school, to work out what the bloody hell we're going to do. Carol has long since given up talking about an abortion – too young in any case to sign the forms without her mother and from her rounded shape beneath the baggy jumpers we all realise it's way too late.

Sally is talking nonsense – about us all leaving school, getting jobs in shops, sharing a flat and bringing up the baby together when our parents throw us out. I have not the faintest idea what to suggest. We have been arguing. Desperate. Terrified. And then the bleeding began.

My mother is already at her charity shop for the day and is going out straight after her shift to celebrate a colleague's birthday. My dad is away in Essex for a few nights – a sporting event with my brother, Michael, before returning him to his own school.

Carol reckons she's about twenty-five weeks into the pregnancy, maybe more, maybe less. We really have no way of knowing for sure. The bump has recently become difficult to hide. She's been wearing this stupid girdle thing and has huge breasts and, for the first time, terrible spots on her chin. I remember Sister Veronica staring at the spots one day and Carol's face flushing hotter and hotter above her baggy top as if the spots somehow would give her away.

'You think you're having the baby, Carol? Right now? Is that what this feels like?'

'I have no idea. I don't know, Beth.'

◆　◆　◆

'Are you all right, love?'

I open my eyes to see a nurse near the hospital check-in desk, her voice steady and kind. She reaches out to hold on to my arm with a strong grip just as my legs begin to give way.

'Slowly. Just breathe slowly.' She steers me to the nearest chair right next to the information desk and makes me lean forward, head between my knees.

Tea is offered – but no. I need to find Adam. 'Adam Carter? He's been in a road accident. A hit and run, they said.'

And then the nurse is liaising with the check-in staff over the computer screen. They insist on waiting until I'm steadier and then she's once more steering me very gently by the arm. 'I'll show you. This way. Take it slowly.'

Soon we're on A&E where I turn to the nurse and try very hard to read her face.

'Is he all right? Is Adam going to be all right?'

'This way, Mrs Carter,' she says. 'The doctor will be along to talk it all through with you in just a moment.'

I'm led to this man in a bed and there's a moment of relief at the terrible mistake. This is *not* Adam. This is an imposter. This man is too old. Skin too grey. Much too ill.

And only when he opens his eyes, straining to reassure me that he's all right, do I hear it. The wind at the beach. *Watch the ball, Beth.*

The whistle as I miss it and it passes me through the air, right across the beach.

'Beth. You're here . . .'

I'm hushing him, wanting him to save his energy as I kiss the huge dressing on his head – in my own saying a thousand sorries.

For lying to him. For not sharing the truth. The threats. The blackness of who I really am and what we did all those years ago.

For not paying attention.

For taking my eye off the ball.

CHAPTER 34

BETH – NOW

The following twenty-four hours remain a blur. Doctors. Police. Tests.

Adam has all manner of scans. There's a collapsed lung, broken ribs, swelling on the brain and his left leg is a complete mess. He becomes very disorientated and so they sedate him and then he's taken for surgery for what feels like hours while I pace the corridors and talk to the police.

At first I think there must be some kind of mistake. *A hit and run?* I imagine a young driver who lost control of his car and panicked perhaps? But the facts as they slowly emerge are utterly baffling.

Before his surgery Adam became more and more confused – mumbling about a pedestrian crossing, which made no sense to me. *Which crossing? Where?* And how can you have a hit and run on a pedestrian crossing? Did he get distracted? Step out in front of someone? It doesn't sound like Adam at all.

I remember about the dentist, that Adam said he'd walk there. Wish I'd paid better attention.

Next I discover that Adam is not the only one hurt. There's an older woman in intensive care. They won't share details of her condition but I sense she's in even graver danger.

And then a new police officer turns up with the news that a witness has been found from the door-to-door inquiries – a woman who was at her bedroom window and saw the accident from the end of the street. She didn't get an absolutely clear view because of the distance, but she says that a motorcycle seemed to drive straight at Adam on the crossing at quite a speed. As if *deliberately*. Adam was looking down at his phone and an elderly woman behind him lunged forward to try to pull him out of the way of the bike. But too late. The rider was almost thrown clear but managed eventually to right the machine, get back on and then simply zoomed off.

So on top of the terrifying fear over Adam's condition, I'm told 'off the record' that the elderly woman's condition is now very touch-and-go. This could even become a manslaughter inquiry. There's to be a police appeal in the papers, on the radio, and possibly on the local television news this evening.

In the corridor near the operating theatre, I pace. My mother calls.

'Sorry,' I say, 'no news. We just have to wait. I'll ring you the minute he comes out . . .'

And then my phone rings again and Sally's name flashes on the screen. I stare at her name – Sally – as the phone pulses and I just can't help it. Tears blurring my vision. What on earth to say to her? We haven't spoken properly since the row, just that text I sent about Sam on Facebook. I don't even understand what the hell is going on here.

I put the phone to my ear, hand shaking.

'Beth. I'm so, so sorry, darling. I just got your new message and spoke to your mum. I can't believe it. How is he? What's happened? Shall I come to the hospital?'

'He's in surgery, Sally. Could take hours. We just have to wait. They're putting pins in his leg and they're worried about swelling on the brain. Mum's with the boys.'

'Dear Lord. So you're there on your own?'

'Yeah.'

'Oh, Beth. Can I come? I'm so, so sorry we had that stupid falling-out. I said things I shouldn't have said. Please. I should have been in touch. Please say I can come.'

I look across to a painting on the opposite wall. It's of a night sky with stars and a full moon. Just like that night I met Adam. It looks as if a child painted it – quite a nice picture but all the colours are blurring as tears still cloud my eyes.

The nurses wanted me to wait in the relatives' room downstairs but I want to stay here, nearer the operating theatres. Nearer Adam.

'Yeah, I'd love it if you'd come. There's really bad stuff going on, Sally. It was a hit and run. It's going to be on the news.'

'A *hit and run?*'

'Yeah.'

'OK, I'm on my way.'

◆ ◆ ◆

When she arrives, she looks pale and tired herself. She is hobbling, has done something to her foot, but despite this she moves immediately into the very gear I need – Sally at her best. Everything that I love about her: calm, organised, borderline bossy. She speaks to staff and finds out it will be at least another hour of surgery, maybe longer.

'Right. I need to get a drink inside you, Beth. Hot tea with sugar. You can't just sit here in the corridor. You're trembling.'

In the end, I let her lead me, arm through mine, to the cafeteria on the floor below.

'Sit there.'

I drink my tea in a complete daze. I do as I'm told. I see the love and the fear and the confusion in Sally's eyes across the table and I thank my lucky stars that I have her, so very sorry that I upset her at that stupid and ridiculous barbecue.

'Don't worry, Beth. He's in good hands. We'll go straight back to the ward and they'll tell us the minute there's any news. You won't miss anything. I've made sure.'

Only when I've finished the whole cup of tea, do I say it: 'A witness is saying it looked deliberate, Sally.'

'*What?*'

'A motorbike ploughed into him on a pedestrian crossing. As if on purpose. The woman who was hurt very badly tried to yank him out of the way.'

'But that's completely crazy. Why would anyone . . .'

She tilts her head and frowns. She looks away and then back at me, eyes now wide. I say nothing at first. 'Oh, come on, Beth. You don't seriously think that this could have anything to do with . . .'

'I don't know. I don't know what to think about anything any more.' I'm glad she's said it first. 'I feel as if I'm going completely mad here, Sally – the things I'm thinking. Do you think I should tell the police? About the messages, that funny call to school? The message on Sam's Facebook page?'

'No, no, no. You'd have to tell them everything then. No, darling. This is awful, dreadful, but it's just some terrible coincidence, the timing, Beth. It *must* be. And the police will catch whoever did this, I'm sure they will. But no. This can't have anything to do with Carol. It *can't* have . . .'

CHAPTER 35

BETH – NOW

I know now why lack of sleep is such a perfect form of torture.

Adam comes out of surgery after three and a half hours but is still heavily sedated. They say the operation went well but he's not out of the woods and is moved to intensive care. He's being kept sedated apparently to let the swelling on the brain go down. I refuse to leave his side, dozing a few minutes here and there in a chair by the bed until he's allowed to regain consciousness.

Sally fetches me some things from home and sits with me for the whole of the second day. By the evening there's terrible news. The woman hurt trying to help Adam has died. She apparently had a heart condition and the shock brought on a fatal attack.

I cannot take it in. One part of me truly horrified – the other? I'm ashamed to say I just feel relief that if one of them had to die, it wasn't Adam. What does that make me? I can't bear to think of Adam's response.

It also means the police have stepped everything up a gear. This has become a death by dangerous driving inquiry and could even be escalated to manslaughter. Lots more questions. More pressure to find new witnesses.

Meanwhile, Adam's drugs are adjusted and when he comes round and is finally able to talk, the police want to know what he remembers. The problem is, he's still so groggy and confused, unable to recall much of what has happened at all. I beg them all not to tell him yet about the woman's death. *Not yet . . . please.*

By 11 p.m. the nurses say his readings are all much better and I really should go home to have a shower and get some sleep so that Adam can sleep again too.

I don't want to go. I'm terrified something will happen when I'm not there but everyone tells me he's stable now. And I can see from my mother's phone calls that the boys need me too and so reluctantly I let Sally take me home by taxi. She isn't driving because of the foot. Just a sprain, I think she said.

At home I find two very frightened little boys, despite their grand-mother's reassurances, and realise I should have come home sooner. They've been told there's been an accident and Daddy's going to be fine, but they've seen the TV coverage – tipped off by friends – and they're very confused. *Why didn't the motorcyclist stop, Mummy?*

The police are in touch to say no other witnesses have yet been found. It was a quiet time on the street with most people at work or waiting at nearby schools to pick up their children. Worse – there's no CCTV footage. The nearest camera was faulty. But they feel sure there will be a breakthrough soon. There will be damage to the bike. *We'll find it.*

I try to sleep but it's completely impossible. Even when I do drift off, I have these terrible dreams. All the horrible images blended together. Three candles in a church. The shells on the shelf. Adam on the pedestrian crossing. Carol sitting beside his bed in the hospital instead of me . . .

At 2 a.m., poor darling Sam appears at my door to confess to an accident. He's wet the bed, something he hasn't done since he was tiny. I tell him not to worry, to change his pyjamas and get into my bed while

I take his bedding down to the machine so that no one will know. *I don't want people to know, Mummy.* He means Sally, who's sleeping on the couch in the sitting room.

I smooth Sam's hair and tell him *Daddy is going to be fine* and only when he's finally fallen back to sleep do I creep downstairs to make tea. It's not long before Sally appears in the kitchen.

'How are you doing, Beth?'

'Awful. Can't sleep. I keep thinking about that poor woman and just treading water until I can go back to the hospital.'

'I think it's helped the boys to see you, even for a bit.'

'Yes, yes – you're right.' I do not add that I feel torn in two, that I should be with the boys and be with Adam too. Impossible to get it right.

I make us both tea and sit alongside her on the sofa in the front room. It's cold with the heating off and so she wraps the duvet around both our shoulders.

'Listen. I've made a decision that you're going to find very difficult, Sally.' I don't look at her as I say this. It's all I've thought about since I sat next to Adam in the hospital. 'When he's well enough and when they let him home, I'm going to tell Adam *everything.*'

'Oh, Beth . . .'

'No, please don't try to dissuade me.' I take her hand beneath the duvet and hold on to it tightly.

'But all these years, Beth. The promise . . . All these years.'

'We were wrong, Sally, to make that promise. I know that now. I think I always knew that. And now – Jeez. I could have *lost* him and it may even be my fault. It may have something to do with it all. I'm sorry, Sally. I know you don't think it's connected but I'm not asking your permission. I've made my decision. This is my family and my call. When Adam is home and when he's well enough, I am going to *tell* him. All of it . . .'

CHAPTER 36

BETH - BEFORE

Carol's baby is born very quickly. Very tiny. A girl. For just a second, maybe two, I am sure I can see her breathing but immediately I am thinking that she *can't* be. Too soon. Too small. *She can't be.*

Sally is instantly hysterical and just to get her out of the bathroom – *out of the way, Sally, out of the bloody way* – I shout for her to get a clean towel from the linen cupboard on the landing. *Now, Sally! Now.*

But then as her sobbing leaves the room, there's a terrible crash as Sally collapses. At first I fear she may be concussed – has hit her head on the wall as she blacked out. *Sally! Sally? Can you hear me?* I'm out on the landing, slapping her face. But then – *thank God, Sally, open your eyes, look at me* – she's coming round and I prop her up as quickly as I can. Put her head between her knees. *Oh – come on, Sally. Quickly. For Christ's sake, just sit still. Carol needs me . . .'*

And then when I am finally back in the doorway of the bathroom, it's the silence that strikes me. Carol is now clutching the tiny perfect bundle to her stomach like a child with a favourite broken doll. Absolutely silent now. The baby is blue. No breathing. No movement.

I stare and stare at the baby's mouth, willing it to move again but it does not. And here is the thing: I do not ask and I do not check. I do not try for a pulse or try mouth to mouth or anything.

'I think I put my hand over her mouth.' Carol is staring at me. 'I think I did this . . .'

'Don't say that. Don't even think that. You wouldn't have done that.'

And for a moment everything stops quite still and it's as if the room is full of water and I'm swimming around in it. A mermaid. Unable to hear. Only to see.

I see Carol hugging the baby – blue and completely limp now – even closer to her body, rocking it ever so gently, and I turn to see Sally on the landing still, her head between her knees.

And I twist and turn, swimming around and around to make sure that I do not forget anything. The four little shells that we found at the beach last holiday – lined up on the blue-painted shelf below the mirror. I remember the happiness the day I collected them, and the contrast – my mother moaning about how much dust they collect now and *can't we throw them out, Beth. Get some more next year?*

The blind at the window – permanently down because the mechanism has broken. *It's you children. You tug too hard. Shouldn't tug so hard . . .* The mirror over the sink that I must polish during the holidays for my pocket money. I see myself in the reflection, smiling with my Pledge and the clean duster, bright yellow in my hand, with my mother over my shoulder, and I can smell the normality. Ache for the normality.

But most of all, worst of all, it's the expression on Carol's face – black with something beyond sorrow.

And that is the second, as I try to read Carol's face – the precise moment in time when my life as I had known it stopped and this new one began. A life in which you have to push, push every day to keep this black and terrible picture deep somewhere at the bottom of the ocean so that you can swim above it to find oxygen and breathe. And live. It's the picture in that mirror. The look on Carol's face. The scene that registers what had happened. Not to someone else. But to us.

'*Will I go to hell? Will I burn in hell?*'

And I wish more than anything in my life now that I'd called an ambulance. And my mother. And Carol's mother. Maybe all our lives could have been completely different if I'd done that.

But I didn't.

For a long time we just stayed there – the three of us, in silence and in shock, Carol's back against the bath, Sally finally shuffling along the floor to join us. And then Carol began mumbling about the police. *Should we call the police now?* That she would go to jail. No. Detention centre. Explain that it was not our fault – mine and Sally's. But *her* fault. That she was so very sorry. But she must have got the dates all wrong. Did not realise it would be a proper baby yet. A real, whole little baby. And could we forgive her? Ever forgive her?

And the more pitiful her voice became, the more sure I became that we must help her. I was saying that she was not to blame, that we were all to blame. We'd been stupid. Not wicked. But *stupid*. My fault for not phoning my mother. That it was too late for the baby. That we couldn't have known – any of us – that it would be a proper baby. And no, Carol. She would not go to hell. We would pray. Light candles. Pray.

Carol was mumbling now about limbo. Wasn't that where babies went when they hadn't been christened? I remember saying – no, I did not believe in limbo. That the baby was in heaven. *Heaven, Carol.* And as she carried on mumbling and trembling, I asked if we could call her mother. Truly I did. But she was so afraid. Begged us – no. Please, no. That it would break her mother's heart into pieces. So we gave Carol a bath, me and Sally, and finally persuaded her to let us wrap the baby and all of the birthing mess in the stripy towel. Hid it in a bag in my bedroom. We bought a huge pack of sanitary towels for the bleeding and told my mother late that evening that Carol had a very heavy period.

Carol stayed in bed for two days, and I remember willing my mother to find us out. To wrap her arms around me and make it all better. But she did not. So when Carol was steadier on her feet, we did something truly terrible. We took the bundle in a plastic bag back to the convent. Where we buried it.

A tiny, tiny baby buried in a wood all alone. To this day. Sally vomited. I cried. Carol said nothing at all, her eyes completely dead. It took us an hour to persuade her to leave the wood and then afterwards we all went to the school chapel where we lit three small candles, watching in silence as they slowly burned down in the darkness.

And that's when we made the promise. Holding hands as those candles burned. Never to tell anyone. Ever. To keep it between us. The three of us. To pretend that it had never happened.

Promise.

Promise.

Promise.

CHAPTER 37

BETH - NOW

There is a plant just beyond my kitchen window that is a favourite with ladybirds. I wish I knew the name – keep meaning to look it up. I spend a lot of time watching the ladybirds when Adam finally comes home from hospital. It's so calming, watching their bright little bodies, so busy and so beautiful, waiting for that moment of magic when the fairy wings appear.

How many today, Beth?

Six.

On one plant?

Yes, Adam.

The leg is still very painful and he's on crutches but we've been told that the brain scans are fine. No long-term damage mentally. Despite this, it may take weeks, even months, for him to be back to full strength. Temporarily he is just not himself.

In practical terms, it's as if his brain is tired all the time. Foggy. He says something and then forgets that he's said it – then a little later he'll realise that he's been muddled and gets upset. *I'm going mad, Beth.*

No, Adam. You just need to rest. It'll be OK but they say it'll take time. We have to wait.

Just as I feared, Adam was utterly devastated to learn of the woman's death – the pedestrian who tried to help him. He still doesn't remember the details. Doesn't even recall why he was looking down at his phone as he crossed the road.

The police appeals continue but so far there seems to be no progress.

Given Adam's health, I haven't yet told him the truth – what happened with Carol and Sally in school. I need to wait until he's stronger, more himself. It means that some days I look into his eyes, wondering what on earth he'll think of me when he knows who I really am. What we did. What I did.

For now I just watch. And wait. Counting the ladybirds and belatedly my lucky stars, that Adam is still here with me. Safe.

It's a good place for him to recover, this house. The garden has the most glorious views, the plot backing on to woodland. The property itself is pretty too – rich, red brick sprawling over three floors. We've never had the funds to do it up properly but I don't care. I love its shabby, lived-in feel.

We've fallen quickly into an easy routine, well practised from the long summers of a teacher's marriage. The school run, coffee and papers in the conservatory, a spell apart when I work on my CV for new job applications or run errands for the family. Lunch. Then a relaxed time when he watches me gardening or ironing while reading a book or dozing in a chair.

Cash flow for now is fine. Adam has full sick pay and I have some severance.

One morning I catch him watching me as I think about Carol. The past. The motorbike . . .

'Are you worrying about money, Beth?'

'No, not at all. There's nothing for us to worry about. You need to rest. Concentrate on getting well.'

To try to encourage him to still himself, I am quiet for a time. I just smile and then turn to stare through the window at the laundry dancing on the line – one of Adam's shirts flapping its arms to some imagined beat. I'm thinking about the police and how shocked I am there's been no progress with the hit-and-run inquiry. It was on the TV, the local radio and in the local papers – how can there be no firm leads at all? No CCTV of any real help. Apparently they have now found a shot of a bike on a camera about a mile from the pedestrian crossing but they're not even sure if it's the right bike and rider. There's mud covering the licence plate and the rider is in full helmet and motorcycle gear. Could be anyone, quite frankly.

I really did think it would be all sorted by now. That it would have turned out to be some teenager who just got scared and rode off in a panic. That's what I want it to be. An accident – horrid, yes, but nothing more than that.

I want to shake off the dread that seeps in during the nights, wondering if I should mention to the police about the stupid messages. Give them Carol's name? In some moments I think this would be the right thing to do and then I imagine them seeking her out, turning up at her house in France. Carol, of course, having absolutely nothing to do with any of this – her shock and sense of betrayal when they tell her it was me who sent them. Pointed the finger . . .

'Are you sure there isn't something you want to say, Beth?' Adam asks. 'You have that look on your face when you're holding something in.'

The laundry falls still for just a second as if listening to us, then finds the wind again – straining to one side before dancing once more.

'No, I'm fine. I just want you to stop talking and thinking and just to rest.'

◆　◆　◆

And then – around ten days after his return home – I'm in the garden with secateurs, pruning and tidying, when Adam shouts from the conservatory that *it's the phone. It's for you.*

'I'll ring back.' I'm right in the middle of work on an awkward shrub, pushing a heavy branch aside so I can reach deep into its centre.

'No, Beth. It's Ned. He's ringing from France . . . Carol's partner Ned.'

I lose concentration, let go of the branch and my finger catches the edge of the blade. A neat slice into my flesh, although I don't feel it, not even as I suck at the blood, running across the lawn to the kitchen.

'Hang on. She's on her way.' Adam has his back to me. 'Oh, look – here she is. I'll leave you to it.'

I'm breathless as I take the phone. 'Ned?'

'Beth. I'm so sorry to surprise you like this . . .'

'Is it Carol? Is she OK? Has something happened?'

'So she's not with you?'

'Goodness, no.' I'm still sucking on my finger, willing the bleeding to stop. This is such a shock. I can't remember when I last spoke to Ned. Years. Many years . . . 'Why on earth would you think she was here?'

There's a long pause.

'I'm sorry. I shouldn't have phoned like this. It's just I rang her mother, Deborah, and she gave me this number. Carol mentioned you'd been in touch about some school event. I said it would be good for her to see you guys. But she says she doesn't want to come.'

'Yes. Right. So why is she not there – Carol? I don't understand.' I really cannot process why he's calling. Did he honestly think she would come *here*, when she won't even come to the school?

'Look, I don't want to alarm you and I don't want to tread on Carol's privacy. She doesn't like me talking about any of this stuff.'

'*What stuff?*' I take a tissue from my pocket and press my cut finger into it, clenched in my palm.

There's a longer pause as if he's considering something carefully. 'She'll be angry if she finds out I've rung you, Beth.'

'Please, Ned. I'd like to help if I can. What *is it?*'

'We've had a rough few years, Beth. We've been trying to adopt and we've had a lot of disappointments.'

'Oh my goodness. I'm so sorry.' I don't share that Deborah has already told us this. I can feel my heart beating more loudly.

'As I say, Carol doesn't like to talk about it, not even with her mother. She finds it all very distressing – overwhelming.'

'How dreadful.' I close my eyes and am again wondering if this is a direct result of what we did. *Our fault.*

'And sometimes, if the news is bad, she needs to take some time out. Goes off on her own. I'm used to it. I try to be calm and give her space. She always stays in touch. But I worry about her, Beth. Really worry. She's so frail these days, still doesn't eat as well as I'd like. And the thing is, she's gone off again and this time I don't know where. She hasn't told me. Just a message to say – not to worry.'

'So when was this? How long has she been gone?'

'A couple of weeks back she disappeared for two nights. Kept in touch and came back – but she didn't take her mobile phone. And now she's disappeared *again*. Like I say, just a message to say I'm not to worry. She'll be back soon.'

'Right. Goodness.' I have no idea what to say. What to recommend.

'I'm glad you've been in touch with her. Her mum said, and I've been trying to encourage Carol to visit her mother more. Come to England more. But she gets so upset – closes the whole subject down. She will never say *why*.'

Again I can feel my pulse, feel a slight sickness in my stomach suddenly.

I think of Carol longing for a child, then I think of Carol in that bathroom with the tiny, tiny baby. Blue. Cold. Gone . . . I find that I have to sit down. 'So have you reported her missing, Ned?'

'No – I mean, she isn't missing *technically*. She's been in touch. Just says she'll be home soon. We're right at the top of the list with a new adoption agency and the waiting is doing her head in. She's afraid it'll be another disappointment, so when it all gets too much she just packs her things, takes the bike and heads to the coast . . .'

'*Bike?*'

'Yes. That's the other thing I really don't like. The motorcycling. She says it clears her head. Makes her feel alive and in touch with nature. She's been riding for about ten years now. It's not a powerful bike and she's very safe but it's other drivers I worry about.'

I can hear my pulse in my ear, imagining also the roar of the bike as it ploughed into Adam. A coincidence. Of course. It can't be a link. *Can't be* . . .

'So, anyway, I shouldn't have phoned and she'll go mad if she found out I shared this with you. But when Deborah said you'd been in touch, I kind of hoped she might have arranged a visit or just turned up. Long shot.'

'No, sorry. Look – will you stay in touch, Ned? Keep me posted?'

'Yes, of course. I'll let you know when she's home. But like I say, I won't tell her I rang you. Please don't tell her I rang you behind her back. She'll be angry with me.'

'OK.' Slowly I unfurl my hand to find the finger has at last stopped bleeding. 'Listen, Ned, can I ask you something?'

'Sure.'

'How bad does Carol get? I mean – how worried should I be? She wouldn't hurt herself or . . . I mean – do you think you should let the police know?'

'No, no. I don't think she would hurt herself. Or anyone else. She's not a danger, not Carol. You know that. I didn't mean to imply . . .' He sucks in his breath. 'I shouldn't have phoned. I'm sorry.'

'No, you were right to ring. We still really care about her, Ned. So will you keep in touch. Yes? When she gets back.'

'Sure. And you'll let me know if she gets in touch with you?'

'Of course.'

Adam is staring at me, wearing a deep frown as I put the phone back into its cradle.

'What on earth is all that about? What's going on, Beth?'

'Nothing for you to worry about. I'll talk to you soon, Adam, I promise. But right now I need to ring Sally.' I do not add what I'm really thinking. That before I tell Adam everything, I need to talk this through, not just with Sally but with Matthew. *Urgently.*

CHAPTER 38

BETH - BEFORE

Physically Carol had seemed over the course of the fourth form to recover. There were cramps and heavier periods for a time and one month she ran a fever but we were too afraid to involve a doctor, sticking always to our script. As if the discipline of silence could undo it. Make it un-happen.

Life and exams carried on and we noticed, all of us, that Sister Veronica was especially kind. It was as if she'd picked up some change in the air, an awareness in her that all at once frightened and yet also reassured us.

We'd planted bluebell bulbs at our special spot in the woods – an excuse to visit and a cover to stop others meddling with the ground. Sometimes when we took walks there, I could see Sister Veronica watching us and there was a part of me almost hoping that she would follow and ask questions. I still had this fantasy in my head of one of us breaking down and it all coming out. Adult help. Arms around our shoulders. For a while I longed to be rid of the guilt just as I'd hoped right at the beginning that my mother would find us out.

But no one found us out. The bluebells grew. Spread. The seasons came and went. Life went on.

◆ ◆ ◆

At the end of the fifth form Carol dropped her bombshell – that she was leaving for art college. No sixth form together. She tried the spin that it would be more liberating and more fun, that we could stay with her at weekends to party. But we all guessed correctly from the tone of her voice that it would never happen.

She dropped the news on us over a Chinese takeaway, which we stole out to buy one midweek evening against all the school rules. Ridiculous to think of it now but at the time it felt truly rebellious – exotic and grown up.

We even did a recce one Saturday morning to work out how long it would take to collect, synchronising our watches and timing the walk at a brisk pace (although not a run for fear of attracting attention) from the Convent of St Colman down the High Street, via the town park to the Chinese restaurant. *Twelve minutes. Street lights all the way. Good.*

We knew we would not be able to pre-order but were assured by the woman at the takeaway counter that most orders midweek were ready in fifteen minutes maximum. So that was a total of thirty-nine minutes. There was a shorter route, using the narrow alley behind the cinema, but this was often frequented by drinkers even in the daytime so we decided this might not be wise for sixteen-year-old girls after dark.

Fifth-form privileges meant we were by now sharing a large room on the third floor – just the three of us. The rooms were actually designed for four, but perhaps remembering the debacle of sharing with Melody, Sister Veronica had made the case for one bed to be removed so we might have more floor space. Lights out was still 9.30 p.m. but the 'patrols' by duty nuns rarely ventured to the top corridor as we had supposedly reached the point of being trustworthy.

So this was the plan. We would opt for a Thursday (with Sister Veronica on duty – still the most lenient nun) and as soon as our room was checked at lights out, two of us would then sneak down the back staircase and head for the Chinese restaurant. The remaining girl would stuff pillows into the beds to create the impression of sleeping teenagers just in case anyone came back to check on us.

According to our recce the food should be back by 10 p.m. – and we would triumphantly feast at the end of our exams. We'd bought a bottle of red wine and the order was to be sweet and sour pork, special fried rice, chicken in black bean sauce and prawn crackers. We had never been so excited.

We threw dice to determine who would stay and who would go. I rolled only two and so for the excruciating forty-five minutes of the operation (preparing our order, of course, took *far* longer than we'd been told) I practised explanations and excuses in case our adventure was discovered.

So pleased was I with the elaborate cover story I'd invented, I was almost disappointed when Carol and Sal returned undiscovered – breathless with a white plastic bag, straining at the handle and steaming with food.

We shut the dormitory door quietly and I passed around the crockery and cutlery, borrowed from the dining room, desperately trying to limit the clattering. The food – especially the sweet and sour pork – was an alarming colour and the wine that glowed warm and inviting in our mugs tasted unexpectedly bitter. No matter. We were celebrating. We were grown-up. We had finished our GCSEs.

Only one small thing had been miscalculated.

The *smell.*

It was no more than ten minutes before Sister Veronica appeared, following her nose – the look on her face priceless. For a second we froze, unsure of the outcome, but – mercifully missing the alcohol – she then shocked us by laughing.

'Chinese?' She was reaching for a prawn cracker. 'Last year they went for Indian.' She crunched the cracker and then looked a little more serious. 'Please tell me no one went out on their own.'

'Two of us went. Street lights all the way.'

She nodded, a smile in her eyes. 'OK. You'll clear up and take your plates down in the morning?'

'Yes, Sister.'

She turned and as she pulled the door to, grinned again. 'I sincerely hope it tastes better than it smells.'

As the door shut, we stared in amazement at each other.

'I don't believe that.' Sally was spooning more of the chicken goo on to her plate as she spoke. 'Still, I suppose we'll have so much more freedom next year, she didn't think it was worth getting heavy.'

'Yeah – but there's still a curfew in the sixth, you know.' I was not at all keen on the chicken so took another handful of prawn crackers, weighing up whether to risk more of the bright orange sauce that went with the pork.

Carol was silent, only toying with her food. I poured her some more wine, grateful that I'd thought to hide the bottle in my locker. I suspect Sister Veronica would have been less amenable if she'd spotted the alcohol.

'You OK, Carol?'

'Look, I don't want to spoil this. I was going to wait until the weekend to tell you . . .'

'Tell us what?' My words were distorted by my full mouth.

'The thing is, I'm not coming back for the sixth form.'

The combination of the unfamiliar spices, alcohol and shock made me miss a breath. I started choking and Sally had to thump me on the back as I took a large gulp of wine to recover.

I was still wheezing, unable to fill my lungs properly, staring at Sally who looked as shocked as I was. There had been no clue, not the slightest hint that Carol was considering leaving. And it was only a week until we were to part early for the summer break.

'What do you mean?' Sally turned now to Carol who looked away, still toying with food on her plate.

213

'Is it the money, Carol?' I was remembering the lottery win now. Was that it? Had the fund dried up?

'No, no – at least, not really. Mum says she can afford it but . . . Look, I don't want you to be hurt. To misunderstand. You know how much I love you both. I just . . . After everything that's happened, I've just had enough here.'

'But we've done so well, Carol. *Together.*' I was now both pleading and panicking as I closed my eyes and tried not to see them. The candles. The smell of the wax. *The bluebells . . .*

Carol pushed her fork around her plate. 'The thing is, I'm thinking of art college – or a design course, maybe. They just don't take all that seriously here. There are a couple of really good places nearer home with better facilities and I think it would be nice for Mum. She's on her own, remember.'

I could think of nothing to say.

'So have you told the school?' Sally had put her plate down on the carpet.

'Yes.'

'So, Sister Veronica *knows?*'

'I'm sorry. I wanted to tell you two first but I knew you'd be upset. And with the exams and everything – I didn't want that.' Carol forced a little smile – at both of us in turn. None of us was brave enough to say what we were really thinking. 'The good thing is you'll be allowed to come and stay with me at weekends. We can party a bit. Go out. Have some real fun.'

'Yes.' I did not lift my eyes from the food congealing on my plate, an unattractive orange skin forming.

We scraped the uneaten food back into the containers.

We all guessed it wouldn't happen. The weekend visits. Carol didn't even stay with her mother. Soon after her eighteenth birthday she went on an exchange programme to France and then worked as a chalet girl in Austria at a ski resort. A drifter. We saw her rarely when she was back in Brighton but only when we did the chasing.

Which is how we all shut the lid on Pandora's box and pretended it had never happened. Never spoke of it again. The candles. The promise. The *bluebells* . . .

And although I worried for Carol and I missed her too, I know now that I must tell Adam the whole truth. Which is that I can never quite forgive myself for the most surprising feeling when Carol first pulled away from us. Which was relief.

CHAPTER 39

MATTHEW - NOW

Matthew rolls the first marble across the desk and waits to hear the distinctive *plonk* as it lands in the waste bin. The second does the same, then the third veers off-piste, missing the basket by maybe two inches. Matthew frowns and then sighs. He leans over to again adjust the stack of paper under the rear right-hand foot of the desk. He folds several of the sheets in two to increase the height and thus the angle of the desk. *Yes, that should do it.*

He walks around to slightly reposition the waste bin and moves back to his chair to collect another fistful of marbles from his drawer.

For a moment he pauses, turning the marbles over and over in his hand. Never mind that this ridiculous distraction tactic is not working and never mind that, despite placing several new adverts, he has no new case to work on. He has somehow to resist the temptation to phone her. To make it all *worse*.

Matthew releases another marble and watches it catch the light as it gathers speed and heads for the basket. Plonk. He tries another, which moves even faster. Damn. He's raised the desk too high. The marbles are now running much too quickly. *Oh, stuff it. Stuff everything . . .*

As he kicks the stupid desk in frustration, his phone rings and the name confirms it is at last his best contact still in the force. Melanie Sanders. She's a DS in Cornwall still but has some mates in traffic in Devon who are checking out his tip-off.

'So, any news?'

'Lovely to talk to you too, Matt.'

'Oops, sorry. Out of practice – small talk, niceties. So how are you, Mel?'

'I'm fine, but don't let's pretend you care.' There's a smile to her tone – she's teasing and Matthew closes his eyes. It's only at times like this, when he's chasing a favour from one of his former colleagues, that he lets himself think about how much he misses it. The force. The job. The sense of belonging . . .

'Right then. So the Devon team checked out your druggy motor-cyclist and there's no damage to the bike and no sign of repair. Also he has a cast-iron alibi for the time of the hit and run. Sorry, but they've checked and double-checked. Definitely no link.'

Matthew lets out a long huff of air. He really had thought that Melody Sage's boyfriend might be involved. Matthew was still strug-gling to put a real motive together but he had a hunch, was glad to have passed on the lead and was disappointed that he was wrong.

'So are you going to tell me why you thought this guy might be of interest?'

'Sorry, can't say. Just a long shot.'

'So this is where I say we should have a drink sometime so that I can try to persuade you to reconsider coming back to us . . .'

'And this is where I say, you know I'm done with the police but I'll text you about a drink.'

'Which you won't.'

'Look, really sorry, Mel, but I've gotta go. Bit busy with a big case here. Talk soon.' He hangs up to turn two more marbles over in his right palm, closing his eyes.

He tries so hard not to think about the past. The worst of it in the force. Sometimes he wonders if the memory will fade over time. It's been barely two years and still when he talks to Mel, it all comes back. The smell . . .

No one warns you in training school. They joke about it later. The black jokes to mask the true emotions. But in training school no one tells you that you can't get it out of your nostrils – the first time you smell burned flesh.

Matthew opens his eyes and uses his thumb to scroll through the pictures on his phone. *There she is.* Sally on that first walk around the lake when he got stupid over the swan. There's a smile in her eyes and he can hear her laughter right now.

There's a part of Matthew that wishes he hadn't gone to her mother's, wishes he hadn't had that chat in the kitchen while Sally was upstairs, sorting through some old pictures in her former bedroom.

Sally had told Matthew that she was completely over the idea of marriage and happy families. *Tried that, got the tee shirt, thank you very much. No siree* . . . She'd said it over dinner and he wondered at the time if it was the truth or just something she felt men, and he in particular, wanted to hear. They hadn't been going out long enough to have any heavy conversations but it had come up after the barbecue row because Beth seemed to have some bee in her bonnet that Matthew was not a family type of guy.

Matthew had been straight when she asked. No, he did not want children. It was the truth. Sally had said that was fine by her. They were not serious after all. What did it matter . . .

And then in the kitchen Sally's mother had shared an entirely different story. She'd told Matthew how pleased she was to see Sally with such a nice young man after all she'd been through. There had been oversharing – the truth of how Sally's marriage broke down, not just over infidelity, but over the loss of a child.

Of course she hasn't given up hope. I keep telling her there's still plenty of time . . .

Sally's mother told Matthew that her daughter had come close to a breakdown after the miscarriage. Had drunk a bit too much for a time and then worried that she was taking after her late father. *I told her not to be so silly. But she was always worried it might run in the family. The drinking.*

She confided too that there had been some awful scene in a shop where Sally was almost done for shoplifting. Had put a pack of babygros in her handbag. It was only Beth who talked the security round, got Sally off with a warning by promising to take her to the doctor.

Matthew stole glances at Sally as they drove home and wondered just how much she hid from him. It was early days for them, yes, but she was saying what he wanted to hear. The script that she was not fussed about marrying again ever, about being a mother.

It wasn't true. She was taking his cues, saying what he needed to hear.

After dropping her at home, Matthew had paced his flat for a whole hour. Who was he kidding? He wasn't being fair, should never have started this. He could not deprive Sally of the future she deserved. He had already stolen that from one innocent woman. He could not steal it from another . . .

CHAPTER 40

BETH - NOW

I take my phone into the garden and sit on the grass alongside a patch of ground, dug ready for new planting. It's muddy and uncomfortable – I can feel the damp through my jeans – but need to stay well out of earshot; I can't risk Adam hearing. 'Sally. Good. I've just had a really shocking call from Ned.'

'Ned?'

'I know. I couldn't believe it either. He apparently heard from Deborah that we'd been in touch and she gave him my number. But listen, Carol is *missing*.'

'What do you mean missing?'

'Gone AWOL. Apparently she does it occasionally to clear her head. This business of trying to adopt, it all gets too much for her. The waiting.'

I can hear Sal sucking in her breath. She'll be thinking the same as me . . .

There's a horrible pause and I tap my bottom lip with my right hand. I do not share the questions still booming in my head. *So the fact she can't have a baby now. Is this because of what we did? Failing to get Carol to a doctor all those years ago?*

'There's something else, Sally. I just don't know what to think.'

'Go on.'

'Carol has a motorbike. She uses it to go off when she wants some time out.'

'*A motorbike?*'

'Yeah. I mean, it's a coincidence obviously. I don't seriously think there could be any kind of link. Carol would be incapable of harming a fly. I know that and you know that. And I asked Ned what he thought – whether Carol could ever harm herself or whatever and he really took offence . . .' I'm speaking faster and faster as if rushing the words will make them less dangerous. 'But I wanted to know what you think? If I'm going mad even mentioning this? This *coincidence*. This weird thing that is making me feel so strange. And disloyal for even thinking about it and saying any of this out loud.'

'Dear God. I don't know what to say.'

'I'm worried if we tell the police, they'll hunt Carol down and it will be a final straw for her – tip her right over the edge. So I'm thinking we talk to Matthew. Get his advice? Yes? What do you think? I mean, she wouldn't do anything bad – not Carol. I know in my bones that she wouldn't, but do we have some kind of responsibility to mention this weird coincidence, do you think? *To the police*, I mean. This and the messages on social media? Matthew will be able to tell us. Advise us.'

There's another long pause and I'm shocked to hear what sounds like sniffing. No. It grows louder. Snivelling. Then proper, full-on crying.

'Oh my goodness, Sally. I didn't mean to upset you. I don't seriously think for one moment that Carol has anything to do with this. I'm not suggesting that she would hurt Adam; I'm just worried about whether we're supposed to disclose this without . . .'

'Matthew's dumped me.' The words are gasped through sobbing.

'*What?*'

There's more sniffing and blowing of her nose before Sally speaks again. 'I didn't want to tell you with everything going on with Adam. You have quite enough on your plate and in any case I thought you'd be pleased. Seeing as you didn't approve anyway . . .'

'Oh, Sally, I'm so sorry.' I'm shocked and upset to hear just how distressed she is. It's a while before her crying settles.

'So you *really* like him?' I say.

Sally doesn't answer, just cries some more, again blowing her nose.

'Tell me what happened.'

'That's the problem – I just don't know. We were fine. No, better than fine – we were *great*, Beth, and then suddenly I get this text . . .'

'Text? He dumped you by text? Jeez . . .'

'Yeah, just said it wasn't working. He was truly sorry, blah blah, but it wouldn't be fair to me.'

'Right. Well, I need to see him.' I struggle to stand, smoothing the damp patch on my jeans.

'No, Beth. Please. Leave it.'

'I'm sorry, Sally, but I can't. In any case, I need to talk to him about Carol. And I'm *not* having him treat you like this. *No way . . .*'

◆ ◆ ◆

I drive the way I drove to Sally's all those years ago when she lost the baby. Like a woman possessed. Grating gears. Bashing the steering wheel. Raking my fingers through my hair over and over.

I know that the anger bubbling inside me is both dangerous and hypocritical. Sally's right – I didn't approve of them dating but that was only because Matthew seemed a bit off around the boys. Not the family type. Not the type of man I trust and hence like best myself. But listening to Sally crying so desperately has brought back horrible memories of all that Sally's been through down the years.

I think of that awful day years back, sitting in the back office of the shop with the security officer when Sally went off the rails. They claimed they had CCTV of her putting baby clothes in her bag but Sally had no memory whatsoever of what she had done. She was just mumbling. *They're pretty, the babygros. Aren't they pretty* . . . It took me an age to get them to see sense. To understand what poor Sally had just lost.

I think again of Matthew, realising only now just how much Sally cares for him.

How. Dare. He.

◆　◆　◆

There are no free parking spaces close to Matthew's office and so I have to walk in the rain for five minutes before I'm ringing his buzzer, even crosser.

'Matthew. It's Beth here. I need to speak to you.'

'Oh right. Goodness. I was just about to have a meeting with a client . . .'

'I mean it, Matthew.' I take a deep breath. 'Let me in. This won't keep.'

The steepness of the stairs surprises me again. I can't believe how much has happened since I was last here. This time I'm not nervous, just furious.

The look on his face as he lets me into the office is of a small child who's been found out in something – sort of sucked in as if fearing a slap. He moves behind his desk, which is set up at some kind of odd angle, and I realise that I'd quite like to slap him, actually.

'I've just spoken to Sally. What the hell are you playing at?'

Matthew looks at the floor and then back into my face, pursing his lips together and narrowing his eyes.

'Look,' he says, 'I think, with respect, this is private. Between me and Sally . . .'

'You do, do you? Well – I'm sorry but that's not how I see it, Matthew. I booked you. I introduced you to Sally and then you treat her badly, you play with her feelings and you think you can just get away with it? You send her a *text*? *A bloody text.*'

Matthew scratches at his neck and then fidgets, one hand up to his forehead, again looking at the ground. 'That was very wrong of me. I admit it, that was bad. Cowardly. And you're right to be angry and so is she but you have to believe me, I was just trying to do the right thing, to be—' He pauses as if searching for the right word. '—fair.'

'*Fair?*'

Matthew then lets out a huff of air and closes his eyes. When he opens them, he's almost as agitated as I am. He paces to the side of the room and back, finally sitting at his desk and putting his right elbow down and resting his forehead on his palm.

'I'm sorry but you need to go, please, Beth.'

'I'm not going anywhere.'

We stare at each other. Thirty seconds. A minute.

'I mean it. Please go, Beth.'

'No way. Not until you tell me what the hell you're playing at.' I sit down and put my bag on the chair beside me, a signal that I'm quite prepared to sit this out. However long it takes.

'OK, OK. So, Sally told me when we very first went out that she was done with marriage and dreams of parenting and happy-ever-afters. That she was happy to just live for the day – no strings, nothing heavy. See how things went.' He's now looking away as he speaks. 'And then we went to her mother's. She didn't really want me to go but there was this stupid accident: her foot. Anyway, never mind, I did go and her mother spoke to me and told me the truth.'

'What truth?'

'About the flake Sally was married to first time around. And how she had always wanted to be a mum, still wants that deep down very much . . .'

'And so you run for the hills because you don't like kids. You don't think to talk to her? You know – like a grown-up?'

'I can't talk to her about this. I'm sorry but this is not your place.' Matthew bites into his bottom lip and stands up. 'It's not what you think, Beth. I mean it. You really need to go now, please.'

'What – so I've got this wrong, have I? You're not just some commitment-phobic child, too selfish to imagine losing the number one slot to a baby? Prefer the single life to the responsibilities of family? Er, am I hitting the nail on the head here?'

'No.' His voice is barely a whisper.

'What then?'

He stares right into my eyes, takes a deep breath. 'It's not your business, Beth.'

'Oh, but it is. You hurt my friend and you make it my business.'

There's a very long pause and I wonder if I really am just going to have to leave. No resolution. No point. No chance to ask advice about Ned's phone call either. And then Matthew is suddenly opening the bottom drawer of his desk. He rummages through paperwork to draw out an old newspaper. He looks down at it, wincing. He stares and stares, his eyes narrowing as if he can't quite make up his mind, and then finally hands it to me.

'There.'

It's a local paper from Cornwall. On the front page is a picture of Matthew in his police uniform. Alongside is the image of a child, smiling.

I can't believe it – gasp with the shock. The child's face is so like Sam's. Same colouring. Same freckles.

'This boy. He looks a bit like my *Sam*.' My voice is trembling and I can feel this dread building inside me.

'Yes, that's what threw me when we met. That first day you showed me the picture of your sons. Same colouring. Similar eyes.'

I now read from the front page to the story inside, which continues on page three, the dread growing and growing.

'Oh God, Matthew . . .' I put my hand up to my mouth.

On page three there's an additional picture of the boy with his mother – both of them beaming.

I finish the story, skimming it quickly at first and then going back to read over the awful details more closely. I close my eyes to regroup before I can even speak, tears pricking my eyes.

'I had no idea.' I can't believe how wrong I got all this.

'It didn't make the TV, thankfully. Just the local papers.'

'So this is why you left the force?'

'Yes.'

I find myself glancing at his arm. You can just see the scar, peeping from his shirt on to the back of his hand. I asked Sally about it. She said it was from an accident while working with his father. A lie. I glance back at the story to read over a paragraph from the inquest again. Oh dear Lord. The scar was from *this*.

'I'm so very sorry, Matthew.' I'm still looking at the paper, taking in the horrible details. 'But the authorities – they all say it wasn't your fault. The inquest. The inquiry. They said you were very brave, that you risked your own safety. You need to talk to Sally about this. She'll *understand*. She'll sympathise. Help you . . .'

'He was twelve, Beth.'

A little noise escapes my mouth. A gasp, a huff of air to stop myself crying. It won't help Matthew if I break down. This is his hurt. My mistake. I feel so wretched for misjudging him.

'Outside the inquest his mother actually cursed me. *Cursed me to my face.*'

'She would have been—' I pause and glance to the window, searching for the right words. I am trying not to imagine. My Sam. Dear Lord. If it had been one of mine. '—mad with grief.'

'She said she hoped I would never sleep properly again.' Matthew's voice is flat. I turn back to see his shoulders and head sort of sink as if he's weighed down with the memory. I watch him and feel terrible that I've made him go over all this. He must carry this with him. Every day. And I, of course, know exactly what that's like . . .

'She also said—' He's looking straight in my eyes now. '—that if I ever had a child, she hoped it would die. So that I would know how it felt.'

CHAPTER 41

MATTHEW - BEFORE

The irony? He wasn't supposed to be there. In that spot. At that time.

Two years back – a Thursday – and Matthew was supposed to be in his car driving home. His shift was over and he'd been told to call it a day. He was parked a five-minute stroll from the station but instead of heading straight to the car, he decided to very quickly check on an old guy who'd been having trouble with a gang of youths living next door. Matthew had visited him twice and the poor man, frail and in his eighties, had been very agitated.

He was a nice old guy, ex-army – he'd shown Matthew all his medals. He lived just around the corner from the station so Matthew called by for just a very quick hello, declining the offer of a cup of tea. All was well. The neighbours were away. *Good.*

It was as Matthew walked away from the old veteran's house, past the supermarket, that it all happened.

First the young lad bolting through the automatic doors and then the shopkeeper, waving his arms and shouting, 'I'm calling the police!' He had his phone in his hand but on looking up spotted Matthew.

'Stop him – that boy. He's stolen from me . . .'

Matthew was in uniform and so the shopkeeper was now staring at him, clearly expecting action. 'That boy – that boy . . .'

And so Matthew gave chase. Around the corner, along the next alley. But the boy was fast.

Matthew's plan, once out of sight of the shopkeeper, was to give the kid a good talking-to. A warning. He looked no more than eleven or twelve and Matthew, on the quiet, liked to weigh up on the spot whether a court case and all that went with it was really the right course of action. The shops, of course, always wanted a prosecution.

But Matthew never had the chance to weigh it up, to make that call . . .

At the end of the alley was a dead end with a narrow strip of grass and fencing to the railway sidings. To Matthew's horror, the boy began to climb the fence.

'No – *stop!* Not the railway . . .'

Matthew stopped still himself, hoping this might make the boy change his mind. But he did not glance back – he was nimble and was soon up and over the other side.

'You need to stop – *please!*'

By the time Matthew had then caught up and scaled the fence himself, it was as if everything happened in slow motion.

'No – not the line. *Keep away from the line!* It's live . . .'

Still the boy ran.

'It's live. The line is LIVE!'

The moment of contact comes back in dreams. The jolt to the boy's body. The horror of little swirls of smoke appearing from the child's clothes. At the neck of his hoodie and the cuffs first, then near his waist.

By the time Matthew reached him, he guessed it was too late. The *smell*.

Dear God, he will never, ever get that out of his mind . . .

Matthew used his phone to call it in, demanding urgent backup, an ambulance and the transport police to turn off the power and stop any trains.

He knew the drill, he knew that technically he was supposed to do nothing else. The protocol was that he was supposed to wait. But how could he not try?

He saw a long thick branch not far from the track. It had been raining slightly and so it wouldn't be dry enough to be safe, but what the hell. He used it to prod, ever so quickly, to try to push the boy's sad and pathetic little body away from the live rail.

There was a jolt as he felt the charge trying to pass from the child's body to his own. A flash and a burning to his right arm and hand. Damn. No good. No options.

And so then, phone up to his ear – *how long, how long?* – he just stood there, waiting.

Waiting.

Waiting.

Alongside the boy, who lay face down across the track, Matthew could see two packs of cigarettes. And the awful truth dawned. He had chased him for *this*: for two sodding packs of cigarettes . . .

CHAPTER 42

BETH - NOW

Back home, it's my turn for the truth. So very hard, finally sharing a secret this big, this dark. Like watching a ball of black wool that you've kept wound tight and neat and unseen in your pocket suddenly rolling away down the stairs.

Everything unravels over our promise so very quickly that there's not the relief I hoped for but just this panic, watching the tangle of wool and worrying with every footstep, every noise, every tick of the clock and beat in the room that all the people I love will trip over the strands on the stairs. That it can never be the same, the mess and the blackness never wound back up.

I realise most of all as I watch Adam's face change that I'm afraid he won't love me any more. This real me, the me *who did this thing*.

'You buried the baby in a wood?'

'Yes, Adam. We did.'

We're sitting in the conservatory and I can see the pampas grass behind him through the window, caught in the wind. Waving. Drowning. Waving. I can hardly bear to look at his face, the expression increasingly appalled. I wonder if he's imagining as I have a million times watching the news. The reason I had to *stop* watching the news with him . . . *Human remains discovered in a wood.*

But then his eyes change. He looks at the ground. 'Fourteen? You were fourteen?'

'Yes.'

'Carol gave birth without proper help. At fourteen?'

By the time he looks back up there's the beginning of tears in his eyes. I've only ever seen Adam cry twice and that was with joy when our boys were born.

'Oh, Beth, how terrible for you.' His voice is barely a whisper. 'How truly awful for you . . . *All these years.*'

My own tears come then and for a long time he just holds me while I mumble how sorry I am. How I wish with every ounce of my being that I could go back and do it differently. That I hate I have to share this terrible thing now while he's still so unwell. But he just hushes and hushes, smoothing my hair. Lets me cry.

As he comforts me, I'm thinking of Matthew's confession back in his office. The newspaper story. I feel ashamed now that I didn't know quite how to comfort Matthew. I said I was so very sorry for misjudging him. I tried to be kind. But somehow it was as if my whole world was filled up with too much sadness. I could only think of Sally, of wanting Matthew to go quickly to patch it up with Sally so they would have each other as Adam and I have each other.

Adam, who's so much better at this. Gets it right.

He holds me tight. He kisses my hair. Then he lets me talk for a long time, all the guilt and the pain and the shame rushing out like a flood bursting a dam. The weight of it so great that I simply can't stop once I start. *Why didn't I phone an ambulance? Why didn't I phone my mother? Why, oh why did I make that promise?*

'You were a child yourself, Beth. All of you. You were in shock. You were children yourselves . . .'

I tell him then about the risk with the building work, why we really hired Matthew to find Carol, and I also hint there's been some trolling on social media over the school closure. But I do not mention the direct threats or the detail of the call from Ned. I can't bring myself to believe there's a link with his accident. And Adam is still so very frail . . .

He wants us to go straight to the police, is sure there will be some procedure for this to be handled with compassion and sensitivity. *You were just children . . . but this needs to be reported. It's a crime not to report a child's death.* I say he's right but that I want first to check if the baby's grave is to be disturbed so that we can control the timing. How it all comes out. The media and so on. And especially the impact on Carol in France. I don't want the police just turning up at her home without warning her.

I say that I want still to buy time. That I remember the nuns complaining about the nuisance of tree preservation orders on part of the woods and it's possible that might now prevent development in the area so precious to us. I want to go back to the school and find out for sure if we'll be found out imminently when the builders dig . . . or if we have the option to wait a while. Until Adam is stronger. Until we can, perhaps through Ned, inform Carol what we're going to do.

I tell Adam of my new idea. The cover of filming a little video on the school closure, which will give us free access to the grounds to check what is really happening. I can use a freelance cameraman from *The Meeting of Minds* and sell copies to the old girls to cover the expense.

At first he says *no – don't be ridiculous. You need to go to the police now. It's been long enough.* But in the end I persuade him, beg him actually, to allow me this one last compromise so we can find a way to warn Carol that it's all going to come out. *Please – how can a little longer matter?*

He wants to come to the school too, to support me. But I insist he's not well enough yet and the boys need one of us at home. So I say we'll take Matthew to keep an eye out in view of the trolling but mostly to give us advice on calling in the police if the building work will disturb the child's grave very soon.

I spend the rest of the day contacting the Convent of St Colman to pitch my idea and get permissions in place. The nuns are ridiculously enthusiastic – excited at being filmed. They say they'll dig out old cine film of the school's beginnings to be edited into the video and I feel guilty for lying all over again.

I keep checking my phone for any message from Sally. I told Matthew that he needs to tell Sally the truth about why he left the force. Why he suddenly dumped her. And that if he doesn't speak to her by this evening, I will. I'm praying she'll have Matthew's support, just as I have Adam's, and that she'll agree to come to the convent to face this with me.

Two hours pass. No word from Sally. I feel overwhelmingly tired, as if this confession and the thought of returning to school have sucked all my energy. Adam persuades me to lie down and I find myself drifting in and out of dark daydreams, all jumbled up together.

I keep thinking of all the years in this house. Birthday parties when the children were small. The magnolia tree. Sal's heartache.

I think of the birth of our boys, which made Adam cry. I remember them in my arms. Sam and Harry. And it makes me realise something so terrible and desperately sad that I break down myself.

CHAPTER 43

MATTHEW – NOW

Matthew is sitting in his car, the newspaper alongside him on the passenger seat. He glances at the front-page picture of him in his uniform. Different person. Different life.

There's no answer at Sal's flat and her phone isn't picking up messages. Probably turned off. *Afraid of another text?*

He scrolls back through his own phone to view the message he sent her. He conjures the precise moment standing in his kitchen, in such a panic the morning after that visit to her mother's. He hadn't slept and believed he was doing the right thing by her. He was afraid to see her or ring because he thought he would crumble – that his face would give him away. That he didn't want to lose her. But reading the words now, there's no context that can make them OK.

I'm so, so sorry, Sally. I'm not being fair to you. We need to stop seeing each other.

Beth is right to be furious and Sally too.

A bloody text? What the hell was he thinking . . .

He glances down the street and wonders if he should just sit it out and wait for her car – but then another thought.

◆ ◆ ◆

The drive out to Sally's row of cottages takes about forty minutes and it's completely dark as he turns the final bend – a lurch inside as he spots her car, parked on the little patch of grass alongside the terrace.

The sky is clear, stars just becoming visible, and Matthew takes in the irony of how striking, how beautiful the cottages look with their new thatch. Sally found a guy in his fifties – a real artisan. His signature is to add little straw figureheads to the centre ridge of every thatch he completes and so the animals sit there, high and proud now amid the stars. A squirrel, an owl, a rabbit and a pheasant.

Just last week Matthew had helped oversee the installation of second-hand Rayburn stoves in the kitchen-diners and log burners in each sitting room. He feels another pull in his stomach, remembering Sally gabbling to the stove installer about how often the chimneys would need to be swept. She'd been reading up about safety. Draughts. Was thinking of the insurance and the thatches, no doubt.

The puzzle now is that there are no lights on. He gets out, grabbing the wretched newspaper, and tries the middle cottage, tapping first on the door and then the window. Nothing. He moves to peer through the front window of each of the properties in turn. Still no movement inside. A little bubble of fear escalates in his stomach. They are near the coast path and he worries she may have gone off walking in the dark.

Quickly he takes the path round to the rear of the cottages. The old and rotten fences dividing each garden have been taken down and for now, temporarily, there's just one large plot backing on to the whole row. In the centre is a beautiful magnolia tree that Sally loves and alongside it a bench and a small table that the builders have been using for their tea breaks. Sally is sitting there in her coat with a bottle of wine, a large glass and a single candle in a small tilley-style lamp on the table.

She turns and sees him – and the worst thing of all? No reaction on her face. No surprise. No pleasure. No anger, just a horrible blankness.

Matthew says nothing. She says nothing. Finally she turns back to the table, pouring more wine into her glass, spilling some and mopping it with a tissue from her pocket.

'I warn you I'm on my third glass.' She takes a large slurp of alcohol, rolling her lips together. 'Her father's daughter after all.'

'You're not like your dad.'

'Aren't I? And why the hell are you even here? I don't want you to see me like this. Go away.'

'Beth came to my office—'

'Ah.' She looks towards the coast. 'So you've come to do the break-up in person? Make it neater.'

'No, actually. I've come to apologise for being an asshole. For the text. For being a coward.'

Her head doesn't turn and so Matthew moves forward to place the newspaper alongside her on the bench. For a moment he keeps his hand on the paper, not wanting to let go. He's hating every minute of this.

'I don't talk about this, Sal, not to anyone. The force wanted me to see a therapist but I don't see the point. I don't even want to tell you now. But Beth pushed me and made me promise to tell you. The story, the one in this paper. It's why—' He takes a deep breath. '—it's why I am how I am. Why I felt it was better to break it off.'

She turns, her eyes narrowed and puzzled, to look down at the paper on the seat beside her and Matthew watches her face then alter completely, just as Beth's had.

'You need to read it. The boy who died – *my fault* – was just twelve. He looked like Sam, Beth's Sam.'

She picks up the paper and places it closer to the candle to read, turning the page, her left hand finally moving up to her mouth.

'You need to read what the mother said to me at the inquest. She stood up and shouted at the end of the hearing. She said she hoped that I would never sleep again, and that if I ever had a child it would die so that I knew what she felt like. Look, I'm not going to lie. I'm finding this completely unbearable. But Beth said if I didn't tell you, she would. She also said something cryptic.' He looks away to the stars for a moment to remember the words precisely. 'Tell Sally to *break the promise*. I have no idea precisely what that means but I assume she means about Carol?'

CHAPTER 44

CAROL - NOW

Thursday 8 p.m.

I'm home again and Ned is so relieved. Looks so much happier. He's been incredibly understanding and patient with me; yes. The happiest I have known him in months. It's not just business going so well but something more. Something I can't put my finger on. Maybe it's because I've promised not to take myself off and to keep my phone with me. Also I've been trying to eat more. He so worries when I don't eat enough . . .

He bought me the most beautiful necklace with opals and garnets. I wore it in bed and it was like the times I'd almost forgotten, when we first met and my head was straighter. Different. We sat up talking for hours, with the shutters wide open – watching the stars. There was a breeze blowing and the curtains rippled like waves. Like the seaside back home.

I've promised to try harder not to pin everything on the adoption. Instead we talked about all sorts of things – travelling the world together, plans for the terrace and the gardens. It's so strange because on nights like that I can forget almost everything – as if the past and my unhappiness and my fears are just a dream. In my head only.

And do you know what? I think the tarot cards may be right. Last night I drew The Sun for the very first time. The card of happiness and the card of family. It means that something very good is about to happen for us. Something unexpected . . .

I can't share this with Ned, of course. I've never told anyone why I do this. Need this. How much I would truly love to find proof, to believe that there's a life after this one. That my father is out there. Watching. Listening. That one day I might truly get through to him . . .

Ask him what I need to ask him.

But this special card. The Sun. I feel it's a good sign and I am daring to hope.

Ned meantime has promised to sort out the business of the crows once and for all with Jonathan. Says he will pay for the machine himself – doesn't matter how much it costs. I feel so happy, so relieved that I almost talked to him about the girls – Beth and Sally.

It's at times like this that I feel I don't deserve him and am so very afraid to lose him.

Just like I lost them.

CHAPTER 45

BETH – NOW

Adam has tried over and over to convince me that he should come with us to the convent tomorrow but he's simply not well enough. He tires easily. He's forgetful still and the metal pins in his leg stop him sleeping and so finally he's reluctantly agreed my compromise that Matthew will join us. Advise us. Help us.

Turns out Sally and Matthew talked pretty much all night after I confronted him at his office. They had to camp out at her cottages in the end – too tired and too much wine to drive home. She has no idea if it'll work out between them long term but both seem to want to try, which is good. One day at a time and all that.

I feel so sorry that I misjudged him but as we all learn much too late, guilt is a dangerous bedfellow.

I won't sleep this final night, of course. I remember that when I was little, I used to play a strange game. I used to pretend that I was going to do something outrageous – anything from screaming out loud in the middle of the supermarket to jumping into a raging river. And then I would imagine all the ramifications. The shock of the shoppers. The rescue plan. It fascinated me in a dark and unhealthy way that there are seconds between one whole path in your life and a different one. A split-second choice. *Do it. Or don't.* And tonight it feels just like that. A blink of time between something calm and safe and known. And something else.

I want to know if we are going to be found out very soon. Or if we can control owning up.

I keep imagining how it will feel at a police station: giving a statement, saying it out loud to strangers. Will they press charges straight away? A court case?

For now, my sweet Adam is trying too hard. A white Burgundy three times our usual budget on ice. I have needed to keep busy and so have spent the whole day in the kitchen, making a special dinner. Like some ridiculous last supper? Our final normal family meal?

My mother is coming back to help out while I'm away but I realise, on reflection, that I worry about her in this picture. This mess.

Adam thinks I should tell her what happened all those years ago right now, before we decide about the timing of telling the police. But on this we completely disagree. It would kill my mother. It was our mistake but she would take it on her own shoulders and make it hers. She would find some way to blame herself and I couldn't bear that. Not yet. Not before I face it myself.

In terms of what we need to find out tomorrow, Matthew has been calm and practical. If the builders are actively digging and there's a real danger the grave will be imminently discovered, we'll go to the police straight after the party and he's explained exactly how they'll handle things. Also how long it will take to do all the forensic tests – for the Crown Prosecution Service to decide if any charges will be brought. For the record, he thinks this is highly unlikely. He's said there would probably be very little of the child's remains to help with an inquiry. A DNA test might be possible although not guaranteed but it's unlikely they'd be able to tell how many weeks the child was. Even the gender. He's made some inquiries via contacts and spelled out our options.

If there's no imminent digging – Plan B: we'll come home and make our decision in our own time. I suppose my biggest fear and the thing I'm keen to avoid is the police just turning up on Carol's doorstep in France without warning. Also – the media coverage.

Given this, I do see the paradox of me taking a camera along tomorrow. But I still believe it's the best way to get free access to the grounds and the plans, without raising too much suspicion. My biggest hope remains the long history of the trees – that preservation orders will make the development of the woodland out of the question. I have tried repeatedly to get more detail from the school by telephone but they're being infuriatingly vague, saying we can film all the plans from the display when we arrive.

Meanwhile, I continue to be plagued by flashbacks. A tightening in my chest as I remember it all. Back in that bathroom. The blood. The shells.

Playing that awful scene over and over has made me think more and more of when our own boys were born. Sixteen hours of fruitless labour with Sam and then an emergency caesarean. I remember the relief, that he was unbelievably beautiful with a full head of dark hair and huge eyes and I remember thinking too that he was *tiny* and wondering if all full-term babies were that small?

'Is this normal?' I kept asking the nurse. 'Is this the normal size?'

What I see now is that was how the time bomb began ticking once more for me, how the whole madness was stirred up all over again. By motherhood. Having my own children made me desperate to work out how old Carol's tiny baby may have been all those years ago.

And when Harry was born? It was much quicker. Four hours of labour and then an arrival so fast that the midwife only just caught him.

Again I was obsessed with his size. *Is this normal? He seems so small . . .*

I remember the relief too that it was another boy – unaware until that very moment just how terrified I was of holding a tiny little girl in my arms.

CHAPTER 46

BETH - NOW

'So we're really doing this.' Sal's voice is right beside me and yet somehow not close at all, as if filtered through a haze. We're just a few minutes from the school now and my heart is pounding.

Matthew has an early morning surveillance booked, which he can't get out of, so he's travelling separately. He's to meet us at the hotel later after we've called in to the school to discuss the filming. To be honest, I'm glad he's not in the car.

I'm embarrassed by how jumpy I am. So very stressed. Every time I see a motorcycle in the rear-view mirror, my heart races just like this. Ridiculous.

It's just a bike, Beth. Just an ordinary bike . . .

As we round the final corner, Sal is straining on her seat belt as if to see over the hedge. I'm wondering too when the convent will come into view, willing my heart rate to slow. In the past the school was visible from the lower road but there's a new two-storey building in the way – some kind of industrial unit.

'I feel a bit sick.' It's an understatement, both hands suddenly sweaty as we approach the final road junction. I take a long, deep breath but it doesn't help. True nausea.

'Jeez, Beth, what are you doing? You can't stop here. Someone will run into us . . .'

I can't help it – I'm so desperate to stop the car that I swerve towards the hedge on the nearside, the tyres screeching as I pull on the handbrake even before I finish braking. *Mints.* We lurch and stall at an awkward angle as a white van swerves past, only just missing us – the driver blasting his horn in fury.

Sal is looking around for some imagined obstacle in the road while for me the smell grows stronger.

Mints?

'Speak to me, Beth. What are you doing? Was there something in the road – an animal?'

It's the one thing I hadn't thought about or expected today. With my heart still racing, I can feel my expression twisting into a frown as the smell fades just as quickly as it came – drifting away until it's gone completely, leaving only the sense of someone leaving the room. I'm so confused that I don't know if I've completely imagined it.

'I'm so sorry, Sal.'

'Do you need a bag?' She's scrabbling about in her handbag. 'Are you actually going to be sick?'

'No, I don't know. I don't think so.'

'Too much? Coming back like this?'

I restart the engine. Sal reaches out her hand to stop me but I pull forward just enough to straighten the car into a safer position before I can answer.

Did I imagine it? The mints?

Sally's face is all alarm. 'So, do you want to forget this? Go home? Don't worry, I'll drive. It's too much, isn't it?'

'No. I don't know.'

'I really don't mind if you want to forget it. Change the plan.'

'No, it's not what you think.'

'So what then?'

'I don't know how to explain it.' *Christ*. 'This is going to sound really mad.' And now the picture. Yes – the mint packet on the dashboard with its neat foil spiral. 'My *dad*.' I'm looking at her, suddenly starting to get it. 'It made me think of my *dad*, Sal.'

'Your dad?' Her face is all confusion.

'Yeah – this road. Driving along this road. I thought it would all be about us. About Carol. But it made me think about *my dad* suddenly.'

'Oh, Beth.' Her face is slowly softening and she puts her hand out to gently touch my arm. Sally always liked my father – such a contrast with her own. It was no surprise when Sal's parents divorced while we were in the sixth form and after that her dad just didn't want to know. No contact – not even on her birthday. When he died – abroad (some drink-driving scandal with a young woman from his company, who was also killed) – I'm ashamed to say I was almost relieved, that at least he couldn't disappoint her any more.

It was why I loved to have her and Carol to stay. I felt sorry they didn't have dads of their own.

I place my hands back on the steering wheel. I glance at the mirror and suddenly I'm *really* understanding. Yes. I can picture them exactly – Mum with her tissues in the front and Dad with his faux jollity, grinning at me through the rear-view mirror. Trying to buoy me up for the start of a new term.

'I've never been along this road without them.' I'm looking at Sally as it sinks in fully. 'Mum and Dad. I never thought about it. Didn't occur to me.' All the worrying about Carol and the grave and how I might feel today. And I never thought of this happening. Of it triggering this strong sense of *Dad*.

'Oh, Beth.'

'I even thought I could smell his bloody mints. How mad is that?'

'You want me to take over the driving? Seriously. Or we can forget this? I don't mind. If it's all too much?'

'No, no – we really need to do this. I just hadn't realised how many layers there are to this. I'll be fine in a minute, honestly. Just give me a moment.'

Sally pushes her handbag away from her feet and offers again to take over the driving but my hands feel cooler so I wipe them dry on the little cloth meant for the windscreen and finally we set off again.

Both of us expect the school to come into view once we clear the new industrial unit but instead there's a huge white tent.

'Oh goodness, the marquee for the party. I thought they'd put it on the other side of the building. It never occurred to me they'd put it on the front lawn.'

On the phone Sister Maurice had explained that the orangery used for annual reunions wasn't big enough for this final party so they'd arranged a large marquee for the buffet and drinks. I can see the sense but it feels disorientating for this first glimpse of the school to be so unfamiliar. Also it means that I can't see across to the woodland beyond to confirm if there are any signs of builders about yet. *Diggers?*

I park up, noticing a large skip in the corner of the car park, but it's empty. Unhelpful. As soon as my cameraman turns up, I'll need to recce properly. Yes – find out urgently what exactly the builders are up to and how soon the real work gets going.

And now as Sally finally steps out to stand alongside me, we are utterly stilled. Silent too. The boarding house in front of us looks unchanged. Still that odd shade of salmon. Still the orangery on the side, although it all seems smaller than I remember. The car park is closer too. I find myself inexplicably leaning backwards, like straining on elastic, needing to take in the picture from further away – to stop it feeling so close. It's as if I need a different lens on the camera.

'Girls! *Girls!*' It's Sister Maurice. She has a stick to help her walk, which she waves in the air until we move forward to meet her and then it's all out of our hands. The mood. Crushing hugs.

'Come in, girls, come in.'

'I don't think we quite pass as *girls* these days, Sister.'

'Bah! You're all still girls to me. Come along.' As she hobbles ahead of us, mumbling about her latest hip replacement, I try to work out her age. In her fifties, I reckon, when she ran the kitchen team in the old days so that would make her late seventies? Maybe even turned eighty.

She's chattering about how excited everyone is about the filming, tells us off for snubbing all the reunions in the past and leads us past packing boxes to the kitchen. And now comes a new wave of disbelief. The layout of the kitchen is *exactly* the same – not a thing changed in twenty years. On the wall, the same blackboard where Sister Maurice would write out the menu for the day.

I don't believe it. Look at this, Sal. The same cupboard – where we all kept our cocoa mugs? And the tea urns. *I seriously don't believe it. These are never the same tea urns.* And the stainless-steel trolley that was wheeled into the common rooms with sandwiches and cakes during Wimbledon – the only time we were allowed to eat in front of the telly.

Sister Maurice is now laughing at us as Sal begins helping with the tea.

'We're to pack the kitchen up last, of course. Now then. You always liked Battenberg, Beth. Yes?' Sister Maurice is lifting tins from a shelf to check on the cakes inside. How the hell does she remember this?

'This is surreal.' Sal looks pale as I join them at a small side table. 'So are all the sisters here for this?'

'Most.' Sister Maurice is pouring our tea into white china cups – a grown-up courtesy. Chunky mugs in the past.

'I saw a few workmen on the way in.' I'm sipping my tea. 'So what are the plans, Sister, for the site? Is any work under way yet?'

'Full demolition soon. We try not to think about it. The planning application is for student accommodation for the local technical college, which calls itself a university these days.'

'So is all the land being sold?' Sal shoots a warning glance. 'Sorry, Sister – rude of me. It must be such a wrench for you.'

'To be frank, Beth, I'm quite looking forward to returning to Belgium and seeing Mother Superior. She's not at all well: too poorly to travel. And I'm getting too old for these draughts myself. We all leave in six weeks. Sister Joanne is back in charge. She'll stay on here to oversee the paperwork, the lawyers and the final handover.'

Sally and I exchange a glance. No one much liked Sister Joanne. She was drafted in from Belgium to take over the finances when Mother Superior was first taken ill. Had some fancy business qualification. Made a lot of unpopular changes during our sixth form. Not even sure the other nuns liked her.

Sister Maurice picks up the plate to offer me more cake but I shake my head. 'So, we know all about Beth and her television work – very exciting. What about you, Sally?'

'Property.' Sal is biting into her piece of cake, crumbs falling on to the floor. She leans down to sweep them on to the paper towel we've been given as a napkin. 'I'm a surveyor but I've started a bit of property developing. A small project.' She folds up the paper and throws it into the bin beside the table.

'In this strange market?'

'Well, uncertainty brings opportunity as well as crisis.'

'So they keep telling us.'

I check my watch. 'Listen, Sister. My cameraman will be about half an hour. Is the exhibition all set up? We thought we'd have a really good look around while it's quiet, if that's OK? I'll be wanting some shots around the school and gardens and woods, then a chat with you – here in the kitchen? And any of the other sisters who are here? What about Sister Veronica?'

'Teaching in New Zealand now. Left the Order years back. Didn't you know?'

'You are kidding me.'

Sister Maurice is grinning. 'And don't you go thinking this is some scandalous line for your film.' I blush. 'No scandal, Beth. She just decided on a different path. Rather sad and rather sudden but it happens.' She peers over the top of her glasses. 'We had hoped she might come for the party but the flight costs are difficult, of course. And what of your co-conspirator?'

'Sorry?'

'Carol? Joined at the hip, the three of you, as I remember it.'

Sally looks away.

'Abroad too, Sister,' I say. 'She was hoping to make it but it's tricky.'

'Shame.'

'Yes. So is it all right then to have a look around and plan the filming before my cameraman turns up?'

'Help yourself.'

'I take it they'll have to leave the woods alone, Sister? Weren't there tree preservation orders?'

'Well, actually there's been a bit of a U-turn on that. It was something of a sticking point over the sale price. We thought the same – that about two acres of the plot would be unusable, but then there was this ash tree thing.'

'Sorry?'

'This new disease. Unfortunately, our trees are all affected – mostly ash so they have to come down anyway. So they've put in new extended plans now, including a large part of the wood. Terrible shame if you ask me but it's put the sale price up so I suppose that's good, for the Church, I mean. Sister Joanne is delighted.'

I can't look at Sally as I take this in.

'You would think they might have kept the house.' Sister Maurice shakes her head. 'Are you not surprised they're going to demolish, Sally? I would have thought they might do it up?'

She doesn't answer.

'Sally?'

'Sorry, Sister, distracted. I'm afraid it's just the maths. Building firms don't do sentiment, just sums. Student accommodation is big business these days.'

'Always the sums. *Grand dommage.* Still, there it is. So, then. I expect you need to get on, Beth?'

We visit the marquee first, which has several boards displaying photographs and newspaper cuttings of the school's history, along with a smaller display detailing the plans. The site has around six acres in total and all bar the separate chapel and adjoining garden is being sold. Most of the wood is now included in the planning application for three blocks of student accommodation. From the drawings, it looks as though the area of woodland we so dread will almost certainly be disturbed very soon. The building work is expected to start within the month. We obviously need the *precise date*.

'You want to go there now?' Sal is fiddling with her hair. 'I mean – is there any point? Now that we know what's going to happen. It'll just be upsetting and there's nothing we can do . . .'

'I still think we should.'

The pathway through the hydrangeas seems shorter than we remember. People always say that, don't they? That the memories from our childhood are geographically distorted.

But the foliage, hedges and trees provide good camouflage. Soon we can't be seen from the house and the main school. All those years ago we used the excuse of planting more bluebell bulbs as a cover to return to the spot. We told everyone we wanted a whole bluebell wood but in truth the cover story was unnecessary. The nuns never followed us.

The trees are all bigger and the undergrowth thicker but the path is still passable.

'It's further up, Beth. This way. Through here.'

'Yes, I know.' And then I place my hand on her shoulder. 'I'm sorry. I didn't mean to snap.'

It looks a little different from my dreams but not as different as I'd expected. More overgrown but still familiar. There's a surreal sense of shock that we're truly back here after all these years. And then suddenly they are right in front of us – the three trees close together with the little clearing.

'So they'll be digging here within a month. For the foundations, Beth?'

'Yes.'

'So what do you think. Really. What do you think the chances of it being found?'

'I don't know, Sally. I have no idea. We don't have to make a decision today but it's not good news, is it?'

'No, we need to update Matthew and Adam. See what they think. We'll talk to Matthew when we get to the hotel.'

'Agreed.'

I stare at the trees. I feel my eyes narrowing and a huff of breath escaping as I think back. That awful day. The bag. The digging . . . 'Have we been wrong, Sally? All this time? Should we have come back here before? Sorted it all before?'

And then there's a noise suddenly – from the bushes behind us. A crack of a twig underfoot.

'Sssh. Keep still.'

'What was that?'

'Don't know.'

I'm aware suddenly of my pulse in my fingertips as I clench my right hand. 'Could be Sister Maurice. Sssh.'

We wait. Another crackle. And then she appears on the path, face stony. Older. No smile.

'Sister Joanne. Goodness.'

She hasn't aged well – very lined skin. I hadn't expected to see her. Although she was technically in charge of the school for years, she was forever being sent to sort out the finances in different parishes. I check her steely eyes. Ah yes, the Church would want her here now, to drive a hard bargain over the sale.

'Looking for something, girls?'

'No, no – just wandering. I'm doing this film. Did Sister Maurice tell you? We need to—'

'Oh yes. Sister Maurice has kept me—' She pauses. '—*abreast*.'

'So, goodness. You're handling the sale, they tell us. Must be quite a big deal for you all. Difficult.'

'I'd wondered who it would be.' She's staring at the patch of ground by the trees, glancing between it and the two of us. It's the wrong time of year for bluebells so there's only scrub but she's staring at the precise spot.

I can suddenly feel the breeze on my face as I register in this moment that she's still not smiling. I look at Sal. 'We should get back to the house. Find out if my cameraman has arrived early. You must be tired, Sister Joanne. Such a busy time for you all.'

'I know why you're here.'

That breeze on my face again.

'This spot. I wondered if someone would come. Give themselves away.'

I look at Sal again. She makes a strange sound. A strained breath as if there's something wrong with her throat.

'You're worried about the building work.'

There's a powerful churning in my stomach.

She's moving across the clearing and brushes off a log before sitting on it, face still stony. 'So what now? We talk, do we?' Sister Joanne is staring at me but I don't answer.

'You *know*, don't you?' Sal is wide-eyed. Incredulous.

'Shut up, Sally! You say nothing. Do you hear me? Nothing.'

'It's OK, Elizabeth. Too late for that. I do know. Sister Veronica would never say who she thought it was. But yes – I know, all right. I just didn't know *who*. And so I came back and I came up here to tell you that the child's remains have already been moved. There will be *no* scandal. You hear me? It is dealt with. It is in the past and it will stay in the past.'

There's a pulsing through my veins and a terrible pounding in my head. I'm unable to compute these words.

No, it's not possible.

A bird makes a break for the sky. I look up to the treetops as some leaves fall, and then back at this woman whose face is cold and blank and entirely devoid of the emotions that in me are shooting through the years. Through the dreams and the darkness and all the blood in my veins.

CHAPTER 47

BETH - NOW

We're at the hotel now and have just two hours before our taxi is booked to take us back to the school. My first instinct is to head straight home. But I can't because of the stupid filming. Ed, my freelance cameraman, is already on site. Five messages from him on my phone.

Two long hours in which Sal spends most of the time in her room, talking this madness through with Matthew, and I spend most in mine, talking to Adam.

Still we can't believe it. All this time. All these years watching the news with a cold, empty dread every time the wrong mix of words have spilled from the screen. *A child's body has been discovered in a wood . . .* All these years and the baby was never there.

Never. There.

'I can't believe it, Adam. I just cannot believe it.'

He tries to calm and soothe me. He says that with this horrible shock comes the unexpected option of a full stop. We can now decide what to do in our own time. We even suddenly have the option once more to do nothing.

But I can't feel relief yet. I just feel shock at the way we were told. So coldly and calmly and with such detachment. I find I need to move, am unable to keep physically still, pacing around my room as I talk on the phone, trying to move the pieces. To fit everything together.

Sister Joanne gave us only a few minutes. A cool and brief account. Clinical. Yes, they found the bag with its tragic contents. No, they did not contact the police. Or try to find out who was involved.

Why, Adam? Why would they not try to find out who was involved – such a terrible thing?

Turns out Sister Veronica saw us the evening that we buried the bag. She assumed more teenage mischief initially – a stash of alcohol or cigarettes – and given the saga with Melody, she left well alone, probably fearing the convent would give no more chances if we were found out. She still felt guilty for our suspension – for aligning us with Melody in the first place.

She kept an eye on us throughout school, apparently, believing it was a passing phase –smoking, drinking. Never dreaming for one moment that it would be anything very serious. And then when we stopped going there, to the woods, she let it go. Forgot about it entirely until some work was scheduled by tree surgeons a few years after we left. There was root work planned and some new planting and so Sister Veronica suddenly remembered the buried bag and the patch of blue-bells and began to fret. There was a lot in the papers about drugs and she started to think – what if she'd called it wrong, been naive? What if it was something more than alcohol, our little stash in the woods? What if it was hard drugs – something incriminating to be found by an outsider? A scandal for the school, which was already in spiralling financial trouble. Over time, she'd fretted and fretted until she'd convinced herself that it might be drugs and that she had to at least check that it was gone. Safe.

She did the digging herself and fell apart, Sister Joanne said. Had run to fetch her immediately, hysterical. 'She had some notion we should call the police, the authorities. I was in charge at the time and had higher responsibilities.' And so Sister Joanne had taken over. Made Sister Veronica understand that they had to think first and foremost of the school and the Church – the scandal. *You need to get a grip, Sister Veronica. To listen to me. We have to be practical. The media will have a field day with this.*

And so, unbelievably, Sister Joanne insisted they move the remains of the bag with its tiny and terrible contents to the garden of the chapel, where they reburied it beneath a drystone wall to be sure that it would not be disturbed again. Land that is not to be sold as part of the new development. Sister Veronica was warned to say nothing, not even to any of the other nuns.

'So it is over. And I trust that you will not want this to go further either, that this should never be spoken of again.' She had stood up then – Sister Joanne – and dusted down her robe from the moss on the log as if it were the weather we'd been discussing.

She shared very briefly that Sister Veronica had struggled to adjust after all this happened. There was *something of a breakdown* – and so a fresh start for her was organised abroad.

'And the rest of the Order? None of them ever knew?' I was in absolute shock.

'No, it was my call. And I did what I had to do for the Church.'

Sister Joanne then looked both of us in the eye in turn and walked away. No drama. No raised voices. No sympathy. Absolutely nothing.

I think that is what killed me most and will stay with me always. The anticlimax. Watching her stand and brush down her robe so nonchalantly, knowing what we – mere children – had been through back then but not wanting to discuss it. Not back then. Not now. Not ever.

Can you believe it, Adam? All these years and we have not known this. All. These. Years.

When the message comes from the hotel front desk – Sister Maurice wondering what time we're starting filming – I want to tell them to leave me alone but it's all too late. Ed, the cameraman, is still on site, waiting for me.

'Let's just tell them we're ill.'

'We can't, Sally.'

We argue but in the end Sally agrees we'll do the bare minimum. An hour of filming maximum and then I will feign illness and we will leave.

So we arrive, shell-shocked, back at the school to find Sister Maurice outside the kitchen – her face black with dread.

'There's something going on. Some scene over at the marquee. I think we may need to call the police.'

We hurry across to the patio area near the tent where there is already a little crowd of early arrivals – former pupils and ex-staff shouting at two people on a huge motorcycle. There has clearly been some kind of row. To my horror the bike rider revs his engine and moves forward as if to drive right into the crowd. There are screams of shock as everyone pulls back. I can just make out Ed in the distance, filming. The motorcyclist stops just short of the nearest people, still revving his engine as a threat. The rider then takes off his helmet, one foot on the ground, laughing. He has long hair in a ponytail. I don't recognise him. Thankfully he hasn't spotted Ed and his camera. The pillion rider then takes off a matching helmet to reveal long, fairer hair that is loose and greasy. It takes me a moment to process the familiar face.

'*Melody Sage.*' Sal beside me is the first to say it. 'Dear God, I think it's Melody.'

Were it not for the hair colour – strawberry blonde – it would be hard to believe it. Melody, gaunt face and stick-thin, is a shadow of her former self. Her eyes are wild, bulging, and she's now shouting again at the crowd. 'Stuck-up losers, all of you!'

Again the motorcyclist revs his engine, this time swerving past the crowd, heading along the narrow road that leads to the marquee.

He weaves his way from side to side, Melody shrieking as if this is some kind of rodeo. For a horrible moment, I think they're going to drive right into the tent itself. I imagine them trying to destroy the tables. The displays. Smashing into people already inside. I am praying they will not notice Ed and the camera and target him.

Sal has her phone out and several other people are already dialling the police but suddenly a figure appears to block the entrance to the marquee, arm out in front of him.

'Matthew!' Sally's tone is one of abject horror as the bike rides right up to Matthew, the accelerator roaring until at the last moment the rider pulls up. Matthew then grabs the right handle of the bike with one hand and the shoulders of the rider with the other.

'Right. Off. Both of you – police!'

When they fail to move, there's a scuffle, the bike eventually falling to the ground with Melody and her partner struggling to free themselves. The rider attempts to hit Matthew but misses. Matthew manages to twist the rider's arm up his back as Melody, unsteady on her feet, staggers about, waving her finger.

'You assaulted me. I'll have you for assault. I'm going to sue you . . .'

Sally has run ahead of me and by the time I catch her up, Matthew – still holding on to the motorcyclist – is also on the phone to the police, bringing them up to date and urging them to hurry.

'They're both users,' he says. 'High as kites. Quick as you can, please. And we'll need to take the motorbike away. It may be evidence in another case.'

Melody is now sitting on the ground, leaning forward as if feeling faint. And then being sick on the ground beside her. When the retching stops, she turns to me, takes in my face and then gives me the finger. 'What are you looking at?'

It's about five minutes before we hear sirens and two police cars appear. Matthew talks to the officers, asking everyone else to *move away, please – you all need to step back*, and then it's over as quickly as it began.

Matthew explains very briefly to Sally that he didn't like the idea of us back at the school without support. So he had decided to watch the site 'just in case'. He takes photographs of the motorcycle and wheels it to the parking area, promising to liaise with the local force. He doesn't think it's the same bike he saw before at Melody's flat. He says he'll get on to his friend, Melanie Sanders, to run a check on whether Melody's boyfriend owns this *second* bike and to recheck his alibi. He's more suspicious now that maybe Melody's boyfriend *was* involved in Adam's hit and run.

There's about half an hour of continued shock. Cups of water are handed around. The police arrange to get a copy of Ed's footage and take names and addresses of witnesses who will need to give fuller statements later. Matthew stays until all the official business is sorted.

And then as the police finally leave, there's a decision to be made. Do we carry on with the party?

'Of course we do,' Sister Maurice announces, clapping her hands as if the question is ridiculous. 'Do you have any idea how much food I have prepared?'

Inside the marquee there's at first a strained mood as more guests arrive to be updated on the drama. Everyone's wearing little white stickers bearing their maiden name. The same mutterings across the crowd. *Melody Sage – whoever would have thought she would go this far? What a thing to happen . . .*

But eventually there's a relaxing of the mood and I take in the scene in a sort of daze, on automatic pilot.

There are the Mayhew twins. And Maud Sillito. And Jane Parrot – apologising that her sister, Elaine, had refused to come back 'to that awful place' for the reunions but Jane felt this was different and wished Elaine had made the effort too. *Student accommodation? Can you believe it? The whole place flattened?*

Some of the staff are mingling – Miss Fox who inspired me with my English. Miss Hamper who failed to convince me that physics served any useful purpose.

Every now and then I stand back, watching Sally in the distance with someone I can't quite place, and it's both surreal and so busy that it's somehow almost bearable, so that we stay much later than planned before I make my excuse of a headache.

I return with Sally around eleven o'clock to the kitchen to say goodbye to Sister Maurice. I find myself staring at a stainless-steel trolley parked in the corner. In the old days it was used to wheel the enormous supper dishes to the dining room. After all the chatter and all the stirred memories, I can picture the serving trays. Almost smell it all. Soggy cabbage and unidentifiable meat. Rice pudding and bright pink jam. I continue staring at the trolley, still in some kind of strange daze, when Sister Maurice is suddenly flustered.

'Oh crikey, Beth. With the Melody drama and the police and everything, I completely forgot your *letter*.'

'Letter?' I look at Sally.

Sister Maurice disappears into the lobby next to the kitchen then reappears to pass me the airmail envelope – pale blue with the distinctive striping around the edge. I pause. At first I think it must be from Carol. I'm expecting Carol's writing and my heart begins to race. But no, not Carol.

The letter is from Jacqueline Preer. The girl who slit her wrists . . .

I skim through the pages quickly and then take out the photograph tucked inside the envelope.

'Good God,' I say. Sister Maurice fires a warning glance but I can't help it. 'Sorry for the blasphemy, Sister, but look – she made it. Jacqueline *made* it. Look at this.'

Sal moves alongside me as Sister Maurice feels into her apron pocket for her glasses. I pass the picture to Sally – a large glossy print that shows Jacqueline beaming from ear to ear alongside a tall, rather attractive man and *five* children.

'Not all hers, surely.' Sal passes the picture to Sister Maurice, who presses the crucifix around her neck to her lips.

The letter explains in handwriting I now remember – had always admired. Sloping to the right. Proper ink. I can picture Jacqueline with her expensive fountain pen, hunched over her diary. *Mind your own business.* She heard about the reunions and this final party on Facebook, she writes. Couldn't face coming back. The gossip. The memories. But she wanted to thank me privately, to say sorry about what had happened that awful night in the school bathroom. To let me know how it had all turned out.

Her story is summarised in just a few paragraphs. There was a spell in hospital. Therapy and counselling. Finally she managed to get away – a trip abroad on a voluntary exchange programme – and that's where she met Jean-Pierre. Twenty-three. French. A teacher. She describes him as *insane for hooking up with me* then lists the names of their children with their ages – three daughters first and then twin boys. *Mad even for a Catholic, I know, but Jean so wanted to try for a boy.*

And only now do I feel it rise inside – like a spring that's been pushed down. Held in place for the visit to the wood. Pushed down hard, even through Sister Joanne's appalling revelation. Through the scene with Melody and her boyfriend. Through the stint on automatic pilot at the party.

The coil of metal pushing back now, ripping right up through my body as I stare at this picture of Jacqueline's children – three beaming girls with the boys pulling faces in the front, struggling to sit still. I can imagine the voices. *Keep still, boys. For the picture. Please. For Mummy.*

So that I have to turn away, my legs weakening and my face crumpled as the spring stretches to its full length and I suddenly cannot bear it.

CHAPTER 48

BETH - NOW

The taxi is late. Booked for 11.30 p.m., it finally toots its horn outside at midnight.

'Are you feeling better now, Beth?' Sister Maurice presses a card into my hand with the Order's address in Belgium.

'Much. I was just overtired earlier, Sister. A long day – what with Melody and everything. We'll keep in touch. Let you know about the film.' I kiss her cheek then, embarrassed to have broken down earlier. I hate it when people see me cry.

Soon, from the back seat of the taxi, I watch her waving from the window as the driver circles to the right and begins to pull away, the wheels crunching the gravel in front of the house.

The last time we will see it? I wonder what we'll decide now, given the shocking update. Do we go to the police anyway, me and Sally? Or do we just leave it? Close Pandora's box forever?

The taxi engine purrs and soothes through the darkened streets and by the time we reach the hotel, Sally is asleep so that I have to nudge her gently as I'm paying the driver. There's a picture of two children taped to the car's dashboard – a girl with red hair and big juicy freckles and a boy with a front tooth missing. They beam at their dad as he clears the meter ready for the next fare and I imagine them tucked up in bed, hushed in the daytime so Dad can get his sleep before the night shift. I give him a ridiculous tip and hurry Sal from the car.

The hotel front desk has its lighting dimmed and the air as we walk across to the revolving doors has the sweet smell of the damp, secret hours. Midnight mass. Bonfire night. There's a different girl on the front desk now, yawning as we approach and hurriedly hiding a book with a bright pink cover under the counter. The lights behind the bar across the room are dimmed too – just a couple of businessmen, their jackets and ties discarded, nursing brandy glasses in the far corner, one with his feet up on a low stool, wriggling his toes with his shoes alongside the chair. A hole in one of his socks.

I head to the front desk to check for a message from my cameraman, Ed. He left the convent earlier than us with Matthew to sort the footage of the motorcycle drama for the police. Ed promised a note with an update on the logistics as to how he will get the second copy of the footage to me. He needs to get off early in the morning – booked for a corporate event back home.

The girl on the desk is stifling a yawn. 'A message for room 202? Hang on – yes. There's a note from your cameraman. Also your friend's still up. On the sofas – over there.' She points to a cul de sac of high-backed dark blue sofas by the bar. I imagine she means Matthew? I glance at Sally, who is bleary-eyed, utterly exhausted. Sweet of Matthew to wait for us, keen to check Sal is OK. I plan a quick goodnight and thank you and will leave them to it.

In her exhaustion, Sal drops her handbag and so trails behind me as I reach the sofas ahead of her.

But – no. I stop frozen in my tracks. It isn't Matthew . . .

She's curled up along two of the cushions of the nearest sofa, the one with its back to the front desk, fast asleep. Although her face is hidden by her hair, there can be no mistake. Alongside her in a small tartan carrycot is the most beautiful baby I have ever seen, Carol's arms draped protectively over the top of the little cot – just touching one of the straps.

For a moment Sal and I don't move. Yet another shock. Finally we exchange a glance. I reach out to touch Carol's shoulder but then hesitate, she and the baby looking so utterly content. Then from behind us is a noise and I turn to see the shoeless businessman taking his feet down from the stool as the barman clicks the trellis shutter down in front of him. It's enough, that single click. Carol is screwing up her face before opening her eyes.

Next it is all craziness. We talk over each other so that Carol has to signal with her hand to *Hush, please, not to wake the baby. Please.* I am saying that I have never seen such a perfect child. *Such a beautifully shaped head and so much hair, Carol. And why the hell didn't you tell us . . .*

She explains in whispers that it all just happened – the adoption. Right out of the blue after a string of disappointments. And she was so terrified it would fall through that she dared not tell a soul, not even her mother. Still she can't quite believe it. Couldn't face the school, all the guilt and the nightmare from the past, but wanted us, for obvious reasons, to be the very first to know.

'We had given up hope. Ned has been checking out orphanages in China – so many children needing homes – but that's getting more complicated. And then, suddenly—' She glances lovingly at the sleeping infant. '—*Thomas.*' Her father's name. 'He was supposed to be placed with another family but it all fell through at the very last moment. The couple split up. And so we suddenly got the call. I still can't believe it. I stare at him and I can't believe it.'

We are all gazing into the little cot and I can't find the words either. Carol is babbling that she was nervous about travelling but it went better than she hoped. She's just as I remember her before it all happened – her eyes shining and her face full of hope. I feel this terrible pang of guilt. I should never have mentioned the call from Ned about the bike to Sally. I'm suspecting now that it really was Melody's boyfriend. That the police will be checking his other bike now. I still don't understand the motive but of course it had nothing to do with poor Carol. She could do no one any harm. Just a horrible coincidence . . .

Relief is now beginning to seep through the shock as the barman coughs, keen apparently to get off shift. Carol has managed to get a room – she found out from her mother where we planned to stay. And so Sally texts Matthew in their room to say she's back safe but will be a while yet and we decamp to Carol's room to finally whisper the shock from the school – the news from Sister Joanne – finding brandy to calm Carol down as she shakes.

For several minutes she's white, cuddling Thomas close and sipping at the brandy, but there are no tears between us. Somehow it feels much too late for tears. We tell her that it's possible to visit the chapel garden any time she likes – it won't be developed – but we don't yet discuss what Sally and I think privately. That it's time to own up officially. That is not a conversation for tonight.

Instead we each take a turn holding the baby and Sally says we must look forward now for Thomas's sake. *Yes? We have to look forward, Carol?*

Finally Sally checks the minibar for a small bottle of champagne to toast Thomas's arrival.

Carol's room is slightly larger than mine – but in immaculate order with her small suitcase properly sited on the luggage rack alongside the wardrobe and all her clothes already laid out for the morning – a crisp white shirt and smart black trousers.

I tease that she and Sal were always so much tidier than me. And then comes the shift we all need – like that change of gear at a funeral when everyone starts remembering happier times as nostalgia squeezes the sadness from the room. Very soon we're both teasing Sal about her immaculate nails and her immaculate hair and she's defensive, saying that she's actually quite ropey these days. Getting old. *No, really.* And as if to prove the point, she slips her blouse off her shoulder to display her allegedly *old lady arms.*

'Look, pastry arms. Disgusting.'

To top her, I roll up my trouser leg to show my broken veins. *Bet you don't have these.*

Sally, now giddy on champagne and tiredness, pulls Carol's cardigan off her shoulder to compare arms, saying she bets that Carol's are *hideously and disgustingly toned and gorgeous still.* Next we all freeze as Carol winces and immediately hitches her cardigan back on to her shoulder before staring directly at me. Not at Sally. At me.

'I tripped. Stupid of me.'

'Oh my God, Carol. You poor thing. That looks *so* painful.' Sally's voice is all concern as she moves closer to Carol and gently moves the cardigan down, which Carol, embarrassed, hitches once again into place. 'Must have been a *really* nasty fall. You should be careful, Carol. Imagine if you were carrying the baby? Now, hang on – arnica. Yes, that's good for bruises. I think I've got some in my washbag in my room. Do you want me to fetch it?'

'No, it's fine.'

'It's no trouble.'

'It's fine, honestly.'

Sally needs the loo and so disappears through to the en suite while Carol continues staring at me, saying nothing. Maybe she realises that I will guess first. Which, of course, I do – instantly. I've seen it on *The Meeting of Minds* often enough. And I'm suddenly remembering the bruise allegedly from the skiing – in Paris. A black run, she had claimed. And I am thinking – *no*. Just the word *no* over and over again in my head.

There's the sound then of the flush and the taps from the bathroom as I put the three glasses, slipping now from my fingers, back down on the carpet. Suddenly the baby is stirring and Carol is relieved for the distraction – rushing forward to cradle him and to put on the kettle to warm a bottle that she pulls from the neat tartan bag, exactly matching the carrycot.

As he cries, she puts her little finger gently into his mouth and for a time he's soothed as I help to warm the bottle, Sally still clattering about in the bathroom.

'A friend in France taught me this. A neighbour – worked for both her children. Better than a dummy, don't you think? It worked on the journey really well. Put him straight to sleep.'

'How long has he been hurting you?' I'm shaking the bottle, rested in the little metal teapot on the courtesy tray to help it warm through more quickly. 'From the very beginning?'

Still Carol will not look at me, gently smoothing the child's hair, and my mind is almost exploding. I mean – she can't seriously expect them to let her keep the baby. Not now. Surely. I am astonished she has managed to keep this from the adoption agency. I feel certain they will find out eventually.

'I thought the baby would change things.' She's speaking very quietly as if she doesn't want Sally to hear yet, still smoothing the child's hair – him sucking harder on her finger.

At last the bottle is warm enough and I pass it to her just as Sally emerges from the bathroom – standing in the doorway, at first looking from Carol to me and then back again like a spectator at a tennis match.

As Carol begins to feed the baby, I'm flicking back through the albums with all the colours changing. All the travelling we had envied, all those smart hotels. I can hear the raised voices now behind closed doors. Imagine trips to foreign hospitals. Presents, apologies and fresh starts. I think of my birthday party – oh no, of course. My stupid bloody birthday party.

Carol is looking at me but still saying nothing.

'Did he hit you after my party? My thirtieth? When you came back – for my party? When you only stayed for a blink? When you said you had a headache.'

She doesn't reply, the only sound now of the infant's hearty, happy sucking. Of course. Ned is a clever liar, pretending that *he's* the one who wants Carol to stay in touch. With her mum, with us. That isn't real. Ned wouldn't want her around us, back then or now. He probably feared we would have the power to end it – as we should have done. That's why they were late that night. And that look on her face outside the restaurant. She wasn't bracing herself to face the party, she was bracing herself to face the consequences. She'd stood up to him, made him come. For me . . . All that nonsense from him, pretending he wanted her to stay longer. It was a farce. A trick. An act.

Jeez.

I gasp, hand to my mouth as I remember how badly I'd thought of her when in reality she'd been brave. For me. She'd stood up to Ned, knowing that she would probably pay a price. She had done that *for me*.

'Will someone please tell me what's going on here?' Sally's eyes are squinting now as she tries to make sense of the strained mood through the tiredness and the champagne. Instinctively she kneels down to right a glass that's fallen over on the carpet, the few remaining drops spilling into a perfect little puddle.

'The bruises, Sally. It wasn't an accident. It was Ned.'

'*Ned?*' Sally looks at Carol, at first baffled and confused, and then very afraid. All the relief seeping away through the floor of the room.

The full facts, when Carol finally finds her voice, whispering as she still feeds the child, are more awful than I fear. He loves her, she protests. *No, really, he does, Beth. But she's such an airhead sometimes. And she makes him so angry. It is honestly as much her fault as his – and he's always so very sorry afterwards. Also it's been very hard, with all the infertility and the frustrations over trying to adopt. She's been difficult to live with. She has problems with her eating. And it's not always bad. Sometimes months go by and we're fine . . .*

Both Sally and I cannot believe what we're hearing.

'But why didn't you leave, Carol? You can't stay with a man who hits you? Especially not now. Not with a baby.' Sal's eyes are wide and disbelieving.

Carol's voice is still shaking. 'I know. I know. I did try once – but then he bought this house for Mum. So generous. So good of him. And it gets so confusing. One minute he says he wants me to see family and friends. Then when I do, he suddenly turns up all angry as if I was supposed to know he didn't mean it.'

'But that's manipulation, Carol. Cruel – not normal. You must see that? You *have* to leave him,' I say.

'But he would know where to find me so *how can I?* He says he'll follow me. I can't put Mum at risk so I stay away from her. And I know this sounds mad but I do love him. And he loves me. And I just thought, now that we finally have the baby, it will all be different . . .'

We all look at the child then as he sucks so contentedly, the bottle two-thirds empty, his eyes rolling back with the sleepy pleasure of it.

'But you can't stay with him, Carol. What if he hurts the baby?'

There's a pause as if she's thinking this through and then Carol starts to cry. 'You have to help me,' she says. '*Please.* I couldn't bear it if they took him back.'

My feet are hurting from the awkward way I'm sitting but I daren't move as Carol then confirms ever so quietly what I feared, that she can't have children herself because of an infection. Scarring inside. Something to do with the birth all those years ago.

Next she's babbling incomprehensibly about some woman in Paris, some medium, who predicted a turning point. A new life. She says she's taken up tarot to try to read her future. I have to take the baby from her to burp and soothe him as she talks about how it could still be all right. If we help her. Find somewhere for them to hide from Ned? Both of them.

She says he's in Lyon again on urgent business. He'll be away for forty-eight hours at least and believes she's still in France.

If we will just help her.

To hide.

We have forty-eight hours.

Please . . .

It's hopeless. Madness. There's no talking any sense to her. And so finally I persuade Sally to return to her room while I stay on to support Carol. To try to come up with some kind of plan.

I help her to change Thomas's nappy and then he's at last asleep, tucked up in his little carrycot.

I make us both a cup of tea and we just sit, looking at each other.

'Do you want me to tell you, Beth?' Her head is tilted to the side, her eyes unblinking.

'More about Ned, you mean?'

'No, I don't mean that.' She looks away and then back at me. Her eyes are glistening and I get this terrible feeling inside that I can't explain.

'What do you mean, Carol? Tell me what?'

'I always assumed you wouldn't want to know. That's why I stayed away.'

I sip at my tea, which is too hot. I get this renewed sensation of dread. I feel that I should leave. But I also feel compelled to stay. I don't know what to do. I frown. Tilt my own head by way of a question.

For what feels an age she just stares and then finally blinks. 'You should go to bed, Beth.' At last she looks away.

'No, Carol. You can't just start this and then stop. What is it you think I don't want to know?'

'The father of my baby, Beth.' A single tear breaks her left eye first.

I watch it move down her cheek but she does nothing to acknowledge it. Or stop it. I imagine it rolling down my own cheek and would want to wipe it away.

But Carol does not move. The tear drips on to the front of her shirt. 'It wasn't a boyfriend in the holidays.'

I'm aware that I've stilled my lips. Holding my breath.

Another tear appears from her right eye. 'It happened at your house, Beth. That day you and Sally went to the farm shop with your mum. When I had a cold. Do you remember? That time we came to stay with you and I had a cold.'

I feel as if I'm being sucked back in time. Yes, I do remember. We went on a walk to the farm shop. Me and Mum and Sally – to buy a pumpkin for soup. Yes, Carol stayed behind.

But what is she saying? I feel my brain ache and my frown deepen. I feel myself pull my chin back into my neck.

What the hell is she *really* saying here . . . ?

And then I hear a slap and watch her face turn to the left as I cannot help myself. My hand stinging as I slap her hard around the face . . .

CHAPTER 49

BETH - NOW

In this long and airless night, I cannot sleep.

Instead, back in my own hotel room, I just lie in the dark on the bed, drifting through time. I think I hear an owl toot. Once. Twice. But it's like an echo and I can't be sure if it's for real or from one of the strange, dark scenes playing out in my head.

So I keep getting up. Pacing. Through my shock and exhaustion, I want to open the window wider to listen again for the owl, but there's some kind of limiter on the window frame. It just. Won't. Budge.

I strain, gripping the bottom of the window. I push harder and harder. The room is stifling and I am desperate for cooler air. I want to hear the owl. No – I want to *be* that owl. I want the option to fly far, far away and never come back. I also want to scream. Howl into the night sky.

Finally I give up. I turn and let my back slide down the wall until I'm sitting on the floor. I've cried so much that there are no tears left. It's as if all the moisture has dripped from my body and I'm left shrunken. Dried up.

I look down and am surprised to find I'm still dressed. I feel dirty. Sweaty. Across the room the airmail letter from Jacqueline is sticking out from my bag on the floor. I look at it and want to rewind time, to be the Beth who held it in her hand in the school kitchen. Before I *knew*.

I do not want to be this Beth.

This new Beth who knows what I know now . . .

Carol poured us both brandy after I hit her.

I didn't mean to slap her. I just didn't want her to *say* it. As if stopping her from saying it could make it untrue.

At first I thought – she's *making this up*. This vile and wretched version of my family. She's making it up, although I don't understand why. *To hurt me? To put a bomb in the middle of my life?*

But then, with the tears dripping down her cheeks and the bright pink of the flesh where I slapped her, I realised, looking deep into her eyes, that she had no reason to make this up.

Why would she lie?

The next thought was that it was Michael. And that would have been bad enough: for Carol to say that my brother – back then sixteen, maybe seventeen – was the father of her baby. The tiny little baby who died that day in the bathroom with the blood. And the shells . . .

I tried to process this option. *Michael?* We just sat there in silence while I sifted through the memories. The dates. I could feel my head jerk from side to side because something didn't fit.

No. That holiday visit – the time she came to stay when we went to the farm shop without her? My brother was away. He was staying with his best friend in Oxfordshire.

So . . .

'I don't understand. Michael was away that weekend. What are you saying, Carol? What are you *really* saying here?'

'I didn't mean your brother. It wasn't him.'

'*What?*' I wanted to shake her. I had to clench my fists by my side to stop myself from touching her again.

She winced as if she realised what I was thinking and I felt ashamed, remembering about Ned. The bruises.

'Are you sure you want me to tell you, Beth? All of it? I can go if you'd prefer. I can take Thomas and just go.'

◆　◆　◆

I move into the bathroom and turn the shower to maximum. I strip and step under the hot spray, needing the heat and the sound and burst of needles against my skin as I turn over everything she said to me last night, once I nodded. *Yes, I want to know, Carol.*

She said she'd taken her sketchbook and a hot lemon drink into the summerhouse in our garden after me and Sally and Mum set off for the farm shop for the pumpkin for soup. It was drizzling and my mum worried the long walk would make her cold worse. The summerhouse had a small log burner and was cosy. Warm.

My father followed her into the summerhouse, she said, and at first she was pleased. It wasn't long after the Ouija board debacle at school . . .

I interrupted her and said that she'd got that all wrong about the Ouija board; it wasn't her father trying to contact her but a mean prank by Melody. Carol said – no matter.

The point was it had made her think of her own father and so she had leaned into my father's shoulder in the summerhouse. *Like I used to with my own dad when I was little. Was that wrong of me, Beth? Was it my fault?*

She was telling him about the sketches, what she was trying to achieve – copying the daisies by one of the tree trunks across the lawn. My father said the drawings were very good. But then my father put both his arms around her and was suddenly squeezing her tight. She said she was very shocked and pushed him away. But he was suddenly kissing her, telling her that she was very beautiful.

She was talking as if she was in a trance now. Said there were two crows sitting on the fence, watching the whole time. She struggled and she pushed but she wasn't strong enough. She said there was a horrid smell of beer and mints. And the crows with their awful black eyes shining just watched until it was all over.

I should have screamed, Beth. Afterwards, I thought I should have called out for help. But I was afraid you'd come back. And hear him. You and Sally and your mum.

She paused for a long time before looking across at Thomas, still sound asleep in his little tartan carrycot.

I just didn't know what to do. It was your father, Beth. When I got pregnant, I so wanted to tell someone but I knew how much you loved him. And so afterwards, I just couldn't say anything. I mean, look at you – it's breaking your heart. I always knew that it would break your heart . . .

Back on my hotel bed, I sit swamped in a large white towel – my skin hot and red. I'm trying to clear my head. *Of course, of course.* I'm thinking of the magnets. Push, pull. Push, pull. No wonder Carol pulled away from us. No, not us – from me.

For a long time I just watch the light blinking on the digital clock by the bed. 5.30 a.m. 5.45 a.m. . . .

I find that I feel ashamed, which makes no sense. And then I realise it's because I love my father – loved him . . .

Do I have to stop loving him now? Tear up all of our memories?

He never put a foot wrong with me – was always so lovely with me.

I think of my mother and it's unbearable to imagine how much this will hurt her. I hear the echo of her confession to me when I was feeling depressed. The story of her going to stay with my aunt. *There was a bit of silliness – your dad with some young girl in the office* . . .

Suddenly I need to be dressed, to shake myself out of this and be doing something. I stand up and start hunting for clothes. I realise that I need badly to speak to Adam for his advice, but it's so early still and he's not strong.

Also I simply can't bear the thought of sharing this out loud. Not just yet.

Most of all what is dawning on me is that I am not the victim here. Wallowing like this all night in my own shock and hurt.

I think of Carol – all these years.

She told me last night that she'd confided in Ned. About my dad. About the baby. She broke our promise in those early heady days of love and lust when they were trying for a child of their own. When anything seemed possible. At first Ned was kind and understanding. Angry for her. But then inexplicably angry *at her*. Why didn't she *stop him*? My father. Why hadn't she told the police? Why did she have to *look that way – so irresistible*? And then the paranoia. The jealousy – accusing her of flirting, of looking at men. Encouraging them.

When I didn't, Beth. Truly I didn't. Never. Not ever.

Finally the violence began when she tried to leave Ned. Threats. That he would tell Carol's mother what we did over the baby. Tell me about my father . . .

And I just thought if I could try not to make him angry, if we could have a baby, adopt a baby and be a proper family, everything would change, Beth.

I need to help her now. Carol and her baby. Suddenly I am feeling the weight of what she has shouldered all alone because of me. I need to make it right. I check my watch. 6 a.m. Too early yet . . .

I put on the television, mostly to kill some time and for the sound to block out the voices in my head and for the comfort of the pictures – the faces of ordinary people with ordinary, simple lives. It's still much too early to phone Adam and so I flick to a news channel.

And it's like instant paralysis. A freeze frame. The sound is off but the picture – screaming at me. The presenter's grave face and in the corner of the screen a photograph of the tartan carrycot.

No mistake.

Carol's . . . tartan . . . carrycot.

I try to find the right button to cancel the mute – the headline then spooling silently across the bottom of the screen. The horrible truth dawning . . .

BABY SNATCH LATEST: police extend search after child disappears at Heathrow Airport. Officers say tartan carrycot was left unattended for just a few moments . . .

Within minutes I am outside Carol's room and when she won't answer, I'm banging and banging over and over, shouting her name. *Carol – Carol!*

Frantic that she's checked out, I race back to the front desk.

'Room 117 – I've got to get in. My friend won't answer.'

'It's early. Look, I'm very sorry but we can't be disturbing the other guests like this.' The girl on the front desk dials 117 on the switchboard. The engaged bleep.

Then she checks the computer screen, her face changing. 'Hang on. 117? I remember now. Her husband arrived about fifteen minutes ago. Birthday surprise. Lovely flowers.'

'Her *husband*! Oh, dear Lord.'

'What is it? What's the matter?' The colour drains from the girl's face. 'I gave him the room card. I know we're not supposed to – but he said it was a surprise. Her birthday. What's the matter?'

'Give me a card to the room NOW and phone the police!'

'Oh no – I'm going to lose my job, aren't I?'

'NOW!'

The girl punches a card through the machine. I grab it and run towards the stairs, shouting again over my shoulder, 'Call the police! And security – do you have hotel security?'

What I do next, I do on instinct. Unthinking. It's not courageous. Adam is right in what he says later. It's *stupid*.

I should get help – Matthew, Sally. But I am not thinking as I fly along the corridor. I am not thinking as I scan the card into the door. All I can see is a tartan carrycot. So that I'm not even afraid as I burst into the room and see a framed picture of a nymph, reflected in the mirror – below it Carol's terrified face, with Ned's arms around her neck and her mouth. She's choking. Spluttering. Kicking her legs in wild protest. His face, meantime, is purple with rage. Unrecognisable. The eyes black and wild. Alongside the bed is the carrycot with a pillow pushed inside. No sound from the child . . .

I scream, I remember that. Howl for someone to *help us, please*. But Ned is between me and the baby. I look around for something to hit him with, to make him let Carol go. To let me get past to the child.

As I turn to grab something, anything, Ned releases Carol and takes a couple of swift strides towards me. Then he *punches* me in the face – a full swing to my jaw with his whole body weight behind it.

The shock is unreal. I can't believe that a man would do this. I hear a crack, which I must suppose is my jaw, and then a terrific pain to the back of my head as I fall, bashing into the dressing table on the way down. Then all I register is pain in different parts of my body – stomach, legs and side.

Through the pain and the shock – still I *can't* believe he's doing this – I see Carol drag herself to her knees and in my head I am screaming for her to run. For a moment there's a clear path between her and the door. *Run, Carol, run.*

But she does not do it.

In disbelief, I watch her struggle back across the room towards the cot. She's moving the pillow away and leaning over as Ned turns – his eyes huge and wild – as he starts to shout. *Bitch. Get away from there* . . .

For a few seconds there's blackness and then across the room through a fog I see Ned pounding at Carol's back. He drives her to the floor but she gets back up. And all the time she has her arms outstretched, like some magnificent bird, spanning her wings around the nest.

There's nothing I can do but watch. The pounding. The stretching. Until at last I see this wire dangling down alongside me. I pull hard – once, twice – until a lamp crashes from the dressing table. Suddenly there are more voices in the room. I make out Matthew moving into the room. There's a blur of shapes and voices and the dreadful thudding of flesh on flesh.

And then the blackness again.

CHAPTER 50

BETH - NOW

At first when the black turns to grey, I have no voice to protest. Grey shutters at the window, grey walls and the metallic grey of the hospital bed. I open my mouth to protest but there's no voice. Suffocated by the grey dust.

Nurses come to endlessly plump my pillows – to soothe with water and smiles, comfort and kindness. Sal comes too – to sit alongside me, mostly silent but sometimes crying as I drift in and out of grey dreams, waiting for Adam to take me home.

Has she really said nothing? Nothing at all? I hear Sally whispering to the nurses as I wake and they shake their heads and mutter about shock. *Such a difficult thing, shock,* as if I'm now deaf as well as mute.

Even when Adam arrives and I watch his limp, pleading with my eyes for him to take me home. To please, please, *take me home,* there is no voice.

I can hear them saying that I have a fever, that the morphine for my pain is making me confused. But it's as if I'm in a bubble and can't quite reach them. The doctor tells Adam I have a fractured jaw and a punctured lung. I listen to Adam ask question after question but I can't make out the answers.

I close my eyes to it all. To shut out the voices. Shut out the grey.

And then after a time, I can smell them. Candles in a church. So that I turn my head to try to find them . . . I can definitely smell them but I can't see them and so I blow at the grey dust all around me – *huff, puff, blow your house down* – to try to find my voice underneath.

'Carol. I have to find Carol . . .'

A nurse, checking the machines, offers water with a straw.

'Shh, shh. Drink slowly. You're a bit confused – it's all the drugs. Try not to worry about it.'

Adam is next, whispering into my hair, 'You're not to try to speak yet. Just rest. Everything is going to be fine.'

'No, I need to find her.'

'Shh.'

'Carol. I have to find her.'

'It's all right, darling. She's here. Carol is here at the hospital.'

Here?

Adam glances at the doctor who's entered the room behind him.

'I don't understand,' I say. 'Have I missed it. The church?'

I can smell the candles again. *Promise. Promise. Promise.*

'No, no, Beth. It's the medication. You're confused.' Then whispering, 'Carol's in a coma, Beth. Very poorly. We didn't want to tell you until you were stronger. But the baby is doing really well now. You both saved the baby she took – he's going to be fine.'

I remember the bird then. And the wings spread out wide with someone pounding at its back. For a time I seem to sleep but when I wake there's some kind of argument.

Shouting. It might be my voice. Yes.

I need to see Carol. Please. Will you take me to see Carol?

There's a long discussion. Adam is not happy. Sally is crying. And then finally I'm in some kind of wheelchair – a nurse pushing the trolley alongside with my drips and tubes – and I can hear Adam saying, 'This is not a good idea. Not a good idea at all. I'm not happy with this . . .'

The first thing I see is the back of Deborah's head as she sits in a grey plastic chair alongside the bed. There's a lot of bleeping. Tubes. Wires. Machines.

In the middle – Carol's face. Perfect. Beautiful. She looks so peaceful. Just asleep like on the blue sofa at the hotel. But when Adam wheels me closer, I see her neck. Puffy and purple. Deborah turns and tries to smile – first at me and then at Adam over my head.

'How is she today?' Is it Adam's voice? I'm not sure.

'The same.'

They won't let me stay for very long but it's long enough.

And tonight in my dreams I realise what is happening. I'm the only one who can see it. So when I open my eyes I try to whisper it to Adam, who is curled up in the chair alongside me, but he isn't listening. It's the grey. The grey is *killing* Carol.

No – no! Don't get the doctor. It's the grey, Adam. You have to help me. She hates grey – Carol. If we leave her in that room, the grey will kill her. Suffocate her.

Sally appears then with a nurse and I hear muttering about a sedative. Someone is saying it's a reaction to the painkillers – pressing the little buzzer by the bed. The nurse tries to hold my arm to calm me.

So I start shouting. Don't they see? She's cold. She needs her own blanket. The *pink one. Sally – you remember. Her pink blanket? If you could just get it for her.*

There's a panic in Sal's eyes that I cannot understand. *The pink blanket. You remember, Sally – don't you? It must be here somewhere . . .* I begin feeling around the bed, wondering who's taken it.

Sally begins to cry and Adam is shaking his head, trying to hush me, so I start shouting that I'll get it myself. If no one will help me, I'll *fetch . . . it . . . myself.*

I try to get up out of the bed then, but as I swing my legs the room seems to move – to blur – and then all is black again.

◆ ◆ ◆

When I wake next I can hear Adam and Sally's voices squabbling.

But what harm could it do? Sally's tone is determined but Adam is saying – *no, enough.* And then, when I open my eyes I can see it in her hand. Thank goodness. She has the blanket. Adam's eyes are red and he's shaking his head.

'I could only find a cot blanket, Beth. It's all they had in the shop. But is this OK, darling?' Sally holds it out and lets me touch it. Soft and pink.

Yes. Yes.

She wheels me along the corridor, Adam and a nurse trailing behind, and then she helps me stretch it across Carol's bed.

'Is that OK, Beth? Is that better now?' Sal's voice is very quiet.

The blanket is a little small and at first I have to stretch it up under Carol's neck, to cover the bruising. But *yes.*

I look at Carol – her face brighter already alongside the pink. That's much better. Just like in school. The grey underneath and the pink blanket on top . . .

I lay my head on the blanket and I whisper that she's safe now. And I will wait.

I tell her how very brave she was. How this time we saved the baby. And she was *very, very brave.*

'So brave, Carol.'

I fancy that I see her eyelids flutter. The others in the room don't seem to see it but I tell her that she's not to worry about that. That everything is going to be OK.

That I will wait here. This time we will not desert her.

This time, we will keep her safe.

CHAPTER 51

BETH - NOW

It's six months before Ned's court case. I'm told this is unusually quick. *Really?* Who are they kidding? It has been sheer agony waiting for this.

I know little of court procedure and hate that I'm not allowed in until it's my turn to give evidence. It means I don't know what has been said before. How things are going.

The prosecution team has warned me that cross-examination will be tough. Ned's version of events is that Carol and I attacked him, that he lashed out only in self-defence because he was trying to take the stolen baby from us.

His story is that he adored Carol, that she was the hot-headed one. Goading him. Taunting him. Obsessed with her mediums and her past.

'You must try not to get angry. To stay calm.' A very smart young woman on the legal team gave me the final briefing two days ago. 'He's arrogant and entirely deluded. Pleading not guilty to everything. He's trying to paint himself as the hero – the one who was trying to get the baby back to his mother. Their case is that you and Carol lost control and he acted in self-defence . . .'

'How are you holding up?' Adam is squeezing my hand. We're sitting on a long wooden bench outside the courtroom.

'Nervous. I wish you could come in with me.'

'Me too.' He runs his thumb gently across the back of my hand. Adam is also to give evidence. So many charges. So many witnesses . . .

I glance across the corridor and recognise a few other faces who, like us, are waiting to be called. Sitting on her own is the girl from the front desk at the hotel. She looks down at her feet – won't meet my eyes.

And then at last the door opens and a court official appears. My name first.

Inside it's hot and I wish I hadn't worn long sleeves. The biggest shock is how well Ned looks. Smart and improbably relaxed in an expensive suit. I look over at the jury and at the young women in particular. I worry more than ever that they'll be taken in by his good looks and his charm. Just as we were all taken in by his lies, pretending he wanted Carol to see her mother and us, when the opposite was true.

As I'm led to the witness stand, I try to remember what Matthew told me. That the forensic evidence is sound. Ned's fingerprints were all over Carol's diaries. He'd been reading them secretly all along so knew her every thought and plan. They have pieced together Carol's hospital records to prove years of abuse. *They have Ned's bike.*

But for all the warnings, it's tougher than I expect. I give my evidence for the prosecution. And then Ned's lawyer is on his feet.

'Isn't it the truth that you attacked my client? That you would have done anything to help your friend. To cover up her own crime. Taking that child . . .'

'No, no,' I say, 'that's not true. He was trying to strangle her. And I didn't know what Carol had done until it was on the news. We thought the child was adopted.'

'You really believed that?'

'Yes, I did.'

'It seriously didn't occur to you from the very beginning that a newly adopted baby would be monitored by the authorities? That your friend wouldn't be able to just disappear abroad? That this *couldn't* be an adopted baby?'

'No, no. I didn't think of any of that. I didn't think about rules. She just looked so happy with him. The baby was content. I *really* thought the baby was hers until I saw the news.' I can feel my heart pounding, worrying that I must sound naive. But it's the truth.

I look across at her. *Carol*. She's wearing a dark green dress and looks so tiny and so frail. I can't bear that she's having to go through all this.

In the hospital we so nearly lost her. Twice they had to call the crash team when her heart stopped. You see it on the telly but in real life it's so much more shocking. The doctor's voice. *I need you to leave the room, please. Can you all give us some space . . .*

'She's been through so much. She was unwell when she took that child.'

'Yes, well . . . We're not here to go over the motivation of that other case. We're here to talk about my client who was trying to *save the child*. To get the baby out of the room while you and Carol attacked him.'

'That's not true. He put a pillow over the child's cot.'

'You saw that, did you?'

'No, but I knew that he must have done it . . .'

'So you're psychic now, are you?'

'*Objection!*' The prosecution lawyer suddenly on his feet.

On and on it went. Round and round in circles until I wasn't sure if I had done a good job as a witness or not. On paper, Ned's version had seemed so ridiculous but Carol's crime – snatching the baby – had complicated things. There was a tussle over which case would be heard first. Because Ned was determined to put Carol's crime at the centre of his defence, her guilty plea had to be taken first in a separate hearing.

So it was fair game for Ned's defence team. And my goodness they ran with it.

Awful.

It wasn't until the very end of the trial when the prosecution summed up all the evidence – much of which I hadn't heard – that I felt more reassured. Matthew was right. The team had done a good job. It then seemed fantastic that Ned had had the nerve to plead not guilty.

The prosecution pieced together the confetti of Carol's hospital records down the years. So many different departments and false names, linked by her diary. The cracked ribs. The mystery 'falls'.

Ned's version of 'love' was control, the barrister said – pacing in front of the jury. His biggest fear was that Carol would leave him. That her mother or we – her old and true friends – would turn her against him once we found out the truth about his violence. So he used Carol's vulnerability against her. He pretended to encourage contact with us and then punished her for that contact. And while controlling her utterly with his abuse and his bullying manipulation, he tried to play us too, feigning concern over her eating and so on.

In reality he read her diary and he put a tracker on Carol's phone. He'd been following all the social media coverage on the school party and was terrified of Carol contacting us. He knew from Carol about the lost baby and the bluebells. So he was the one who set up the fake Facebook account to try to scare us. Warn us off.

When that failed, he got his secretary to ring my boys' school with a fake pickup message. The poor woman had no idea what it was about.

And finally in desperation? The unthinkable. Targeting my lovely Adam. Still I struggle to understand it. *Why?* a voice screams in my head every time I watch Adam cross a room. His limp.

The counsel for the prosecution sets it out now. When Carol took off for a few days without her phone, Ned flipped. He thought she might visit me. Took his bike on the ferry. Watched us all for a time. Made himself more and more angry. Followed Adam from his school . . .

When Ned phoned me that day, the records show he was actually in England himself. He made up the story of Carol riding a bike to taunt me. She's never ridden a motorbike in her life. It was *him*.

I still can't process it. What had Adam ever done to Ned? I remember sitting with Matthew just last night, turning it over and over.

'But *why*, Matthew?' I kept asking.

'Sometimes it's just pure madness, Beth. He'd got away with hurting Carol for so long, maybe he felt invincible. That he could get away with anything.'

◆ ◆ ◆

It's nearly the end of the day when the jury retires, so we have to return the following morning. None of us has slept. Carol, on bail herself and awaiting her own sentence, is ghostly white.

It's only as the jury returns guilty verdicts on all of the charges against Ned that he loses control. Finally gives himself away – shouting and cursing. That other version of him.

'*You* made me do this. All of it.' He's pointing at Carol. 'Always scribbling in your stupid diary about *Beth and Sally, Beth and Sally*.' He uses this vicious, taunting sing-song tone as he spits our names. 'Bitches, both of them. They would have taken her from me. Poisoned her against me!'

The judge calls for him to be removed but still he rants as the court security staff move in. Ned struggles hard, glaring at Carol who collapses forward, head in her hands. 'If only I'd found someone more like Adam. *Gentle like Adam*. You remember writing that, eh? *Adam and Beth this, Adam and Beth that*.'

It's such a shock to hear him use Adam's name. Sally is sitting next to me and clasps my hand tightly for support. But Ned is still in the dock, shouting and trying to fight off the staff. Mad, jealous raging, glaring at me this time.

'I wish I'd driven faster at your husband!'

'Remove this man from this court. Now!' The judge sounds furious at how long it's taking to get Ned out. Still Ned glares at *me*, twisting and turning and kicking as the handcuffs are finally on and he's dragged away.

'I wanted you to know what it feels like. To fear losing someone that *you* love . . .'

◆ ◆ ◆

That evening Carol stays at our home. She sits in the conservatory as if in a daze, still deathly pale. I bring her a tray with tea and biscuits that I know she won't eat.

We sit for a long time in silence and then she turns to me.

'I did write in my diary about you and Adam. I did wish we could be more like you. Ned more like Adam, I mean. I had no idea he would *read that*. Come looking for me at your place. Watch you and Adam. I'm so, so sorry, Beth . . .'

'Don't you say sorry.' I take both her hands to make her look at me. 'None of this was your fault. You did nothing wrong. Ned's mind is—' I can't find the right words. I want to say – *mad, evil*. '—twisted.'

'But I did do wrong, didn't I? The little boy . . .' Her voice is quieter now, almost a whisper. 'I honestly never meant to take him, Beth. I didn't plan it.'

'I know that, of course I know that. That's why they're doing the psychiatric reports. Into your health. Into all of it. They'll be told everything you've been through before they sentence you. It's nearly all over now.'

And then she explains something else – the final missing piece in this sad, sad puzzle. 'It was the spiritualism, all the readings and the tarot, seeing mediums and all of that stuff that made Ned so angry with me.' She's let go of my hands and is looking out on the garden, a breeze making the longest magnolia branch tap on the roof of the conservatory.

Tap, tap . . .

Ned's defence team had pressed her several times on why she was obsessed with it all, but Carol never properly explained.

'The truth is, I really do want to believe there is something after this life, Beth. Not heaven exactly. I don't think I mean heaven. But *something*.' She turns to look at me directly again. 'I gave her a name, Beth.' She's whispering now.

'What?' I'm not following and it's hard to hear her.

'My baby. I *did* give her a name.'

I can't help it. I suck in air. A gasp of genuine surprise. All those years ago when we lit candles in the chapel after burying the bag, Sally had said we should give the child a name. So that she would go to heaven and not be in limbo. Carol was weeping and she insisted, *No, no name. No name.*

She tells me now that she was afraid at the time that naming the child would make it more unbearable. More real. But later she kept dreaming about the child and so she secretly changed her mind . . .

'I called her Rebecca.' Tears are now dripping down Carol's face. 'And I started to think more and more about the afterlife – heaven, hell, limbo, spirits and all of that. It started with that Ouija board. I genuinely thought my dad was trying to talk to me.'

'But you know that wasn't real. That was just Melody being unkind.'

'Yes, but it *felt* real. I wanted to know what he had to say. And later, after the baby died, it became so much more than that, Beth. I didn't tell the court because it makes me sound as mad as Ned.'

She wipes the tears with her palms, her stare burning into me. 'But I can tell you, *can't I, Beth?*'

'Of course you can. You can tell me anything.'

'I wanted to believe it possible. To contact my dad . . .' She's speaking very slowly and stretches out for my hand once more. 'I wanted to ask *him* something . . .' Her voice again so quiet I can barely hear her.

I lean closer. 'Ask him what, Carol?'

Still she's staring right into my eyes. 'To look after my little girl.' She squeezes my hand.

A pause.

'I wanted to ask my dad to look after Rebecca.'

EPILOGUE

BETH
SPRING 2016

Thursday the twenty-sixth and I cannot remember a more beautiful dawn. Such a waste that half the world still sleeps – missing the sweetness of this early air. The softness of this light. The forecast got it right. Good visibility and I'm so grateful, not wishing to miss a thing today.

My biggest worry is still altitude sickness – the one thing you can neither prepare for nor predict. It's something predetermined, apparently, with no link to fitness, size or age. It's stamped on your lungs at birth to be discovered only when you test it.

How cruel would it be? To dust a person with the magic of the mountains then snatch the dream away. But I must be brave; today I find out.

Across the camp, others are slowly stirring and soon there will be tea and hopefully porridge to warm us before our trek. There are twelve in our party. Some are fundraising – others like me just ticking the bucket list. One named Lucy called up my YouTube video on the school closure, which the convent posted. She's impressed. She thinks working in television must be glamorous. I don't tell her the truth behind it all.

Lucy is just twenty-four and, although she won't admit it, is smitten to the point of gauche embarrassment with a marine biologist in our party called Sol. They steal glances, both still unsure of the other's interest, and I have to bite into a smile, remembering it all: the canvas of youth awaiting the colour of our dreams.

The boys and Adam are in Beijing waiting for me and tomorrow night I take the train to rejoin them. We will then celebrate my birthday together – the big four-zero – with these scenes locked in my camera. My own version of the photographs and the views that have haunted me all these years.

I have the book in my rucksack: the photographic journal that I so fell in love with in the school library. It was out of print but Adam found a second-hand copy online. It's in remarkable condition and last night I read it all again, marvelling at each picture as I remember enjoying them for the first time all those years ago.

Guilin is every bit as beautiful as I'd hoped. We trek high and far today and then we descend to a plateau to the second campsite from where I hope to take my own shots. The guides tell me the view is mesmeric, still exactly as the book's cover depicts – the men with their flat, raft-like boats and lanterns reflecting on the water. The mountains shrugging their amusement all around us.

◆　◆　◆

I've sent my postcards already.

To my poor mother, who still clucks over our health – thinks my lungs and Adam's iffy leg may not be strong enough for this and was a mess at the airport when we left.

To Sister Maurice, who came to the hospital after Ned's attack with flowers from the garden – peonies – and prayers. Day after day. Week after week.

To Sally and Matthew, who have finished the final cottage at last. Dearest Sally – never so nervous but, to me, never so beautiful. Theirs was the easiest card to pick – a tiny Chinese child with inkwell eyes (boy or girl, I can't tell), beaming with a basket of melons, plump and green with flashes of yellow, alongside the dust of the long tourist trail to the Great Wall.

I sigh to think of them. My happiness for Sally and Matthew is at the centre of everything now. I was so pleased to be wrong about him. Not a man who did not want a child but a man too afraid of the fact that he *did*.

They're already choosing names. Amelie if it's a girl. So beautiful. And although Matthew's eyes are still fearful some days, I see more hope and love, happiness and healing there with every passing month.

Sally is well into the second trimester and I've never seen a woman's complexion glow with such grace and joy. They got engaged quickly and married straight after the court cases – a simple and gorgeous ceremony at a tiny register office with Sally wearing a pink silk dress.

I remember watching them both, all nervous and excited up at the front, and when it came to the vows Sal was suddenly frozen, her hand actually shaking. And then Matthew did this lovely thing to steady her – leaning in close and staring right into her eyes until she finally let out a little breath. Like relief.

I'd wondered what they would do by way of reception. So many opt for sausages and mash in the local pub these days but Sal and Matt came up with this sensational idea – a picnic in the gardens of their row of cottages. They set up tables under awnings and rugs on the ground for the children by the magnolia and then shared out wicker baskets with stunning picnic treats of sandwiches and lemon-herb chicken and proper home-made scotch eggs. There was champagne for the grown-ups or home-made lemonade for the children and the drivers. The weather was kind – not sunny all day, but dry with a lovely, soft light and a gentle breeze off the sea. We had strawberries and cream and then coffee was served from large picnic flasks, which made Sally giggle, sharing a story about their first picnic. Matthew and a swan.

And the best part for me? Beautiful Carol – still so fragile but who managed to stand up to make a wonderful speech. About friends. And love. And new beginnings.

My goodness – what a long, dark journey for her.

Ned is in prison now. It should be many years before they even consider parole. Carol is finally safe. But it's her own demons she must battle now.

Facing the mother of the child she took in court was the hardest thing. I had some moment of insanity when I decided I would write to the mother to try to explain the mitigation. The appalling context of what Carol had been through. But Adam and all the lawyers were right. Naive of me.

You should have seen the woman's eyes. In court.

We'd already been to the police ourselves. Carol's child was recovered from the chapel garden. Just as Matthew had warned, the tests were able to confirm very little. Very premature and most likely stillborn but they couldn't say for sure. In the end we had to work out the child's dates from the school calendars, matching the date we visited my home – the farm shop walk – and the date of that later stay when my father was away and the child was born.

Twenty-seven weeks.

I cried when we found that out. Twenty-seven weeks is viable. Just. With the right care . . .

The Crown Prosecution Service decided there was no evidence that we were responsible for the baby's death, also that a charge of concealing a birth would not be in the public interest, given the other charge against Carol. In her statement, she said she had put her hand to her baby's mouth to check for breathing but had always feared she'd left it there too long. That it was her fault . . .

I told them that I thought I saw the baby breathe, but I couldn't be one hundred per cent certain. It was all so terrible. Such a blur.

I think I put my hand over her mouth . . .

Don't say that. Don't even think that. You wouldn't have done that.

Carol was given a custodial sentence for snatching the little boy – suspended for two years when her medical records and the story of the assault by my father and her lost child were finally put before the judge. She decided to have her baby's remains cremated – told us she couldn't bear the thought of another grave.

No surprise that the mother of the child Carol took was unmoved by my letter. Livid at the leniency of Carol's sentence, spitting her fury in interviews outside the court. 'My child could have died. That woman should have gone straight to jail . . .'

◆ ◆ ◆

Belatedly I understand now why Matthew was so badly affected by the mother's outburst after the young shoplifter was killed. It stays with you.

And I do see that there's no rationale for defending Carol as fiercely as we do – me and Sally. Only love. Like a parent who continues to love a child who has done wrong.

We have shared everything now – with Deborah and my mother and Sally's mother too. No more secrets.

The DNA tests on Carol's baby confirmed all she told me. My father was the child's father. It was beyond terrible, having to break the news to my mother. She was so shocked, she nearly passed out. Then she went into a spiral and it was my turn to take her to the doctor for sleeping tablets. Next she blamed herself . . .

I should have kicked him out. When he had that first fling with the young girl in the office.

No, Mum. You are not to take this on yourself. We didn't do this.

We have counselling. All of us. My mother and I both struggle to know how we're supposed to feel about my father. Shame? Guilt? I still haven't worked it out. Hating him so much one moment. Remembering happy days the next. So confusing and terrible.

And so now we just take it one day at a time – living in our new bubble. Helping each other. Deborah and my mother have let their own properties and, for now at least, are moving furniture into one of Sal's cottages. They need the company, they say, and Deborah wants to be as close to Carol as possible. Sal's mum visits sometimes too to support her through the pregnancy.

For herself Carol chose the cottage with the squirrel on the roof and the best view of the sea. She's done up the spare room for her young friend Emily, who is sometimes allowed to stay. Emily's family were wary after the court cases, but she's a lovely young woman with a mind of her own. Begs to visit, swims every day in the sea, rain or shine, and is so fond of Carol.

Sal and Matthew are next door – the cottage with the magnolia. Technically they talk of selling one or more of the developments down the line, but I wonder.

'All a bit *too* close for comfort, don't you think?' was Adam's worry but not mine. For we are still learning how to breathe again.

And there's the word.

I saw the baby breathe . . .

She would be twenty-six – Carol's child. My half-sister. And yes, it's far from certain she could have lived – twenty-seven weeks. I've perhaps read more than I should on the chances . . .

The truth is, we can never know for sure how it might have turned out if we had sought help.

So every day I simply do what I must do – I remind myself we were all too young. Not bad. Just young. And for my boys, for Adam and for my friends, I push myself up from the bottom of that ocean – the place in that bathroom all those years ago with all the blood and the sadness where the baby is not breathing and I can't breathe myself and I come right up here for the air.

For this beautiful world where across the valley right this minute the mist looks so close that I can almost believe I could stretch out a finger to stir it into a different picture.

It reminds me of that photograph from the Downs. The three of us lying on the grass all those years ago: Carol with the wind blowing her hair into her mouth, smiling up at me.

You love it up here, Beth – don't you? Her voice just a whisper on this same wind.

I think of us frozen in time: three girls so innocent, hopeful and happy with no idea of what lay ahead for us. I think of the Carol she was and the Carol she might have become.

But most of all I think of my new dream. A new haunting in which we do it right. We tell our mothers. We get help. And the story has a different ending. A girl in a field with a fistful of bluebells.

In the dream, I walk up to the girl to ask who the flowers are for. She looks up to smile with Carol's eyes and tilts her head as if it's a foolish question.

Of course it is. This is *Rebecca*.

And I know the answer so I close my eyes to whisper it on this mountain wind.

The flowers are for your mother . . .

AUTHOR'S NOTE

Thank you so much for reading my third psychological thriller *The Promise*. The first thing I want to say is that I really did go to boarding school . . . and had a very happy and uneventful time there! In fact, I still meet up with boarding-school friends and really treasure our get-togethers. These loyal friends followed my difficult decade, dealing with rejection in the early days when I was trying to get published. And they were there cheerleading when my first novel finally came out.

So my apologies to those dear friends and lovely staff at my real school . . . for coming up with such a dark story in my fictional one. The reason I decided on boarding school for this novel was simple. I needed my trio to develop a credibly *intense* friendship. I needed them to live together but I didn't want to make them sisters. So boarding school, where I made such good friends myself, seemed the perfect solution.

Sometimes I'm asked why I put my characters through so much. Make them walk in such dark shadows? Decades in journalism is the answer. I was lucky myself to have loving parents and a happy childhood. I knew nothing of sorrow until I lost my mother in my teens to cancer. But through many years in newspapers and television, I covered some truly shocking stories. Over and over I saw bad things happen to good people. But I also learned, through those most difficult and sometimes harrowing stories, to admire courage. Resilience. The healing power of love and the eternal hope for justice. And recovery.

So while I would never base my fiction on real stories or real people, I do use the *emotional landscape* from those years as a journalist. And I don't shy away from difficult themes precisely because we should not pretend these kinds of things could never happen.

My thanks again for reading *The Promise*. I hope new readers have enjoyed meeting PI Matthew Hill on an early case and that readers familiar with Matthew are pleased to understand more of what makes him the man he is. If you have enjoyed the writing, I would greatly appreciate a review on Amazon. They really do help other people to discover my books.

I also love to hear from readers, so feel free to get in touch. You can find my website at www.teresadriscoll.com and also say hello on Twitter @teresadriscoll or via my Facebook author page: www.facebook/TeresaDriscollAuthor.

Warm wishes to you all,

Teresa

ACKNOWLEDGMENTS

As I work on the edits for this book, my husband is downstairs cooking us all a Sunday roast. You'll guess where this is going! Writers often have to hole up in their 'writing cave' for long stretches and we can be a tricky species when things are going awry. The truth is, I honestly could not do what I do without the support, love and patience of my gorgeous family.

My next thanks go to my readers. With every book, I tend to hit a phase of doubt. Am I getting it right? Will this work? Should I change that? Through these inevitable ups and downs, I am always cheered by the lovely messages I receive every day from readers all around the world.

I am forever grateful to my publisher Thomas & Mercer for the whole team's flair and energy. Also to my patient editors Jack Butler and Ian Pindar for their ideas and insight to help me shape and polish this story.

And finally, as ever, a shout out to my wonderful agent Madeleine Milburn and her team, without whom none of this would have happened.

ABOUT THE AUTHOR

Photo © 2015 Claire Tregaskis

For more than twenty-five years as a journalist – including fifteen years as a BBC TV news presenter – Teresa Driscoll followed stories into the shadows of life. Covering crime for so long, she watched and was deeply moved by all the ripples each case caused, and the haunting impact on the families, friends and witnesses involved. It's those ripples that she explores in her darker fiction.

Teresa lives in beautiful Devon with her family. She writes women's fiction as well as thrillers, and her novels have been sold for translation in nineteen languages. You can find out more about her books on her website (www.teresadriscoll.com) or by following her on Twitter (@TeresaDriscoll) or Facebook (www.facebook.com/teresadriscollauthor).